Valentine

By the same author

Elizabeth the Beloved
Kathryn, the Wanton Queen
Mary, the Infamous Queen
Bride for King James
Joan of the Lilies
Flower of the Greys
The Rose of Hever
Princess of Desire
Struggle for a Crown
Shadow of a Tudor
Seven for St Crispin's Day
The Cloistered Flame
The Woodville Wench
The Peacock Queen
Henry VIII and His Six Wives
Jewel of the Greys
The Maid of Judah
The Gallows Herd
Flawed Enchantress
So Fair and Foul a Queen
The Willow Maid
Curse of the Greys
The Queenmaker
Tansy
Kate Alanna
A Child Called Freedom
The Crystal and the Cloud
The Snow Blossom
Beggar Maid, Queen
I, The Maid
Night of the Willow
Ravenscar
Song for a Strolling Player
Frost on the Rose
Red Queen, White Queen
Imperial Harlot
My Lady Troubador
Lackland's Bride
My Philippa
Isabella, the She-Wolf
Fair Maid of Kent
The Vinegar Seed
The Vinegar Blossom
The Vinegar Tree
Lady for a Chevalier
My Catalina
The Noonday Queen
Incredible Fierce Desire
Wife in Waiting
Patchwork
Minstrel for a Valois
Witch Queen
Much Suspected of Me
Proud Bess
The Flower of Martinique
England's Mistress
A Masque of Brontës
Green Apple Burning
Child of Earth

Valentine

MAUREEN PETERS

ROBERT HALE · LONDON

First published in Great Britain 2000

ISBN 0 7090 6597 3

Robert Hale Limited
Clerkenwell House
Clerkenwell Green
London EC1R 0HT

2 4 6 8 10 9 7 5 3 1

Typeset by
Derek Doyle & Associates, Liverpool.
Printed in Great Britain by
St Edmundsbury Press Ltd, Bury St Edmunds, Suffolk.
Bound by WBC Book Manufacturers Limited, Bridgend.

ONE

At dusk the gas-lamps spilled pools of honey over the cobbles, mellowing the dark stone. A gust of wind rattled the window-panes and sent a flurry of soot down the chimney to remind her that it was getting late. Tansy Clark let the plush drapes fall into place and turned to survey the room that had been familiar to her for most of her life.

The carpet that covered the greater part of the floor was faded now, its original florid design muted and blurred, and the curtains she had just held had faded in sympathy from crimson to a brownish rose. The well-polished furniture stood in the accustomed places, the high-backed chairs for visitors, the miniature armchair she had used in childhood, the low, fireside chair where her mother had sat, usually with a piece of sewing or a half-finished knitted garment in her hands while opposite her, pipe-rack at his elbow, her husband had read aloud to her – not from the novels of Mr Dickens or Miss Austen, but from the pages of the latest police report on some crime of murder or robbery. Her mother, Tansy recalled, had always relished the murder cases most.

Tansy could see her now, her crinoline spread over her seat, lamplight-glinted pins holding her hair in its demure net, her fingers never ceasing in their placid rhythm as she remarked, 'But Laurence my love, if the blows were delivered with such force then the blood must have spattered quite considerably, surely?'

Books filled the shelves that occupied one entire wall and the wall at each side of the double doors. Old, well-thumbed volumes of the classics and of poetry mingled with bound copies of the *Police Gazette*, accounts of famous trials, atlases and, on the bottom shelf, the big, illustrated volumes of exploration, botany and biology from which she had gleaned her own education.

'Laurence, my dear, I'm sure you feel as I do that a school which refuses to instruct its pupils in the realities of life is not suitable for our Tansy. Neither am I impressed with a curriculum that fails to include some strenuous physical activity. Would not Tansy be happier if she continued her studies at home under your auspices?'

Much happier! Tansy, whose formal education had ended when she was eleven, had happily left the local day-school where little girls were being turned into demure young ladies and plunged with gusto into her father's library, reading anything and everything, encouraged to join in the sometimes lively arguments between her parents concerning the merits of this or that author.

There had been regular trips to art galleries, to stately homes and museums. There had been trips to the theatre and long rambles through the parks, and an occasional boat trip down the Thames, with her father making the past come alive as he pointed out various landmarks. Best of all though, had been the evenings when her parents had talked through the current case engaging the attentions of the police department where Laurence Clark had been a much respected inspector.

Over the mantelshelf an oval mirror was tilted slightly to show the room in its slightly foreshortened entirety. The flat-topped desk which was still piled with papers, pens sticking up out of jars, bottles of the brown ink her father liked, small, lead paperweights and cuttings from various newspapers that had caught his eye.

In the mirror also Tansy could see her father, straight backed in his wheelchair, his grey hair still plentiful despite his fifty-six years, pipe in hand, the flames in the fireplace glinting on the heavy gold ring on his well-shaped hand.

'It's getting late, Pa,' she said. 'I ought to be making a move.'

'Do you want Finn to call a cab for you?' He spoke somewhat absently, his mind clearly on the newspaper cutting he was holding.

'I'll get one at the corner. It isn't raining and I could do with a bit of a walk.'

'Whatever you want, dear.'

He was frowning slightly, smoothing out the cutting, taking the pipe out of his mouth and tapping it on the edge of the big, square ashtray at his elbow.

Tansy took her cloak and hat from the walnut hallstand just outside the door and put them on. When she went back into the room her father had laid the pipe aside and was sorting through the pile of uncut newspapers on the desk.

'Going already?' He looked up in faint surprise.

'Pa, ever since I arrived your mind's been elsewhere,' she complained, laughing. 'What's in the newspaper that distracts your attention from your cherished only daughter?'

'Cherished?' He raised an eyebrow. 'Flighty more like.'

'Pa, I'm thirty!'

'Thirty and impertinent,' he retorted.

'The newspaper, Pa?'

'Probably nothing, but take a look.' He passed over the cutting.

' "His Royal Highness the Prince of Wales will be opening an Exhibition of French Art at . . ." Oh, you mean this?' Tansy slid her eyes to the item beneath and read it aloud. ' "Have you personal problems? Consult Valentine who will give advice based on a lifetime's experience of the human heart. Many satisfied clients from the highest echelons of society." Have you got a problem, Pa?'

'Nothing I can't handle.'

'Then what d'ye find so interesting about this advertisement?'

'I don't know.' He grimaced slightly. 'It jogged something at the back of my mind.'

'Old habits die hard?' She shot him an affectionate glance.

'It's not a regular item.' He took the cutting from her. 'It's been in before though. I wish I could remember when.'

'If you clipped the cuttings together according to date . . .'

'I'd miss the pleasure of looking for specific items. Now, when? Lord, yes! I must be getting old. Three months ago, next to that item about that poor young girl who was murdered in Kensington.'

'We never discussed that one, did we?'

'You took yourself off to the seaside for a couple of weeks and nothing much was made of the affair.'

'Ellie Watson. Wasn't that her name? They never arrested anyone, did they?'

'No suspects and no clues. If Ellie Watson had been some society lady it would've made your head spin to see how fast they'd've picked someone up, but she made matches for a living – if you can call it a living!'

'So what's the connection between the advertisement and the murder?'

'There wasn't any as far as I'm aware,' he said. 'The advertisement was in the adjoining column, that's all. As I recall it had been in for about a week. After the murder was reported I didn't see it again until it appeared yesterday.'

'Meaning?'

'Probably nothing at all,' he admitted. 'Just a feeling at the back of my mind. In a female it would be called intuition.'

A quality, she thought, that had greatly assisted him in his career. Numerous criminals were now lodged at Queen Victoria's pleasure because of her father's flashes of insight. It had been a great relief to many intending law-breakers when his career had been cut short by two bullets that had entered his spine five years before, confining him to the wheelchair and the upper floor of the house where he had lived since a promotion had enabled him to move his wife and daughter to a nicer neighbourhood.

'Wasn't Ellie Watson hit over the head or something?' Tansy mused.

'From behind. Tansy, take a look in the corner cupboard. Finn put some old cuttings there last week. The desk was getting slightly overcrowded.'

Tansy knelt to open the cupboard door, thereby dislodging a thick sheaf of newspapers and sundry cuttings.

'Three months ago.' She leafed through them rapidly. 'Here it is!'

Finn, whose ideas of what constituted order and tidiness frequently ran counter to those of his master, had put the papers in rough chronological order.

'Read it out! Refresh my memory,' her father said.

Tansy perched on the arm of the horsehair-padded sofa and obediently read.

' "Park Tragedy. At six o'clock this morning Constable James Howard of the Metropolitan Police, at present stationed in the district of Kensington, was beginning his accustomed morning round when he came upon the body of a young woman, lying face down on the path outside the Public Library. She had evidently been struck over the head and had fallen from the bench on which she was seated. She had been dead for six to eight hours as far as the medical physician could ascertain." Then what was she doing sitting on a bench in the middle of the night?'

'And outside the library. Hardly the usual place for ladies of easy virtue is it?'

'I thought you said she made matches.'

'She may have supplemented a somewhat meagre income,' Laurence Clark said drily. 'Go on.'

' "The body was later identified as that of Ellie Watson, aged about seventeen, employed at the match factory owned by . . . blah, blah, et cetera. Murder weapon not yet recovered. An early arrest expected."

'I don't know why that's still said,' her father reflected. 'Not even the most credulous member of the public believes it any longer.'

'There isn't anything more,' Tansy said, 'but you were right. The Valentine advertisement is right by it in the next column. That doesn't indicate any connection though, does it?'

'None at all. There were a couple of later items about the killing but it tailed off fairly quickly. Not much public interest. Why have you got your hat on?'

'Because I was on my way out. Honestly, Pa!'

'Then get along with you child! Don't let my meandering thoughts delay you.'

'Well, Mrs Timothy frets when I'm late getting in,' Tansy reminded him.

'Mrs Timothy is an admirable housekeeper,' her father said with a grin. 'Finn is an admirable man-servant. I am resolved the twain shall never meet!'

'See you soon, Pa.'

Raising her hand in farewell, she went out onto the landing in time to see Finn mounting the stairs with a tray, his long, thin shadow stretching across the ceiling.

'Going already, Miss Tansy?' He reached the top of the stairs, set the tray on a side-table and gave her a reproachful look.

'I have things to do.'

'Your pa don't 'alf look forward to you coming over,' Finn said. His long, mournful face conveyed reproach for a daughter who had left an invalid father to fend for himself.

Tansy, who knew perfectly well that Finn would have been horrified had she suddenly decided to move back home and start interfering with the routine he and her father had established, said cheerfully, 'If I was here all the time he'd have nothing to look forward to. You didn't make supper for me, I hope?'

'A nice bit of beef, Miss Tansy, with a madeira sauce.'

'You eat my share. Mrs Timothy is bound to have prepared something for me.'

'One only 'opes you eat nourishing, Miss Tansy,' Finn responded. 'Not a spare ounce of flesh on your bones can I see.'

'I'm wiry. 'Night!'

'Shall I call you a cab?' Finn enquired.

'Take in the supper before it gets cold. I'll walk part of the way,' Tansy said, starting down the stairs.

'You look out for yourself, Miss Tansy!' Finn called down the stair-well as she reached the front door. 'The streets are full of villains these days!'

There being one less in the fifteen years since Finn had served his last term for burglary and decided to go straight, she thought, closing the front door behind her.

Pausing on the steps to draw on her gloves she looked up and down the quiet street. From the far side of the park opposite the crescent of tall, narrow houses the sounds of the city echoed faintly. This had been her home since childhood. She had bowled her hoop in the park, sailed her boat on the pond, met Geoffrey by the weeping willow that shaded one of the benches where people met to chat during long summer afternoons.

As Geoffrey's name came into her mind she braced herself, but the stabbing pain of loss was reduced to a sad nostalgia. Ten years since she had met Geoffrey, nine since he had asked her to marry him, seven since he had died of yellow fever a few days before he had been due to sail home from his father's plantation in Jamaica for their wedding.

'He has left you his house in London,' the solicitor had informed her, 'and an income derived from a third of the profits on the Jamaican estate. You will be an independent woman of moderate means.'

The bequest had meant little to her at the time. She had installed a tenant in the house and continued to act as her father's housekeeper until the bullets had smashed his spine, forcing him into early retirement.

It was Laurence who had insisted she carve out a separate existence for herself.

'If you're picturing yourself as the devoted daughter tied for life to an invalid father you can dismiss it from your mind,' he had said briskly. 'I couldn't bear to have a woman fussing round me. Your mother knew that and never subjected me to petticoat government, and in those days I could've resisted. You must strike out on your own, my dear – live in the house that Geoffrey left for you, employ a sensible housekeeper and find some useful occupation. Take a course in something or other. They admit females to many courses these days. Or do some voluntary work somewhere or other. What I don't need is someone fussing around me. Finn and I will manage very well together.'

'Best do as he suggests, Miss Clark,' the doctor had advised. 'He'll adjust to his condition more comfortably if you don't treat him as an invalid.'

So, the tenant having departed, Tansy had spent several weeks in the redecoration and refurnishing of her inheritance and, albeit with some misgivings, had packed her belongings and moved to her new home where Mrs Timothy, whom she had engaged as housekeeper, waited to receive her.

In the beginning she had visited her father daily until Laurence had given her one of his quizzical looks, remarking, 'When I suggested voluntary work as a possible outlet for your energies, I didn't mean to elect myself as your good cause, my dear. Finn and

I are managing very well together and becoming quite accustomed to a bachelor life.'

The problem was, Tansy reflected, that she wasn't sure how to expend her energy! She had enrolled for a course in drawing only to discover that she had neither talent nor inclination for trying to copy vases of flowers and the occasional fully clothed model – life classes being forbidden to the female students. She had done her share of fund-raising, of helping out in East End soup-kitchens and of hospital visiting, with the growing conviction that the recipients of organized charity rather resented it than otherwise. And her one foray into a home for 'soiled doves' had convinced her that the doves in question had no desire to be cleaned up.

The trouble was that she was bored, she thought, crossing the park road from force of habit and returning the keeper's greeting.

'Half an hour to lock-up time, madam.'

'Thank you. Good-evening.'

Tansy nodded and went on along the path that wound in a pleasantly casual fashion between the bushes and flower-beds and led to the bench under the weeping willow where Geoffrey had asked her to marry him.

'It's a year and a day since we met at the museum.' He had taken her hand, idly separating the fingers as he talked. 'We are agreed, I think, that we're in love?'

'Yes,' she had answered simply.

'Then I hope this fits.'

The ring had been an emerald, almost matching her eyes.

She was jerked out of her memories by a stifled snuffling sound and, in the same instant, discerned a small figure, seen dimly in the light from a lamp that gleamed through the drooping branches of the willow.

Tansy hesitated, then seated herself at the other end of the bench, let a moment or two elapse and then said carefully, 'You seem to be in some distress.'

'So much,' said the figure, revealing itself to be a girl by the light, pretty voice, 'that I may throw myself into the lake!'

'The lake? Oh, the pond,' Tansy said prosaically. 'It's less than four feet deep and you'd merely get very wet and muddy. Here's a handkerchief. Why don't you wipe your eyes and tell me what's wrong?'

A small hand accepted the proffered square of linen, and a good deal of sniffling and blowing of nose ensued.

'Thank you,' the girl said timidly.

'You may keep the handkerchief,' Tansy said hastily. 'Now what's the matter that makes you want to jump in the lake?'

'I lost my situation,' the girl said, adding with a touch of pride, 'I was tweeny in the household of the Honourable Sir James Edge, working my way up to housemaid, and then Cook said I had to leave.'

'The cook dismissed you!'

'Not exactly.' The girl spoke with slightly more confidence now. 'She went to Mr Hawkins, the butler, and told him that I was in the habit of tasting the soup before it was taken to table and he had no choice but to take her word for it and let me go. He did give me a very good reference, but it was such an elegant household, only the Edges are away on holiday so I couldn't appeal to them.'

'Surely it's possible for you to get another situation,' Tansy said.

'Not in a really good place,' the girl said, turning a dismal little face towards Tansy. 'All the best families are out of town and not hiring until next month.'

'What's your name?'

'Tilde Miles – short for Mathilde.'

'Mathilde? That's French, surely?'

'My mother was French,' Tilde confided. 'Well, not exactly French, but she'd visited Paris once with a very amiable gentleman. They had a falling out and she came back to England.'

'I see,' Tansy said.

'She never saw him again,' the other said mournfully. 'I expect he was a duke or an earl whose family would've disapproved of his marrying a commoner. Mother was always anxious that I learn how to read and write and speak nicely in case he ever came back. He never did. Perhaps he was killed in a duel or something.'

Tansy mentally discounted dukes and duels. Tilde's mother must either have had a vivid imagination or been incredibly naïve.

'Your mother,' she prompted.

'When she died I couldn't manage for very long on the money that was left so I got a job in the match factory,' Tilde continued. 'That was dreadfully hard labour, so I looked for something else and was taken on as tweeny and I never in my life tasted anything before it was taken to table, Mrs . . .'

'Miss. Miss Tansy Clark.'

'Tansy.' Tilde clasped her small hands together tightly. 'What a perfectly lovely name! How did your parents ever come to choose it?'

'Because the first time they went walking together in the country my mother picked some tansy flowers from the hedge and my father helped her put them in her hair.'

'How perfectly romantic!'

'Yes it was, but the point is,' said Tansy, bringing them both firmly down to earth, 'that you're without work and presumably without a bed of any sort for the night.'

'I'll find somewhere,' Tilde said, choking back a left-over sob.

Tansy surveyed the girl thoughtfully. In the feeble flare of the streetlight she could discern a cloud of dark, curly hair and a face which, when cleared of the ravages of tears, would be very pretty.

'How old are you, Tilde?' she asked.

'Seventeen, Miss.'

Seventeen, pretty, educated above her station and with an innocence about her that would attract a certain type of predator. It was fairly obvious where Tilde Miles would end up if she were left to roam the streets.

'I'm in need of a housemaid myself,' she said. 'Not a tweeny. Can you dust, wait on table, mend linen?'

'I can do fancy work,' Tilde said eagerly, 'and everything else needful I can learn. I've a very good memory. And I know lots of poetry. Shelley, Keats, Lord Byron – "So, we'll go no more a roving so late—" '

'I don't think you'll be required to recite poetry,' Tansy said, repressing a grin. 'Have you got any luggage?'

'I've a bag here.' She bent and tugged it from beneath the seat.

'Come along then. We will find the gates locked if we dawdle. There's a cab-stand just through the gate there. I live on the outskirts of Chelsea.'

Tansy rose and suited action to words with Tilde trailing obediently after her. Her unquestioning trustfulness was touching and slightly alarming.

Twenty minutes later Tansy paid off the driver of the cab she had taken and led the way up the short path with its borders of night-scented stock.

Fitting her key into the lock she entered the passage which widened into a central hall.

'Mrs Timothy, I'm home!'

The words were only half-way out of her mouth when Mrs Timothy appeared, grey hair coiled into its customary doughnut bun, apron crackling with starch. As usual she was as trim as if she had just stepped out of a china cabinet, hands clasped at her ample waist as she surveyed Tansy briefly, then slid her gaze to the small figure at her elbow.

'Who's this then?' she enquired.

'This is Mathilde Miles, Tilde for short,' Tansy said. 'I've engaged her on probation as a maid-servant.'

'Have I complained about the amount of work that I'm expected to undertake in this household?' Mrs Timothy asked.

'No more than five times a morning,' Tansy said.

'Complaining is the right of the working woman, Miss Tansy,' Mrs Timothy said with dignity.

'Granted, Mrs Timothy, but you have frequently wished for a girl you could train up into your methods, now haven't you?' Tansy coaxed.

'I may,' said Mrs Timothy, with even greater dignity, 'have mentioned it. This one looks like a gallivanter to me. Are you?'

'I don't think so,' Tilde mumbled nervously.

'Tilde was unjustly dismissed from her last post,' Tansy said. 'She has not, I believe, had any supper.'

'Supper can certainly be provided,' Mrs Timothy granted. 'Where is she to sleep? You will not expect me to give up my bed-sitting-room and bath to a complete stranger, I hope?'

'Tilde can sleep in the small bedroom and use the scullery to wash in,' Tansy allowed.

'I shall make up the bed there,' Mrs Timothy said in a relenting tone. 'Have you had supper yourself, Miss Tansy?'

'I'll have a sandwich and a cup of tea,' Tansy said. 'Tilde, go with Mrs Timothy and mind you do exactly what she tells you.'

Tilde, looking far too alarmed to give tongue, went meekly in the wake of the housekeeper's formidable bulk into the kitchen.

Tansy hung up her cloak and hat and went on into the long room that spread itself across the back of the house.

This was, in her own mind, the heart of the house, its walls pine panelled, bright rugs covering the polished floor, floor-length windows curtained in green damask, giving access to a narrow terrace from which the garden ran to the river. Geoffrey had bought the house for the two of them, leaving her to decorate and furnish it while he sailed to Jamaica to oversee his affairs there. He had died just after she had completed her task and for months she had not dared to enter the rooms that Geoffrey had never seen. The knowledge that he never would now see them had been too hurtful to bear.

After the departure of the tenant she had used some of her legacy to make the interior of the house as different as possible, determined that she would not live in a place originally designed for a married couple.

So the long room carried no memory of what might have been, but displayed her own interests in the closely packed bookshelves, the Du Maurier cartoons framed on the walls, the brass-bound globe on which she and her father had traced the adventures of various explorers.

She sat down in the big, leaf-brown armchair and pulled off her shoes as Mrs Timothy came in.

'Did you require the fire lighting, Miss Tansy? I dare not trust a complete newcomer to do it correctly, but I have no objection to seeing to it myself,' she said, still very much on her dignity.

'I don't need a fire,' Tansy said. 'Are those the sandwiches? You've been very quick.'

'I took the liberty of making them a little earlier,' Mrs Timothy said. 'Of course if they're not to your liking. . . .'

'They look delicious,' Tansy said. 'Mrs Timothy, she was sitting crying on a park bench. I couldn't just leave her there, could I?'

'Knowing you, Miss, I suppose not,' Mrs Timothy said, somewhat placated. 'Mind you, some extra help would be welcome. As you know, I never complain, but my back does.'

'Exactly.' Tansy seized the advantage. 'You ought not to be bothered with the shopping and the heavy cleaning. And she seems very biddable.'

'I've set a cup of tea and a large slice of chicken pie before her,' Mrs Timothy said. 'I only hope that she won't rise in the dead of night to admit her confederates who will murder us in our beds and steal the silver.'

'She doesn't look like that kind of person,' Tansy protested.

'Criminals don't wear labels,' Mrs Timothy opined.

'Pa would certainly agree with you,' Tansy said, drinking her tea. 'He always asserted that the more wide-eyed and innocent the suspect, the more likely they were to be guilty.'

'Your father is right as ever, Miss Tansy. What that man does not know about criminals can be written on the back of a postage stamp.'

Mrs Timothy had never met Laurence in her life but she quoted him as if he were the world's foremost expert on every subject. Now, unbending more as her mood mellowed, she enquired, 'May I ask how the inspector is? Well, I hope?'

'Very well but bored,' Tansy informed her. 'At present he's thinking about the Ellie Watson case and wishing he was still in the force.'

'The match girl who was murdered in Kensington. I read about the affair.' The housekeeper pursed her lips. 'What a respectable young woman was doing sitting on a bench in the middle of the night with pink ribbons in her hat I cannot imagine.'

'She can't possibly have been waiting for the library to open,' Tansy mused.

'You mentioned you found Tilde Miles on a bench,' Mrs Timothy said with a questioning look.

'In the park opposite Pa's house. She was in great distress.'

'Well, we shall see how she turns out,' Mrs Timothy gave her final word. 'Good-night, Miss Tansy.'

' 'Night. I'll lock up.'

Mrs Timothy made her stately way back to the kitchen and Tansy finished her sandwich.

Rising, she stepped over to the windows and drew back one long curtain. Outside, moonlight whitened the terrace steps leading down into the garden. Creamy honeysuckle hung over the walls, and at the far end of the lawn the river was a ribbon of silver beyond the box hedge.

Ribbons. Now what had ribbons to do with anything? Yes, of course. The murdered girl had worn pink ribbons in her hat. So what was it about pink ribbons that had skimmed the surface of her mind and vanished again?

Newspapers were delivered regularly and kept in a box in the kitchen to be used for kindling and the stuffing of wet shoes. Would there still be one from three months before?

Tansy drew the curtain across the pane again and went through and across the hall to the kitchen. The newspapers were stacked in a box near the stove where a fire still glowed faintly, with drying-up cloths ranged round on the brass-railed fire-guard.

She knelt and went rapidly through the pile, marvelling at the contrast between Mrs Timothy's nearly perfect tidiness and the apparent chaos in which her father's thoughts moved most logically.

'Here we are.' Finding the relevant issue, she drew it out and sat back on her heels. ' "Police are still seeking the killer of seventeen-year-old Ellie Watson, killed by a blow to the back of the head while seated on a bench outside the Public Library in Kensington. Miss Watson was described as a quiet girl who was five feet two inches tall and slender. Her complexion was pale, somewhat freckled, her hair ginger. If anyone can offer any information. . . ." '

That was the query which had touched the surface of her mind. Would any girl with ginger hair put a pink ribbon in her hat?

The Valentine advertisement wasn't there, as her father had noticed.

'Is anything – Oh, it's you, Miss Tansy. You gave me quite a turn.' Mrs Timothy, still in black silk and starched apron – did she, Tansy wondered, wear them in bed? – had emerged from her bed-sitting-room.

'I was just looking up something in the newspaper,' Tansy said, uncurling her long legs and standing up. 'Where's Tilde?'

'Settled for the night, one hopes.' Mrs Timothy sniffed. 'She did show me a reference from a Mr Hawkins, the butler at her last place. Nicely written and gave her a good character – if, of course, it is genuine.'

'Was there no address?'

'Near Grosvenor Square.'

'I'll check it out when I have time,' Tansy said. 'Mrs Timothy, if you had ginger hair would you wear pink ribbons in your hat?'

'No, and neither would any female with any sense,' the housekeeper said decidedly. 'If you were contemplating wearing pink ribbons, Miss Tansy – not that your own hair is ginger, but it is—'

'Dark red,' Tansy said.

'Unless a gentleman friend gave a girl a ribbon, in which case she might wear it once or twice to please him.'

'I do believe you're right, Mrs Timothy. Thank you.'

'Then I'll bid you good-night again.'

Being far too dignified to display any vulgar curiosity, Mrs Timothy bade her good-night and withdrew in stately style.

TWO

She must have been dreaming about something pleasant because the voice in the street below her window dragged her reluctantly from sleep. Tansy, scrambling into a dressing-gown, pulled back the curtains and opened the window wider.

Below in the pale morning light a newsboy was still intoning the words that had penetrated her consciousness.

'Read all abaht it! 'Orrible murder at Kew! Read all abaht it!'

The front door opened and Mrs Timothy sallied out, voice raised and chin pugnacious.

'I'll thank you to cease that caterwauling, young man! It's enough to wake the dead at this hour of the morning! And I'll take one copy if you please. Now move on.'

Tansy hastily withdrew from sight lest her housekeeper be further affronted by witnessing her employer in full view and wearing only a dressing-gown.

The newsboy's cry diminished along the crescent and Tansy contented herself with a quick splash of cold water over face and hands, brushed her teeth and pulled on the light grey dress with the striped green bustle and the green collar and cuffs which was attractive and practical since it didn't require very tight lacing. Her heavy hair she twisted into a pleat at the nape of her neck, taking her customary swift glance in the mirror to ensure she was at least presentable. Geoffrey had thought her beautiful, but Geoffrey she considered to have been biased by his feelings towards her. Her own opinion of her looks, on the rare occasions she even thought about them, was that though her eyes were a striking green and her red hair plentiful, her height and lack of curves detracted from any charms she might boast. Ladies were supposed to comport themselves as feminine and delicate blooms of womanhood, which was rather difficult to achieve when one stood five feet eight inches in stockinged feet and had strongly marked features, with a mouth too wide for current masculine tastes.

In the small dining-room her place was laid and the newly purchased newspaper was folded on the table. Mrs Timothy came in with the coffee and a look of apology on her face.

'I hope that dratted newsboy didn't disturb you, Miss Tansy,' she said. 'I've told him a hundred times not to go waking the neighbourhood but he never minds me.'

'How is Tilde this morning?' Tansy was dying to feast her eyes on the somewhat smeary column beneath the lurid headline but the courtesies had to be observed.

'She seems to be willing,' Mrs Timothy said with an air of reserving judgement. 'Will you have sausages or kippers?'

'Scrambled eggs and toast, please.'

'Right away, Miss.'

Mrs Timothy withdrew and Tansy's fingers leapt upon the newspaper.

HORRIBLE MURDER IN KEW

At midnight last night a police constable patrolling the riverbank at Kew found evidence of a foul and heinous crime. The unlucky victim, who as yet remains unidentified, had been struck from behind with a heavy instrument of some kind which has not yet been located. The body was lying face down on the path, having clearly been feloniously struck down while sitting on a bench nearby.

The deceased is described as a young woman with fair hair and delicate features. She was clad in a respectable grey costume and a blue hat with bright pink ribbon tied round the brim.

A purse discovered near the victim contained only a few coins and a handkerchief. The body has been conveyed to the morgue for forensic examination and the case is now under investigation by Detective Inspector Jarrold. Anyone recognizing the above description or having any information to impart should contact their nearest police station. Our readers will, of course, recall the as yet unsolved killing of Ellie Watson three months ago. This latest affair displays some striking similarities, but we understand from Inspector Jarrold that any link between the two dastardly crimes has not yet been established.

There was more about the advisability of females not venturing out unescorted after dark and the rising crime rate.

Mrs Timothy came in with the scrambled eggs on toast.

'I took the liberty of glancing at the headlines while I was making the coffee,' she said. 'It makes one's blood run cold.'

'Bad news makes large profits,' Tansy said, quoting Laurence.

'That's as may be, Miss Tansy, but we needn't agree with it,' Mrs Timothy said severely.

'I am beginning to be thankful that I brought Tilde home with me last night,' Tansy remarked, starting on her breakfast. 'Not that she was anywhere near Kew, but she was sitting on a bench.'

'There seems to be a positive craze for sitting on benches in the middle of the night,' Mrs Timothy disapproved. 'Could the same man have killed both girls, d'ye think?'

'I've no idea. Pa would say that it's too soon to tell.'

'The inspector will be in the right of it.'

'I think I'll call on him this morning,' Tansy decided. 'Can you manage with Tilde?'

'I shall appreciate some time in which to acquaint her with our ways,' Mrs Timothy said. 'Please give my regards to your father.'

Tansy finished her breakfast and scanned the rest of the newspaper. There was no sign of the Valentine advertisement but that, she recalled, had appeared in the evening editions.

'I've finished with the newspaper, Mrs Timothy!' she called down as she went upstairs to put on her jacket and hat.

'If my duties permit,' came the reply from the kitchen door, 'I may just glance over it.'

Outside the sun was shining and the pale morning had warmed into life. Tansy hailed a cab and was amused to see, as the vehicle entered the crescent, that Finn was hovering on the front steps, obviously on the outlook for her.

' 'Orrible business,' he said with a certain relish. 'The boss reckoned you might drop in. Go right up, Miss Tansy.'

Laurence had drawn his wheelchair to the window and swivelled it around to face her as she came in.

'Another pink ribbon!' he said.

'You remembered. Has Inspector Jarrold been here yet?' She removed her own sober, grey hat.

'Jarrold doesn't trouble to consult anybody these days,' her father said testily. 'He's far too important. Yes, after you'd gone last night I set myself to running over what I'd read about the Ellie Watson case. The girl had ginger hair and a bright pink ribbon in her hat – an odd choice, unless fashions are changing.'

'Not to that extent,' Tansy said. 'But I can't think of any explanation.'

'Would a very poor girl trouble herself about style?'

'Even the poorest girls go out of their way to look attractive,' Tansy said.

'And this latest victim had on a blue hat with bright pink ribbon tied round it. Could be a coincidence I suppose.'

'They were both struck on the back of the head while sitting on a bench in the middle of the night.'

'In respectable areas of the city. Well, I'll await events with patience.'

'Not you, Pa. You're longing to get involved,' Tansy teased.

'I like to keep my brain active. I spent some time last night going through old cuttings and newspapers. You know the advertisement?'

'Consult Valentine if you have a problem.'

'It was in the evening papers for a week up to and including the first murder. Then it disappeared for three months. Now, for the last five days it's been in the newspaper again. It may be a coincidence. It's easy to find connections where there are none.'

'Will you take coffee, Miss Tansy?' Finn had entered with the tray.

'I can manage,' Laurence said with a touch of irritability as he released the lever which enabled him to move his chair short distances over smooth surfaces. 'Pour yourself a cup too.'

'I took the liberty of bringing three cups,' Finn said.

'What d'ye think of this second murder, Finn?' Tansy enquired. 'Have you any ideas about it yourself?'

'Ask me about burgling and forging and I'll bring you experts,' Finn said, pouring coffee. 'Murderers ain't in my circle.'

'Then we shall have to rely on our own wits,' Laurence said. 'Hand me that list of girls reported missing over the last year.'

'You think Ellie Watson may not have been the first then?' Tansy asked.

'I don't think anything, my dear. I ferret about for my own amusement.' He scanned the list that the man-servant had handed him and frowned, shaking his head.

'Do many girls go missing in the course of a year then?' Tansy asked.

'Too many,' her father said. 'I think we're almost certainly on the wrong track here. These two girls were killed and left where they had fallen. If any of these were also killed the bodies haven't been found. Killers follow the same *modus operandi* as I've frequently told you. They don't kill and hide a person one week and leave another victim for anyone to find the next week. Not that I really expect anybody on this list to have been the victim of foul play. Girls run off with smooth-tongued charmers and feel too ashamed to go home, and others lose their jobs and—'

'Which reminds me,' Tansy broke in. 'I have engaged a new servant.'

'The admirable Mrs Timothy having eloped with the fishmonger?'

'No, of course not,' Tansy laughed. 'No, on my way through the park after I left here yesterday evening I came across a girl in great distress. She had been dismissed from her job as tweeny for a spurious reason and—'

'The whole story, please.' Laurence tapped his fingers impatiently. 'I do so dislike potted histories.'

Tansy obediently related the entire episode.

'Seems a bit rum to me,' Finn commented.

'You will check her reference?' Laurence said.

'Yes, of course, but I'm sure she was telling the truth. Now, Pa, is there anything I can do for you?'

'Someone ought to go round to the morgue and nose abaht a bit,' Finn suggested.

'Which morgue?' Tansy enquired.

'The Kensington one. Just nose around and come back for lunch. As I've no official standing I can't go making direct enquiries.'

'Inspector Jarrold will be round here picking your brains before you know it, Pa,' Tansy told him.

'I'll call you a cab, Miss.' Finn insinuated himself through the door.

'You don't make a habit of wandering around in the park after dusk, I trust?' Laurence glanced sharply at his daughter.

'No, of course not, Pa. Anyway I'm hardly a poor but respectable young girl. I'll see you later on.'

Finn, who could conjure cabs out of thin air on the rainiest day, was waiting to hand her in.

'This 'asn't 'alf stirred up your pa's interest,' he commented. 'Keeps 'is brain lively so to speak. Let's 'ope there's a third.'

'Let's hope nothing of the kind,' Tansy said severely as the door was closed and the horse pricked into action.

The morgue was a square, stone building, set back from the road with a yard before it and a discreet sign announcing its function. A small crowd had already gathered outside, though it didn't appear that there was anything to be seen beyond a couple of uniformed policemen planted firmly by the entrance.

Tansy paid the cab-fare and made her way to the edge of the crowd which was largely composed of women, some with shopping baskets, others clutching toddlers, and a sprinkling of men.

'Tansy, how are you? It must be months since we met!'

The man who shouldered his way through the crowd in order to shake hands with her was tall with thick, fair hair and vivid blue eyes, clean-shaven in defiance of fashion and attired more casually than was usual in town.

'Frank Cartwright, how are you?' Shaking hands with the journalist, she added, 'I hope you didn't write that piece in today's *Record*.'

'Give me credit for having more respect for the English language.' He showed blunt, white teeth in a smile, his eyes crinkling at the corners. 'No, I've been up in Scotland for the past few weeks, doing a series on Balmoral. I'm as much in the dark about this as you are. How's your father?'

'Bored out of his skull most of the time. They should've kept him on at the Yard in an advisory capacity at least, instead of pensioning him off. However, he seems to take an interest in this case. Have they found out yet who the poor girl was?'

'I've only just arrived myself,' Frank told her. 'There's a tea-room over there. If you'd like to grab a table while I see what I can find out. Unless you want to go into the morgue?'

'No. Not at all.' Tansy grimaced as a slight chill ran through her. 'I'll wait for you in the tea-room.'

Crossing the road and entering the subdued interior of the tea-room with its brown decoration and small, shiny tables covered with white cloths, she chose a window seat and informed the waitress she was expecting a friend.

Friend was a word that applied more to the Frank Cartwright she had known in former years when he had been a cub reporter on a local newspaper and Laurence, spotting him hanging around in the police station, had taken him under his wing, giving him the odd titbit of information and inviting him home for the occasional meal.

'Smart young fellow. Keen as mustard and has the art of drawing out the right information from people,' he'd told his daughter. 'Good-looking too.'

Which meant, of course, that he had hoped the two of them might take a romantic fancy to each other. Laurence Clark had frequently bemoaned the fact that with her mother dead Tansy's social opportunities were limited.

In fact she and Frank had liked each other from the start. The liking might have ripened into something warmer had she not gone along to an art exhibition at the local museum and met Geoffrey, who had paused briefly to pass a comment on a particularly amateurish piece of sculpture and was still deep in conversation with her two hours later.

After Geoffrey's death Frank had sent flowers and condolences and had had the tact not to rush into the breach and start inviting her to go to various places with him, but she still saw him now and then, usually on his way to or from some assignment, often with a pretty young lady on his arm.

She wondered if she regretted not having encouraged him more. Her father would have approved certainly, believing that an engaged girl whose fiancé dies should, after a decent interval, start looking round for a successor. On the whole she decided that a casual friendship was more suitable than a second-best romance and, in any case, Frank himself had never made any definite advances.

'Someone just claimed the body.'

Frank had entered abruptly and sat down opposite her. The waitress brought the tea-tray and went back to her station by the window where she could watch the people wandering about in the hope of seeing some action.

'Then they know who she was?' Tansy said.

'A milliner's assistant. Name of Frances Jones. Welsh origin and no known family in London. Apparently her employer read the description of the victim in the paper and connected it with a girl who hadn't arrived for work today. She's just made a positive identification.'

'Could we talk to her?' Tansy enquired eagerly.

'I'm not sure how anxious she will be to get further involved,' Frank said, 'but I told her that I'd be here. She may shy away from the press. Most respectable women do – Ah! She's the exception. Here she comes now.'

He rose, gesturing to the waitress to bring more tea, and ushered in a well-dressed woman in early middle age.

'Miss Tansy Clark. Mrs Mainwaring.' Frank made the introductions and drew up an extra chair. 'Miss Clark is the daughter of one of our most distinguished police-officers, now retired due to an injury suffered in the line of duty, but still very active behind the scenes. You'll take a cup of tea, Mrs Mainwaring? Your recent duty must have been harrowing indeed. To be called upon to identify somebody one has known – upsetting.'

'Very upsetting, Mr Cartwright. You speak rightly.' Mrs Mainwaring, whose cut-glass accent sounded more learnt than natural, nodded solemnly as fresh tea was brought.

'What can you tell us about the girl?' Frank asked.

'Not really very much, sir,' she answered. 'As I told the gentlemen at the morgue, I took on Frances Jones as an apprentice two years ago. She is – was, a very quick learner and a hard worker. Very nimble fingers too. I promoted her to assistant only last month. I treat all my young ladies very fairly. No reason for her to try to increase her income by other means, if you follow my meaning?'

'Meaning she was unlikely to have been seated on a bench near Kew Gardens in the middle of the night?'

'Quite out of character, Mr Cartwright, I assure you,' she said.

'Are you absolutely positive that it is Frances Jones?' Tansy asked.

The older woman nodded her head on which was perched a handsome black hat which was probably one of her own creations, as a flash of genuine grief sped across her face.

'There is no mistake,' she affirmed.

'Was she still wearing her hat?'

'No, but it was on a table at the side. A blue one to perch on the head, with grey ribbons to match her dress and two little grey plumes.'

'No pink ribbons?'

Frank had leaned forward slightly.

Mrs Mainwaring looked slightly affronted.

'There was a pink ribbon tied round the brim of the hat,' she admitted. 'Rather a vulgar shade of pink and certainly not part of the original ensemble.'

'What kind of person was she?' Tansy enquired.

Mrs Mainwaring looked surprised, as if she had never considered her late assistant in the category of person at all.

'She worked very well,' she said at last. 'She had a real eye for colour and design.'

'Could I possibly talk to one of your young ladies?' Tansy ventured.

'Are you also working for a newspaper? I'd not wish—'

'As Mr Cartwright said, my father is still keenly interested in the solving of crime. I merely help him,' Tansy said.

'Well, in those circumstances . . .' the other hesitated.

'Where did Frances Jones lodge?' Frank asked.

'She had a room three doors away from my establishment,' Mrs Mainwaring informed him. 'Most of my young ladies have rooms in the same building, just off Oxford Street. May I offer you my card?'

'Thank you.' Taking the card, Tansy slipped it into her bag.

'You will wish me to accompany you, no doubt,' Mrs Mainwaring said.

Tansy shot Frank a quick, imploring look.

'Perhaps you and I might sit here a little longer,' he said smoothly. 'To a lady of taste and refinement the recent experience must've been most distressing.'

'Her face wasn't marked you know,' Mrs Mainwaring said. 'But the back of her head was – there was a white cloth wrapped round it, all stained with blood.'

'Let us have more tea – this time with a tot of brandy in it. You do need something to strengthen your nerves I'm certain,' Frank said with his most persuasive smile.

'Well, if you insist. . . .' Mrs Mainwaring was melting fast.

Tansy slipped away, hailed the first cab she saw and gave the address off Oxford Street which was printed on Mrs Mainwaring's card.

The address proved to be the shop itself, Mrs Mainwaring having perhaps earmarked her as a potential customer. The premises looked respectable, with the name lettered over a plate-glass window in which four very pretty hats were perched on four plaster heads.

A police constable already stood at the door, looking somewhat *de trop*, as well he might, Tansy thought, since it was highly unlikely that the murderer would stroll in to purchase a hat. She hesitated. After all, she had no official standing and the policeman looked like the kind who wouldn't be impressed by her father's name and past reputation.

A girl emerged from the shop, spoke briefly to the constable and hurried past Tansy down a side-street. Tansy hastened after her.

'Excuse me!' She raised her voice slightly the moment they were out of sight of the constable.

'Yes?' The other turned, revealing a sharp, pale face under a neat, black hat.

'My name is Tansy Clark. You've obviously heard about your work-mate.'

'About Fanny. Yes.' The girl wiped her eyes with a crumpled bit of lace. 'Madam took me with her earlier on while she made the identification and then sent me back to tell the others. What do you want?'

'My father is a retired police-officer who's interested in the case,' Tansy said. 'I'm making a few enquiries on his behalf.'

'My name's Sal Finnigan and I haven't got no – any father,' the girl said. 'If you're official you'd better come in.'

'In' was a dingy passage which culminated in narrow steps rising between walls that couldn't have seen a lick of paint in years. In contrast, the door which Sal Finnigan opened on the second landing gave on to a room which, though small, was clean, with net at the window and a bed with a bright blue quilt on it against the wall. The floor was covered with a thin, patterned carpet, and apart from a brass rail on which a few garments hung limply, the only other items of furniture were a wash-stand with basin and ewer, a stool and a shelf along one wall on which a shabby Bible lay next to brush and comb, a jar of hairpins, a jar with a toothbrush in it, a bar of soap cushioned on a face-flannel and a bust of the Queen.

'This is Miss Jones's room?'

'This is – was Fanny's room, yes.' Stepping inside Sal looked round in a woebegone manner. 'She had a room to herself on account of being promoted. Before that she shared a room with me on the next floor.'

'She was Welsh I understand?'

Tansy also stepped inside.

'Came up from Wales,' Sal informed her. 'Her dad knocked her about when he was in drink and her mam died so she ran off.'

'And you both work for Mrs Mainwaring?'

'I does trimmings,' Sal said with a touch of pride, her careful accent slipping slightly.

'Does Mrs Mainwaring own this house?'

'One of her gentleman friends does.'

Sal drew a ragged breath and stared miserably at her hands.

'And you girls do only sell hats?' Tansy enquired as delicately as she could.

'Madam won't allow no funny business,' Sal said, jerking up her head. 'We ain't – are not even allowed followers unless she looks them over first. Very particular is Madam.'

'Did Fanny have a follower?' Tansy asked.

'Not her!' Sal said emphatically. 'She was that plain and small no gentleman would've looked at her once, leave alone twice. All she did was work and go to chapel on Sundays.'

'Which chapel?'

'The Sion Chapel, along Wellinburgh Street. She said the singing was nice there.'

'Methodist? Baptist?'

'Methodist I think.'

'Have the police been here yet?'

'Not seen any coppers,' Sal said.

Her father would have had a detective there immediately after the identification, Tansy thought. Aloud she said, 'Did Fanny go out last night? Are you permitted. . . ?'

'Oh, we're not locked in or anything,' Sal assured her. 'We each have our own key and Madam has a master-key but she's not the snooping sort.'

'And each room is separate from the rest?'

'The house was divided off for lodgers. Most sleep two to a room but the ones that can design hats get a place to themselves. We can go out if we want but by the end of the day all we're fit for is a bit of supper and a kip.'

'Where do you cook? Is there a kitchen?'

'Bless you, but we ain't got time to cook,' Sal said with a kind of weary amusement. 'We eat over at the pie-shop. They do a good breakfast and a sandwich for dinner and suppers too – very cheap.'

'What time d'ye finish work?'

'Start at eight, finish at eight. One hour for dinner. Half-day Saturday. We get the whole of Sunday off.'

'Did you see Fanny last night?'

'She came over and had a bit of pie and a cup of tea with the rest of the girls,' Sal said.

'What was she wearing?' Tansy asked.

'Her grey dress and jacket and the blue hat with the two grey feathers in it. When we're done for the day Madam likes us to take off our work dresses and put on something else.'

'Including a hat, just to walk across the road and have a bit of pie?'

'Madam likes us to wear some of the hats,' Sal explained. 'It acts as an advertisement she says.'

'And Fanny was there with you last night?'

'I just said. None of us had anything to do with what happened to Fanny.'

For the first time Sal sounded slightly aggrieved.

'Of course you didn't but you do want to know who did it, don't you?' Tansy said soothingly.

''Course I do,' Sal said. 'We all do. It comes to something when a girl can't take a walk without getting her head stove in!'

'Did Fanny say anything about going out anywhere while she was having her supper?' Tansy asked.

Sal shook her head.

'She came into the pie-shop at about half past eight,' she said slowly. 'Sat next to me, ate her pie, drank a cup of tea, went out around nine o'clock.'

'She didn't tell you where she was going?'

Sal shook her head again. 'She just upped and left. I took it she was coming back here. We don't do a lot of talking at the end of the day. Too tired generally.'

'And you didn't see her again after she left the pie-shop?'

'No. We just thought she'd come back and gone to bed same as usual.'

'And this morning she wasn't at breakfast?'

'Sometimes she didn't bother with breakfast,' Sal said. 'She had a cup of coffee and a bit of toast mid-morning with Madam. But when she wasn't at the shop, Madam sent me round to find out if she'd overslept.'

'And?'

'Her door wasn't locked. That was a bit unusual that was. I mean anyone could've come in from the alley and climbed the stairs to any of the rooms. We always keep them locked.'

'So Fanny went somewhere last night and left her door unlocked?'

'Maybe someone snatched her up and carried her off.'

'Outside the pie-shop with people coming and going? It doesn't seem likely does it? Was her room like this when you came over this morning? You didn't look in any place?'

'I ain't a cutpurse!' Sal's hard little face had crimsoned angrily. 'We don't go rummaging about in other folks' things, Miss Clark!'

'Of course you don't under normal circumstances,' Tansy said hastily. 'I just thought that you might—'

'Well, I never did,' Sal said flatly. 'I went down to tell Madam she wasn't there and just as I was telling her the newsboy came past crying the murder. Madam got a paper and went to the morgue.'

'Not straightaway though?'

'She went to change into her black silk,' Sal said. 'And her new hat. Very elegant with a little veil trimmed with jet to match the bow on her bustle. She said it was right to show respect even if it wasn't Fanny lying in the morgue and in any case the body wasn't going anywhere. I went with her.'

'Did you go in?'

'I waited for her. She come out and said it was Fanny and I was to get a cab back and tell the girls and then she went back inside for a bit of a sit down,' Sal told her. 'I did what she wanted. The girls are all pretty upset.'

'Fanny was popular then? Nobody was jealous because she'd been promoted?'

'Not jealous enough to hit her over the head,' Sal said wryly. 'She was, well, there weren't no harm in Fanny if you know what I mean.'

'And she didn't take anything with her?'

'Only what she was wearing.' Sal stooped and tugged out a long cardboard box from under the bed. 'Mind you, I haven't looked in this.'

Under the cardboard lid clean bodices and pantaloons, a laced corset, two petticoats and three pairs of stockings were folded neatly with a few handkerchiefs and two night-dresses.

'No letters?' Tansy asked.

'She never wrote any. Never got any either.'

'There's writing-paper there.'

Tansy indicated a cheap block of paper and a couple of pencils at the bottom of the box.

'So there is!' Sal picked up the pad, turned it over and handed it to Tansy. 'I ain't seen that before.'

There were faint indentations on the top sheet as if someone had pressed fairly hard with a lead-pencil on a page above it. A minute roughness at the top of the pad showed where a page had been carefully torn off.

'Better put it back.'

Tansy surrendered it and stood musing as Sal closed the lid and pushed the box under the bed again.

'What I don't figure out,' Sal said, straightening up, 'is what she was doing at Kew. Just outside the gardens on a bench the newspaper said.'

'Mrs Mainwaring doesn't take any of you on trips or outings?'

'She employs us. She ain't our nursemaid,' Sal said.

'Perhaps she went to meet somebody?'

'She might have done,' Sal said doubtfully. 'She might have gone to Buckingham Palace and sat on the throne there. She might have done anything for all that I know. Kept herself very close did Fanny.'

'But she told you her father had beaten her.'

'When he was in drink. Right at the start when she first came to work for Madam she told us she'd run off after her mam died. But she never wrote home or let him know where she was.'

It was possible, Tansy thought, that a drunken father in a rage might've discovered his daughter's whereabouts and come after her, but it seemed highly unlikely that he would have lured her out to Kew and actually killed her, and even more unlikely that Fanny would have agreed to go.

She stared round the small, bleak room, trying to imagine what it must be like to sleep in such a place, to keep all one's belongings in such a small space, to sit day after day designing, stitching and selling hats for fashionable ladies. Yet Mrs Mainwaring was clearly a better employer than many.

'She read her Bible every day,' Sal volunteered. 'Not that it did her much good in the end but she took religion serious like.'

The Bible was next to Queen Victoria's bust. Tansy picked it up from the shelf and opened it. On the flyleaf, printed neatly, was the name Frances Mair Jones. The columns of small print were in a foreign language – Welsh, she presumed. Flicking through the pages she saw they were well thumbed with here and there the corner of a page turned down. Fanny had clearly made good use of her holy book.

Something fluttered down from between two pages and she caught it before it reached the carpet, guessing what it would be before she read the neatly snipped cutting: 'Consult Valentine who will give advice. . . .' It was dated three months previously.

'What's that then?' Sal demanded.

'A cutting from a newspaper. Have you seen it before?'

'No.' Sal scanned it briefly and handed it back. 'I don't read much anyway and when I do it's a nice romance from the Circulating Library. Who's this Valentine then?'

'That's what my father would like to know.'

Tansy returned the clipping to the Bible and put the book back on the shelf.

'How come your father don't come round asking questions himself?' Sal said.

'Some years ago he was crippled by a bullet in his spine when he was investigating the Flower Street gang. Now he does the thinking and I do the walking.'

'Official?'

'Not precisely. He is retired.'

'Makes no matter to me,' Sal shrugged. 'I'm not over keen on the busies anyway. Is there anything else you want because I ought to be getting back to the shop. Trade don't stop because someone died.'

'I can't think of anything else,' Tansy said. 'You've been very patient.'

She stepped onto the landing and took a last look at the room. The previous night Fanny Jones had come here after work, changed into her grey dress and jacket and the blue hat and gone out again to have a quick bite of supper. And she'd left the door unlocked, which could mean either that she wasn't intending to return which wasn't likely since she'd left everything including her beloved Bible behind, or she had had something on her mind so weighty or exciting that she had forgotten. Of the two, Tansy preferred the second option.

They descended the narrow staircase between the unpainted and dingy walls.

'Would any of the other girls know anything more?' she enquired as they reached the street.

'Not very likely,' Sal said. 'I was the only one she was anything like friendly with, on account of us sharing a room when she first come. She was a bit of a mouse was Fanny.'

'It was good of you to let me look round.' Tansy took some coins from her purse and pressed them into a not unwilling hand. 'One last thing. Fanny was found with a bright pink ribbon tied round her hat. Would she have been likely to do that?'

'That makes no sense,' Sal said vigorously. 'I couldn't credit it when I heard it from Mrs M. She was a Methodist was Fanny. Methodists don't never wear bright colours.'

'No, of course they don't. Thank you, Sal.'

Avoiding the eye of the policeman still outside the shop she retraced her steps along the street, a thoughtful frown on her face.

THREE

Laurence leaned back in his chair and sipped the brandy that Finn had just poured.

'Two young working girls,' he said thoughtfully. 'Quiet, respectable, not overly attractive, killed in each case by a blow to the head while they sat on a bench in the middle of the night. One outside a library, the other three months later outside Kew Gardens. Both wearing bright pink ribbons.'

'So there is a definite link between the two murders?'

Tansy, having enjoyed a light but tasty lunch, set down her coffee cup.

'It seems likely,' her father said cautiously.

'The Valentine advertisement?'

'Could be a sheer coincidence but – what is it, Finn?'

'Mr Cartwright to see you,' Finn announced. 'Would you fancy a brandy, sir?'

'Just a coffee if there's any left.'

Frank, entering, brought with him a tang of the world beyond the book-lined room. His thick, fair hair was slightly ruffled, his blue eyes had a hunter's gleam.

'Sit yourself down, Frank.' Laurence nodded towards a chair. 'You've been a stranger for too long.'

'Up in Scotland penning a series on Balmoral. How did you get on, Tansy?' Taking the chair and accepting the coffee he glanced at her enquiringly.

'You first,' she said.

'Well, I persuaded Mrs Mainwaring to have a spot of lunch with me,' Frank said. 'That lady never uses one word where three will do. In the end she hadn't much of value to tell me. Frances Jones was shy, hard-working, skilful with a needle and quiet. Went to chapel on Sundays and hadn't any gentlemen friends.'

'I talked to a girl called Sal Finnigan,' Tansy told him. 'Frances – she was known as Fanny by the way – had a room to herself in a house that Mrs Mainwaring apparently rents from a male friend. It's been converted into separate apartments all opening off a communal staircase.'

'And you saw the room?' Frank looked slightly surprised. 'Weren't the police there?'

'There was a constable outside the shop but the room hadn't been examined so—'

'Trust Jarrold to leave loopholes,' Laurence said with satisfaction.

'By now he'll probably have got around to looking there,' Tansy said. 'Anyway it's a very ordinary little room, just a place to sleep and keep a few belongings in, that's all. According to Sal Finnigan nothing was missing. But there was a block of writing-paper there with indentations on the top sheet as if she'd written a letter on the sheet above, and a Bible with the Valentine cutting in it.'

'The what cutting?' Frank asked.

'There was this advertisement next to the report on the death of Ellie Watson,' Laurence told him, producing the folded newspaper. 'It'd been in for about a week. It didn't appear after that until about five days ago.'

'Coincidence?'

'It struck Pa as odd,' Tansy said. 'Then I found the cutting in Fanny Jones's Bible.'

'Was any cutting found on Ellie Watson?'

'If there was then it wasn't reported,' Laurence said.

'Fanny cut the advertisement out of the edition in which the first murder was reported,' Tansy said. 'It didn't appear again until five days ago.'

'So she kept the cutting in her Bible for three months? She might've just used it as a bookmark.'

'And perhaps she answered it,' Tansy said. 'If she was very shy she might have taken three months in which to pluck up her courage. There's a box number at the end. Do people who insert advertisements go down to the newspaper office to collect their replies? If so then someone must've noticed him.'

'Not necessarily.' Frank shook his head. 'Letters addressed to Valentine would be put in the pigeon-hole corresponding to the box number. He could slip in and collect them without attracting any attention at all.'

'Advertisements generally go in for a week at a time, don't they?' Laurence finished his brandy.

'And they don't have to be personally placed,' Frank said. 'One can simply write a note and hand it in at the reception desk. No need to give a name. Unless this Valentine is of particularly striking appearance nobody will have remembered him. Look, I can make a few enquiries if you like but I don't anticipate any great results.'

'Couldn't we go and sit in the office and wait for someone to come in and collect whatever's in the pigeon-hole?'

'If there are any letters for him and he's the killer it's unlikely he'll pick them up over the next few days,' Laurence said. 'The killing of this unfortunate girl will have satisfied him for the moment.'

'To kill for no reason.' Tansy shivered, feeling the darkness of a world unknown invade the warm, bright room.

'Oh, he'll have some motive that makes sense to him,' Laurence said. 'Not that we must confine ourselves to the advertisement. But Finn and I did some checking this morning and there were no similar murders before the Valentine message appeared and none in the three months since until now.'

'When it was in the newspaper again,' Tansy said. 'Pa, there must be some connection!'

'I'll go down to the office and hang around for an hour or two anyway,' Frank rose.

'You're not on an assignment at the moment, Frank?' Laurence asked.

'At present I'm a picker-up of unconsidered trifles,' Frank said. 'Will I see you soon, Tansy?'

'When you're next in the vicinity of Chelsea come in and pay your respects to Mrs Timothy,' she invited.

'Your dragon of a housekeeper? I'll do that. Hopefully I'll see you later, Laurence. Thanks for the coffee, Finn.'

Coat over his shoulder he was through the door and running lightly down the stairs before Finn could move to open it.

'What that young fellow needs is a good, steady wife,' Laurence said.

'He's an old friend so you may wipe that hopeful look from your face,' his daughter said severely.

'It's a long time since Geoffrey died.'

'And even longer since mother went. Do I nag you to take a wife?'

'My situation is quite different.' He looked up at her with affection. 'You're a handsome woman, Tansy.'

'My nose is too long and my mouth too wide; my hair's red and I'm tall. Only a father would call that handsome.'

'Geoffrey thought you beautiful.'

'There was only one Geoffrey,' Tansy said shortly. 'Get some rest.'

'He does fret about you sometimes,' Finn confided as he accompanied her to the front door and hailed a dawdling cab.

'He reared me to be independent,' Tansy said. 'He can't start grumbling about it now. 'Bye, Finn.'

It would do her father good, she reflected as she was borne towards Chelsea, to have something else to occupy his mind other than her own prospects. In that sense, this second killing, though unlucky for the poor girl, was a godsend for him, even though his involvement would necessarily be unofficial since Inspector Jarrold was jealous of his own position.

Tilde, clad in a neat, print dress with a white mob-cab confining her dark curls was polishing the stair-rails when Tansy let herself in.

'Miss Clark!' She left off humming a tune and bobbed a curtsy. 'Have you had a nice morning?'

'A busy one.' Tansy divested herself of hat, jacket and gloves. 'Where's Mrs Timothy?'

'Her back was that chronic she had to go and lie down,' Tilde said.

'Come into the sitting-room for a moment.'

Tilde obediently put down the beeswax and the cloth and followed.

'Has Mrs Timothy told you what wages you're to receive?'

Tansy sat at the flat-topped desk in the corner.

'Yes, Miss Clark. Thank you,' Tilde said.

'And you may have a half-day off every week in addition to Sunday morning. Do you attend church?'

'Not since my mother died,' Tilde confessed. 'I fell out with God because he didn't spare her.'

'Did you indeed?' Tansy repressed a smile. 'Well, Mrs Timothy would find it eased her mind, I'm sure, if you attended some place of worship. On your half-day you can meet your friends.'

'I haven't got any friends,' Tilde said mournfully.

'Surely you must have some?' Tansy protested. 'You and your mother lived together – where?'

'In Wilborough Street. Mother rented two rooms there. We kept ourselves to ourselves,' Tilde said proudly.

'How did – do you know how she earned a living?' Tansy asked, feeling slightly awkward as the inevitable question entered her head.

'She embroidered shawls and scarves and sold them,' Tilde said. 'I can do a bit of fancywork but nothing like hers. She got quite good prices for them too but when she became sick it became harder for her. I'm ever so grateful to you, Miss Clark, because if I'd stayed on that bench I might've been murdered like that poor girl in the newspaper this morning. I keep wondering who she was.'

'Her name was Frances Jones,' Tansy said. 'She worked in a milliner's off Oxford Street – Tilde, what's wrong?'

Tilde's delicate little face had whitened so abruptly that for a moment she looked as if she might faint.

'Would that be Mrs Mainwaring's establishment?' she asked faintly.

'Yes. Do you know it? For heaven's sake sit down for a minute. Shall I get you a glass of water?'

Tilde, sinking into the chair from which Tansy had just risen, shook her head and took several deep breaths.

'I'm ever so sorry,' she whispered. 'It's just that Mother sold some of her work to Mrs Mainwaring – embroidered scarves and hat-trimmings, and got very fair prices for them. After she died I tried to get a place there but Mrs Mainwaring wasn't taking on any more girls at that time. If she'd given me a position I might be murdered right now!'

'Well, it wasn't you,' Tansy said sensibly. 'Did you know any of the girls who work for Mrs Mainwaring?'

Tilde shook her head. 'Mother took the pretty things she made to the shop herself,' she said. 'I only went there the once after Mother died. Mrs Mainwaring met me at the shop-door herself. She was very nice but she couldn't offer me any work. Oh, I've gone all over cold, truly I have.'

'Why don't you go and make yourself a nice cup of tea?' Tansy urged. 'Mrs Timothy will be up and about soon and she'll appreciate one too, I'm sure. Off you go.'

'Do you want one, Miss Clark?' Rising, Tilde dabbed at her eyes.

'No, not now. Off you go.'

Tilde went, still stammering gratitude at her fortunate escape.

Tansy sat down again, seized a sheet of paper and a pencil and began to jot down a few notes. Laurence had often spoken of the importance of making notes as quickly as possible.

'The memory can play tricks no matter how carefully we listen and observe. It really is vital to get the known facts down as soon as possible.'

She wrote the name 'Ellie Watson' – short for Elizabeth? It probably didn't much matter. She hesitated, then wrote on: 'Aged seventeen. Worked in match factory. Frances Jones. Aged seventeen. Worked at Mrs Mainwaring's. Tilde Miles. Aged seventeen. Worked in match factory and as tweeny in the Edge household. Her mother sold scarves to Mrs Mainwaring.'

Clearly there was more than one connection here.

Underneath she wrote: 'Valentine advertisement appeared in evening newspaper for a week up to death of Ellie Watson. Same advertisement appeared again for five days before the death of Frances Jones. The relevant cutting was in her Bible.'

She read through what she had written; put the paper away in the desk. Somehow it was impossible to settle to anything. She went upstairs and changed into a simple, brown skirt and creamy blouse, the brown bolero neatly trimmed with brown ricrac, and perched a small straw hat on her hair.

Mrs Timothy had risen from her nap and appeared at the door of her room with an apology on her lips.

'Miss Tansy, you ought to have woken me! The truth is that my back was complaining something chronic so I was constrained to lie flat.'

'Very sensible, Mrs Timothy,' Tansy approved. 'Now that Tilde is here you must make full use of her services. Oh, I may not be home for dinner this evening but if I am then salad and some cold cuts would suit me very well.'

'Tilde seems to be shaping up quite nicely,' Mrs Timothy allowed, 'though she has an unfortunate habit of quoting poetry too often. Have a pleasant afternoon, Miss Tansy.'

Hailing a cab to Fleet Street Tansy allowed herself a few moments' pleasant reflection on the anticipation of seeing Frank Cartwright again. In the weeks of his absence she'd hardly thought about him at all, but his return had brought something vital back into the days. It was, of course, because he could speedily jolly her father out of his occasional depressions and had nothing to do with any intrinsic quality that appealed to her personally.

Fleet Street was one of her favourite thoroughfares. She never went there without marvelling at the bustle, the sense of purpose, the motley of editors and reporters and writers on the verge of success.

Dismissing the cab, she went on foot in the direction of the relevant office and spotted Frank at once, occupying the end of a bench in the outer-office.

He rose as she entered, his voice lowered slightly after the initial greeting.

'There are a couple of letters in the pigeon-hole for Valentine,' he said. 'I had a few words with the desk-clerk. Anyone coming to put in an advertisement is given a box number and a key with which to open the box. He can't recall what Valentine looked like. Indeed he may not even have been on duty when the item was paid for.'

'And nobody's called in for the letters?'

'Not since I've been here.'

'I thought I might relieve you if you want to take a break,' she said.

'I'll go and earn an honest living for an hour and then treat you to tea,' he promised.

'With cream-buns?' She glanced at him teasingly.

'Lord, yes! The first time we took tea together I was so overawed at whose daughter you were that I wolfed down three cream-buns to avoid having to talk.'

'Go and earn your living,' Tansy said, taking his place on the bench and opening the newspaper he handed her.

There wasn't much to hold the attention. The Russians and the Japanese were making threatening noises at each other again; questions as to how long Her Majesty intended to bury herself at Balmoral were being mooted. There was nothing further about any murder. She folded the newspaper so as to partly conceal her face and glanced round the office with its broad counter at one end, its rows of numbered pigeon-holes occupying one whole wall, the double doors through which a variety of men, some with shades over their brows, others with shirt-sleeves secured by black bands, others in top-hats and formal attire came and went. Among them was the occasional young woman, hair swept severely back, whalebone holding her collar stiff and no more than an apology for a bustle. Laurence had commented on the fact that, increasingly, females were being employed as secretaries.

'I approve. If a girl's had an education and wants or needs to work she can do worse than take dictation,' he'd said.

Tansy smiled at the recollection and hastily switched off the smile as a messenger-boy, pill-box jauntily on the side of his head, favoured her with a wink. Being noticed was the last thing she needed at this moment.

The elderly man who had occupied the space next to the one she sat on had taken out his watch, put it to his ear and risen. His place was taken immediately by a young man who removed his hat and placed it on the bench between them, darting her a swift, apologetic look before taking from his pocket a small sketch-pad on which he began to doodle rapidly.

For a moment Tansy wondered if he was sketching her, but a glance showed her that his hand, tanned by some sun fiercer than that which rose in London skies, was depicting a series of meaningless circles and interlinked crosses.

Obviously he had leisure to spend doing very little. Yet he seemed not to be at leisure. He constantly shifted his position, crossing now one leg, then the other over its neighbouring knee. He looked round at every footfall and then sketched more furiously and aimlessly than before.

His profile, judged out of the corner of her eye, was classically handsome, his dark hair with a definite tendency to wave, his face as tanned as his hands, his suit conventional and slightly shabby. Certainly he was difficult to place in any category.

He tore off the top sheet of the pad, crumpled it into a ball and thrust it into his pocket before renewing his doodling. His fingers flew as if fuelled by some nervous energy, and another sidelong look showed Tansy a fragile sketch of a female face. Assuredly not her own, she thought with a twinge of amusement, for in the few lines delineated the nose was tip-tilted and the eyes more slanting than her own.

He smoothed out the drawing, stared at it, then put the pad back into his pocket and stood up, reaching for his hat. Tansy riveted her gaze to her newspaper.

The young man stood for a moment as if undecided, then turned and went with his quick, nervous step to the pigeon-hole where the letters to Valentine lay behind the glass partition. Bending, he scrutinized them closely and then straightened up again, the fingers of one hand beating a rapid tattoo on his pocket.

From beneath her eyelashes Tansy saw him turn, glance again in her direction, then leave the office, his slim, tallish figure quickly swallowed up in the general crowd. She was on her feet in an instant, leaving the newspaper on the bench and making her own way into the street.

For a moment she feared she had lost him, but the passing of two dray-horses across the street had slowed his progress and with his hat still in his hand the waving black hair, lifted now by the breeze, made him a fairly conspicuous target for continued surveillance.

Tansy accordingly followed him, remembering the games that she and her father had played when on off-duty afternoons he had taken her walking in the streets of the city she longed to explore.

'If you're following a suspect then you don't need to disguise yourself,' Laurence had instructed. 'A pair of spectacles or a different hat is the most I ever use, even when the suspect knows me by sight.'

As the young man didn't know her at all then no disguise was necessary, Tansy thought.

The horses had passed and the street was clear again. Tansy pulled her mind back to the task in hand and followed as the stranger crossed the road and strode on, not looking back or hesitating.

He turned into a side-alley so abruptly that Tansy, who had allowed a less than discreet distance to elapse between them, was brought up short at the corner, unsure whether to wait or follow immediately.

She decided on immediately and cautiously rounded the corner under the overhanging sign of a tavern where several young gentlemen with their hats on the backs of their heads and loud voices were teasing the barmaid. A glance through the open door assured her that Frank wasn't among them, and she walked on, keeping the slim, dark-haired figure just in sight.

There were fewer people here, a fellow sweeping up rubbish and shovelling it into a barrow, a tired-looking woman with a small child clinging to her skirt. Underneath her feet the flat paving-stones yielded to cobbles and the pavement disappeared.

The young man turned another corner. Tansy counted five slowly under her breath and turned the corner herself into a short, narrow alley which brought her into a mews with a patch of grass and a wooden fence at its end. At each side eighteenth-century buildings, once elegant but now increasingly dilapidated hemmed her in and muffled the noises from the surrounding city. Her own footsteps clacking on the stone sounded disproportionately loud.

The ground floors of many of the buildings were still used for their original purpose of stabling horses. As she went by, several large, patient heads looked out over the doors of their stalls. There was no sign of the quarry she was following. Obviously he had entered one of the buildings, mounting one of the staircases that twisted up out of the stables below.

Tansy paused and looked up at the windows that overlooked the mews. There were curtains at some of them, pieces of grubby lace tacked up at others. Window-sills and doors were largely in grave need of a coat of paint. One or two were window-boxed, the flowers in them a brave protest against the prevailing shabbiness.

A horse in a nearby stall whinnied softly as if it craved company.

'Hello, boy.'

Tansy crossed to the stall to rub the velvety nose thrust towards her and produced from her pocket a short stick of twisted sugar-candy, it being her invariable but seldom-admitted habit to chew on one in times of extreme stress. The horse accepted the offering with equine grace at the precise moment she heard a footfall behind her and something hard was jabbed into her back.

A voice in her ear, soft and with a slight brogue flavouring it, said, 'Walk ahead of me if you please. Up the stairs.'

Her first instinct was to cry out but a further warning jab silenced her intention. She bit her lip in frustration, remembering too clearly her father's instructions when they had played the game.

'When you're following somebody remember they may double back and come up behind you, or have a confederate waiting, so always protect your back.'

She recalled too her mother's laughing protest.

'Honestly, Laurence, anyone might imagine that Tansy was a lad and you were training him for the force!'

'Up,' the soft voice repeated.

Tansy went up, lifting her skirt as she mounted the narrow stairs that spiralled up out of one dim corner, inwardly kicking herself for not having provided herself with some means of defence. Not that she could have used a weapon anyway she reflected wryly. She had learned years before to fire a pistol at the heart of a target, Laurence taking pride in her quick and accurate eye, but she had never actually carried a pistol in her life.

At the top of the staircase was a door, unpainted.

'It's unlocked,' the stranger said.

Trying not to imagine what grisly end might be imminent, Tansy opened the door.

Ahead of her a low-ceilinged chamber stretched beneath a narrow skylight through which the sun poured its afternoon rays. The wooden floor was bare but well swept, the glass in the windows uncracked and clear. She looked round at the few pieces of furniture, the easel set up in the best light, the shelves on which small pots of paint, bottles of turpentine and a variety of brushes jostled for position.

The pressure in the small of her back was withdrawn and she swung round to face the man, her voice pitched higher than usual as she tried to control her nervous reaction.

'So that wasn't a gun in my back!'

'The ferrule of my walking-stick. Do sit down.'

He indicated a chair and she sat down cautiously, raising her eyes to a fine-boned, handsome face, the eyes dark beneath winged brows.

'What on earth do you imagine you're doing?' she demanded, some of the panic draining out of her.

'My turn first. Why are you following me?'

'How did you know?' Tansy retorted, fear becoming a sickening sense of disappointment. Laurence, she thought, would have been scornful of her amateurish efforts.

'I was on the North-West Frontier until only a few weeks ago. One learns there to sense when one is being followed.'

India? That accounted for the tanned complexion.

Tansy said uncertainly, 'You don't look like an army man.'

'I'm not. I went out as a non-combatant to illustrate aspects of frontier life for the War Office.'

'Why should I believe that?' Tansy sat straighter and stared at him.

'Because it would be a foolish thing to tell lies about when it can be easily checked out, now wouldn't it?' he said.

Tansy found herself breathing rather more easily, the young man's words having implied that she would survive to make enquiries.

'Who are you?' she asked.

'My name's Patrick Denny. You?'

'Miss Clark. Miss Tansy Clark. You went over to look at the letters in the pigeon-hole for Valentine. Are you. . . ?'

'If I were Valentine I'd've had the key with which to open the box and actually read the letters. I'm looking for Valentine.'

'So am I.' Tansy felt herself relaxing more. 'Look, wouldn't it make good sense if we joined forces? Exchanged information?'

'The matter concerns my sister,' he said.

'Your sister?'

'Mary Denny.' He took a few steps up and down as if seeking to marshal his thoughts, then sat down abruptly on a stool. 'We're both from Ireland as you've probably guessed. Mary is ten years my junior – not yet eighteen. Since our parents died I've tried to supply the lack of them but she's a headstrong girl and it's not easy. We had a small farm in County Wicklow but the crops failed and the cows got murrein and in the end we were forced to sell at a loss. The truth is that I'm no farmer. Art has always been my passion. Anyway, we decided to try our luck in London and came over with the intention of setting up house and—'

'Here?'

'The neighbourhood's run-down but the rent's cheap and Mary has a fine way with making a place clean and homely. I've contrived to support us both in decent comfort by selling my illustrations to the magazines and I've sold a couple of paintings too. Then I had a great stroke of luck.'

'The War Office commission?'

'Someone at Whitehall liked some of my illustrations and offered me the job. It meant my leaving Mary in London for several months and I wasn't happy about that, but we talked it over and agreed that I should take the commission. I sent money home regularly for Mary and I wrote to her often.'

'Did she write back?'

'Not very often, but Mary never relished writing letters anyway and the overseas-mail deliveries can take weeks and then arrive in the wrong port.'

'Or when you were absent?'

'Surely. I went on hill treks, met some of the tribesmen – anyway back in February I received a letter she'd sent out in December.'

'Yes?' Tansy encouraged. Her terror had vanished. There was no mistaking the sincerity with which the young man spoke.

'Read it.' He took it out of his pocket and gave it to her, before resuming his restless walk up and down the long room.

The letter was written in a small neat hand. Tansy read it with interest.

Dear Pat,

I don't know exactly when this letter will reach you. You mustn't dream of coming home early on my account because if the gentlemen at the War Office approve your illustrations then you may be on the way to becoming a famous artist. Of course I do miss you very much and long to see you again, but you must be quite easy in your mind about my welfare. I have been making myself a new dress to wear at the Valentine Ball. I am to be escorted there by a splendid new friend of whom I'm sure you will approve when you meet. I shall write again very soon and give you more news. I look forward very much to hearing from you and learning something of your adventures in a foreign land.

Your affectionate sister,

Mary

'I didn't receive any letters after that,' Patrick Denny said, taking the sheet of paper from her and folding it back into its creases.

'Not since December? You must have been worried!'

'No, not really.' He put the letter away and recommenced his pacing.

'But surely – your sister was alone in a strange city.'

'Not so strange to her,' he said, defensively. 'We had been here for almost a year when the War Office commission came, so she was quite capable of managing the shopping and the cooking and she's a resourceful girl. Anyway, this was an opportunity I'd've been mad to reject. Mary urged me to take it. And letters did take a long time to reach me. I received that one in February.'

'By which time the Valentine Ball would have been held.'

'Are you familiar with the event then?' he asked eagerly.

'I never heard of it,' Tansy said frankly.

'I'd been up in the hill country,' Patrick said. 'If you could see some of the wonderful native faces that I sketched—'

'When did you come back to England?' Tansy broke in.

'About three weeks ago. I booked passage on a clipper and brought my sketches and paintings with me. They were accepted and greatly praised.'

'And your sister?' Tansy, who was growing a little tired of hearing about Patrick's drawings rose and went over to the narrow window below the skylight, tapping her fingers on the sill.

'Mary wasn't here,' he said simply.

'So what did you do? Surely you didn't just sit back and wait for her to return.'

'No, of course not! I waited for a day or so because I hadn't sent word of the exact day of my landing – didn't know it myself. She might have gone to stay with a friend.'

'You'd made friends then?'

'Not many,' he admitted. 'The city isn't a giving place, is it? We kept ourselves to ourselves, but after I went to India Mary could have made some friends on her own account. After all, she had obviously met someone who was going to escort her to the ball.'

'Were any of her clothes missing? Did you check?'

'I'd been gone since last October. She might have purchased new clothes and taken those with her. A few things were missing. Some toilet accessories and her brush and comb and two nightgowns. Slippers too, I think. Look, Mary's my sister! How many brothers know exactly what their sisters wear?'

'I haven't any brothers,' Tansy said shortly.

It seemed to her that his attitude had been casual to say the least. It was one thing for her father to encourage her to lead an independent life – she had Mrs Timothy and now Tilde for chaperonage and help, and Laurence was only a cab-drive away. And she herself was a woman of thirty, whereas Mary Denny was not yet eighteen.

'Everything was neat and clean,' Patrick was continuing. 'Mary always took pride in keeping the place nice.'

'Did anyone see her leave?'

'We haven't really become well acquainted with the neighbours,' he told her. 'Some of these apartments are empty, others occupied by transients – foreigners many of them. The rent's cheap which is partly why we took the place. I did make a few enquiries but nobody remembered.'

'Have you reported her missing to the police?'

'I'd not shame her by doing any such thing!' His face flushed angrily. 'Now wouldn't I be looking the fool if I went running to the police and she turned up a few days later saying she'd been on a trip somewhere with a couple of new friends?'

'Were you not in the least bit concerned about her having a male friend who was going to take her dancing?'

'Now hasn't my sister the right to have a gentleman friend?' he said. 'She's not the flighty sort and if she found someone to her taste then I for one would be glad of it.'

'Have you made enquiries about the Valentine Ball?'

'There are several Valentine events going on at that season. Some private affairs that are reported in the *Court Circular* – not that I think Mary likely to have been invited to such a function. Public balls, some children's parties funded by various charities.'

'So she is more likely to have bought a ticket for one of the public events?'

'Surely her new friend will have bought the tickets?' he said.

'Probably.' Tansy frowned, her hand diving automatically into her pocket until she recalled that the pony had enjoyed the last of her sugar-candy. 'He would not be so entirely new a friend since she had formed an acquaintance with him by December, only two months after you left.'

'She wrote me two brief letters before Christmas. There was nothing in them about any new friend.'

'Would she accept an invitation to a ball from someone she hardly knew?'

'She would not,' he returned briskly. 'Mary has never shown much interest in young men until now. She generally mocks them and calls them great loons to be sighing after a petticoat.'

'Then this was someone very special,' Tansy said broodingly.

'Doesn't she say that now in the letter? A "splendid new friend". He must be very splendid for Mary to give him the time of day.'

'You still haven't explained,' Tansy said, stopping in her own slow pacing to swing on her heel and face him, 'exactly what you were doing in the newspaper office.'

'Didn't I say?' He shook his head slightly. 'After a few days with herself remaining invisible I looked through her drawers. That's not something I'd usually do for we respected each other's privacy but I felt justified under the circumstances.'

'Do get on with it,' Tansy said.

'There was a cutting from the newspaper under some of her clothes – I wasn't sure if it was anything to do with anything. Mary often cuts out bits and pieces that she thinks might amuse me when we sit together in the evening. I can show you.'

He opened an inner door into a small room with a single bed and a chest of drawers. It was in size and basic decoration uncannily like the room where Frances Jones had slept, but there the resemblance ended. Mary Denny had sewn pretty green curtains and hung them at the window and made a cover for the bed to match. A rug woven in shades of green and blue covered the floor and a portrait of two people, man and woman, stood on the chest of drawers, the two faces gazing out solemnly.

'My parents,' Patrick said. 'I painted them both as a present one year and the next they were both gone – typhoid. There was an outbreak of the fever in our village. That's another reason why I wished to bring Mary away. Typhoid can linger and break out again.'

'Your mother was pretty.'

Tansy looked at the heart-shaped face with the puffs of dark, curly hair round it and the wide eyes.

'Mary takes after her,' Patrick said. 'Surely every lad was eyeing her up and down from when she was fourteen, but Mary just laughed at them.'

Tansy suddenly found herself wishing fervently that she could be sure that Mary Denny was still laughing.

'The cutting's here.' He lifted a pile of handkerchiefs and showed her.

'No date on it,' Tansy said.

'Would that be important?'

'It might be. When did you start going down to the newspaper office?'

'The advertisement appeared in the newspaper again about a week ago. I thought it wouldn't do any harm to go down and see who came to pick up the letters. I was going to give it a week and then, if I heard nothing, I suppose I ought to tell the police though Mary would hate it.'

'What's this?'

Tansy had plucked something from the drawer and held it up.

'It's a ribbon,' he said in some bewilderment. 'Surely a lady'd know that!'

'A bright pink ribbon,' Tansy said. 'Did Mary ever wear bright pink?'

'She wore green a lot. I can't remember whether or not she wore pink. Now and then perhaps, but not that shade. Why? Is it important?'

FOUR

'It could be,' Tansy said slowly.

Patrick Denny shot her a sudden keen look. 'I've explained what I was doing down in the newspaper office,' he said, 'but all I know about you is your name. What interest do you have in my sister? Why did you follow me?'

'My father is a retired police inspector,' Tansy said. 'He retired early due to injury but he still takes a keen interest in crime – puzzling crimes that is, not uninteresting robberies.'

'Mary hasn't committed any crime!' There was indignation in the soft Irish voice.

'I'm sure that she hasn't, but three months ago a young girl called Ellie Watson was murdered—'

'Murdered!'

'She was hit on the back of the head while sitting on a bench outside the Kensington Library in the middle of the night—'

'Surely that's an odd place for a—'

'She was a respectable girl who made matches for a living. I do wish you would stop interrupting! She had a pink ribbon in her hat though her hair was ginger. It was one of those queer, out of place things that always engage my father's attention.'

'But surely another poor girl's just been found.'

'Frances Jones. She was a milliner's assistant. She was found in Kew, again with a bright pink ribbon tied round her hat. The advertisement concerning Valentine was found in a Bible in her room. It was the only lead we had so we decided to wait around in the newspaper office in the hope someone might turn up who had a key to the pigeon-hole.'

She wondered uneasily how she would explain her knowledge of the cutting in the Bible but Patrick had other things on his mind.

'We?' he queried. 'Your da and you?'

'My father's confined to a wheelchair. No, I have a friend who's a news-reporter. Frank Cartwright. He's interested in the two cases as well.'

'Are you trying to tell me that my sister might've been. . . ?' He paused and took several turns about the long room.

'She had the Valentine cutting in her drawer,' Tansy reminded him. 'You went down to the office yourself.'

'What about the first girl? Ellie. . . ?'

'Ellie Watson. The advertisement had been in the paper for about a week before her death was reported. It didn't appear again until a week ago and now that Fanny Jones has been killed I'd wager it won't appear again for a while.'

'All this could be coincidence, nothing to do with the two killings. It isn't what your da would call evidence, now is it?'

'No, but the indications are there,' Tansy said. 'Both girls were seventeen, respectable working girls. Fanny Jones was a Methodist and would never have worn bright pink. Both were found lying on the ground near benches on which they'd evidently been seated. Your sister—'

'Mary might be seventeen but she isn't a poor working girl!' He gave her a hard stare. 'I've provided for us both ever since we came into England. I arranged for money to be transferred into her bank account while I was in India.'

'Has she drawn any of it from the bank?'

'I checked that,' he said. 'She drew a fairly large sum out in February – fifty pounds.'

'And nothing since?'

'Mary isn't a spendthrift. The money would've lasted her a good while.'

Tansy was silent. It hadn't apparently occurred to him that a young woman carrying fifty pounds in her purse was unlikely to remain unmolested in this somewhat seedy neighbourhood.

'Have you considered advertising for her?'

'Mary isn't a dog or a lost piece of property!'

'A discreetly worded notice inviting her to communicate with you would do no harm,' Tansy argued. 'I also think you ought to inform the police. Since your sister's so young I assume you're her guardian?'

'We're a quiet couple.' He had reached the window and stared through it with a furrowed brow. 'Miss Clark, perhaps we don't have much money but we do have our pride. Since you and your da are—'

'We have no official standing whatsoever,' Tansy broke in. 'My father gets depressed sometimes since he can no longer get about as he used to do. He finds interest in studying the occasional police inquiry and from time to time his former colleagues do consult him, but we could guarantee nothing.'

'Perhaps for a few days we could delay informing the authorities? She does seem to have left of her own accord.'

'Can you tell me exactly what is missing?' Tansy asked briskly. 'You say she took some toilet articles and a couple of night-gowns?'

'She kept her toothbrush and flannel in a waterproof bag tied with a draw-string,' he said. 'Her two brushes and her comb are missing too, and a little china box for hairpins. Some – nether-garments. . . .'

'If you mean chemises, drawers, corsets and petticoats, for heaven's sake say so,' Tansy said amused. 'This is eighteen seventy-one, you know, not the Middle Ages.'

'I'm not sure. There's a small carpet-bag missing – cream coloured with shamrocks printed on it. Her green day-dress isn't on the rail and neither is her shawl. The shawl's plaid.'

'It sounds as if she went away for a few days meaning to come back. Can you think of anywhere she might have gone?'

'Perhaps to the Valentine Ball?'

'Taking two night-gowns with her? I hardly think so. Is it possible she returned to Ireland? Have you still relatives there?'

'Some distant cousins. No, she was sometimes homesick but she knew that the best way of getting on in the world was to come to London, and if she'd chosen to go back she'd've written to tell me.'

'Such a letter might've arrived after you'd sailed for England. Would it be sent on?'

'Yes. Yes, I made arrangements before I returned, though only a letter from my sister was likely to arrive.'

'Was the door here locked when you returned?'

'Yes. We both had a key.'

'And the rent was paid up to date?'

'I paid six months' rent before I left.'

'Did you ever paint a portrait of your sister?'

'There are drawings. I never did a full painting. Mary never would sit still for long enough.'

'May I see them? Unless you have a photograph?'

It had been too much to hope for. Patrick shook his head and leaned to leaf through a series of sketches on the table.

'Photographs are expensive,' he said. 'These are all I have.'

These were two charcoal studies, one full face and one in profile. Tansy gazed at them in silence, noting the tip-tilted nose, the dark eyes with the upwards slant, the cloud of dark, curly hair round the heart-shaped face.

Even allowing for a brother's partiality Mary Denny was, or had been, a very pretty girl.

'I think we should go back to the newspaper office,' she said. 'Frank Cartwright will be there. I'm supposed to be taking tea with him. You can tell him about your sister.'

'Then you agree to help?'

'I think we should discuss the matter first,' Tansy said.

Being interested in a particular case in a purely academic way was not the same as becoming personally involved. Her father would not have tolerated the meddling of amateurs during his own career and Inspector Jarrold wasn't likely to tolerate them now.

'May I keep one of these?' She indicated the sketches.

'Yes. Yes, of course.' His mobile face was suddenly grave and quiet.

They went out, Patrick carefully locking up behind him. Tansy, descending the spiral staircase, enquired, 'You left it unlocked when you went out before.'

'Yes. I've rather made a habit of that since I came home,' he admitted. 'I keep thinking that Mary might arrive unexpectedly and have forgotten her key.'

And if anything dreadful had actually happened to Mary Denny someone else could easily have slipped in to remove any traces of a crime committed, she reflected.

'It would be wiser to lock the door in future,' she said carefully. 'I'm sure that – that when your sister returns she will have her key.'

'You're being very kind.' He spoke suddenly as they emerged into the alley. 'I really did suspect you of – I don't know exactly of what, but when I became aware of being followed – I must have frightened you a great deal.'

'Not beyond repair,' Tansy assured him. 'I'm just not accustomed to being held up at gunpoint, that's all.'

She would have liked to linger, to find out who lived in the surrounding buildings but she could hardly keep Frank waiting for ever. She therefore walked as swiftly as the cobbles would allow until they had reached the main street again, where a few minutes later they walked into the newspaper office and found Frank seated on the bench there and scribbling.

'Just making a few notes. When this is solved I might make it the first of a series of pieces on true crime – I don't think I know. . . ?' He had risen and was looking a question.

'Frank, this gentleman is Patrick Denny. His sister is missing, and he fears some connection with the other girls,' Tansy said. 'Mr Denny, Frank Cartwright is a journalist and a most useful ally. If you don't mind I'll leave the two of you to talk and go over to see Pa. He'll be anxious to know how matters are shaping.'

'Will I see you later, Tansy?'

Frank had put a faint emphasis on her Christian name as if to underline their being close friends.

'Come and have dinner with me tomorrow evening,' she said on impulse. 'You will give Mr Denny my address, Frank?'

'Yes, of course.' Frank bowed slightly. 'About this evening?'

'Give me the chance to talk with Pa by myself,' Tansy said. 'Tomorrow at eight then?'

'Thank you kindly, Miss Clark.' Patrick Denny was also bowing. 'When Mary returns she'll add her thanks to mine.'

Frank went with her to the door, his tone lowered as he asked,

'What the devil's going on? Why am I saddled with a complete stranger when you and I were going to have tea together?'

'Because I'm going to be busy seeking information elsewhere,' Tansy said, equally low. 'Take him to your club or something and find out as much as you can about him before you come to dinner tomorrow.'

'What about Valentine?'

'Nobody turned up?'

'Not a soul.'

'I think that Pa was right,' she said. 'Once a murder has been committed something is satisfied for a time in the murderer until the urge to kill begins to grow again. Anyway, you can't be in two places at once. I'll see you tomorrow.'

She turned away, glancing back to ensure that the two men were engaged in conversation before retracing her steps towards the mews.

The information that Patrick Denny had volunteered had sounded convincing but the sober truth was that he had proved nothing. She had only his word that he'd spent months in India on a commission for the War Office, only his word that Mary was his sister and that he'd left her alone in London. If the last was true then either he was a careless brother or Mary Denny had a strong, independent streak. Tansy suspected the latter but there was still no proof.

'Instinct can set you on the trail of a criminal but proof is needed to bring him to justice,' Laurence was fond of saying.

She reached the cobbled mews and paused, looking up at the surrounding windows. At one a curtain twitched slightly and was still. Next door but one to the building where the Dennys had their lodging. She went into the open stable area with the customary staircase leading up to the floors above and made her way up with some caution, the treads being worn and the rail broken in places.

At the top a door opened suddenly and the elderly woman framed in the gap said, 'You have come to tea, perhaps? I tell myself over and over that one day someone from the Old Country will come to tea. Please to come in.'

'I – thank you. Some tea will be very welcome,' Tansy said.

The room into which she was ushered was in size much like the room she had seen that the Dennys rented, but in every other respect it was a complete contrast. Somewhat bemused she looked round at the shawls and bedcovers pinned round the walls, the huge cushions scattered on the floor, the long table on which a multitude of bowls and dishes gleamed eerily in an atmosphere heavy with dust.

The woman who had admitted her was as curiously attired as the room was furnished, her head swathed in a kind of head-dress from which long veils floated over a black gown that had lost its sheen and would have given an unrelieved impression of shabbiness had it not been for the crimson and peacock-blue sashes wound round and round a thin but upright frame.

'Please to take a seat, boobla! I will make the tea,' the apparition said in a heavily accented voice that had once been musical but was now as rusty as her gown.

'Thank you.'

Somewhat at a loss Tansy looked round, spied two high-backed and rather handsome chairs set at a side-table and took one. The other was busily coaxing a low fire into a blaze, placing an already steaming kettle back on the hob and, still on her knees, diving beneath the table to emerge with several pots of conserve.

'If you had given me warning then everything would have been laid out as if fit for a princess,' she said, rising with unexpected agility. 'Had you come at Eastertide there would have been Easter cake, but we must make do only with tea. Are you comfortable? Another cushion for your back?'

'I'm quite comfortable,' Tansy said. 'I don't believe I know. . . .'

'The young forget very soon.' The old lady – despite her appearance some indefinable quality in her manner proclaimed her as such – was on her feet now, opening a tin with hands that were covered with bright rings. 'It is, I believe, one of the blessings of youth. Ah, the kettle boils!'

'Let me help you,' Tansy said, rising hastily as the water bubbled over the lid.

'Such a kind child to help her babushka.'

Tansy, pouring the boiling water gingerly into an enormous gilt teapot, suppressed a start. Babushka was grandmother in Russian. This lady evidently mistook her for somebody else. If her mind was clouded then it was unlikely that any useful information could be obtained from her, but kindness demanded that she stay for a little.

The old lady had found some thin, sugary biscuits and carefully counted them on to a long dish. She was now putting spoonfuls of variflavoured conserve on to several small saucers. Her movements were deft, even graceful.

'So drink your tea. You never learned the old tongue so we must speak in English, but still. . . .'

She gave an eloquent little shrug and passed across the table a small straight-sided cup with two handles into which she had poured the dark, honey-coloured liquid, innocent of milk or sugar.

'Let us drink first to the old times.' She was on her feet again, pouring a clear liquid from a dusty bottle into two thick glasses. 'This last half-bottle of vodka I kept to celebrate your return. Come, drink!'

The first sip almost took the top of Tansy's head off. She swallowed convulsively and set down the glass.

'How are you keeping?' she asked awkwardly.

'Well enough, though my rings were all sold long ago,' the other said. 'The ones I wear now are only paste, alas. But jewels are not flesh and blood. One does not mourn their loss overmuch.'

'No. No, of course not.'

It was, Tansy thought, like finding oneself on stage with no idea what play was being performed.

'So.' The old lady took a spoonful of the fruit conserve and washed it down with tea. 'Tell me how you are. You have grown.'

'I'm well, very well. And you?'

'Oh, well enough, though the days are sometimes long. Nothing to occupy myself with except to sit by the window and watch the comings and the goings of the neighbours. They are good enough people but not of our class.'

'You must know them all,' Tansy said encouragingly.

'Not socially!' The proud old head was raised. 'However, I must admit that when the weather is very wet or cold there is usually someone who will agree to buy what I require to eat that day. Yes, people are often kind.'

'Do you know the Dennys?'

'Where do they live?' the other asked.

'Next door but one to you. A brother and a sister? Irish?'

'The young man who knocked at my door the other day and asked me if I had seen his sister?'

'Yes, that would've been him.'

'I did not, of course, invite him in,' the old lady said haughtily. 'One does not, even at my age, invite in a person of the masculine gender of whom one has no knowledge. And we had not been formally introduced. So I informed him, politely of course, that I had not seen the young lady for some time.'

'You know Mary then?' Tansy sat up eagerly.

'That, I believe, was the name he mentioned.' The old lady nodded her head graciously several times. 'I told him that as I had never been formally presented to the young lady I could hardly interest myself in her doings. He thanked me and went away again.'

'But you do know something of her movements?'

'One sees things when one sits at the window.'

'What kind of things?'

The tea forgotten, Tansy leaned forward.

'The young lady came and went in the evenings. I often saw her pass by beneath my window.'

'Alone?'

'Usually. Always hurrying with a parcel underneath her arm.'

'But not always alone?'

'My dear child, this curiosity about someone unknown to us hardly befits a lady!'

'I wondered if she had a suitor, that's all.'

'Ah, you are approaching the age at which love begins to play a part in your thinking!' The other laughed, showing still pretty teeth.

'She had a suitor? A gentleman friend?'

'I saw her once with a gentleman,' the other said. 'Some months ago – in January I believe. I saw them pass arm in arm.'

'Beneath your window?'

'On the other side of the mews.' The old lady looked affronted. 'I am not in the habit of hanging out of windows in order to spy on people, my dearest.'

'No, of course not,' Tansy said hastily. 'I only wondered – did you see the man clearly?'

'At night? In the winter, with only one streetlamp at each end of the mews? I saw only that he wore a silk-hat and an opera-cape, and came from a different level of society than his companion. He walked like an aristocrat.'

'How can you possibly tell?' Tansy demanded.

'I did not live most of my life in St Petersburg without learning how aristocrats conduct themselves! If your grandfather, God rest his soul, had not so gravely offended the Tsar we would live there still and you would not ask such foolish questions.'

'I'm very sorry,' Tansy said as meekly as she could contrive.

'It is not your fault. You cannot recall the old ways. The young man I saw only once but his way of walking reminded me – well, no matter.'

'And Mary Denny? Did you speak to her?'

'I believe she said good-day to me once or twice when I went out to make a few purchases. I bowed to her in return. One should never ignore a civil greeting, my dear. It is the mark of a true lady to condescend to those who are not – shall we say in possession of such advantages as we possess?'

'Surely she is a respectable girl?' Tansy pursued.

'She seemed very neat and quiet,' the old lady admitted. 'Her brother I never spoke to until he came to my door, asking so many questions that my head began to spin. Why do you ask me so much about this girl?'

'As her brother probably told you she seems to have disappeared.'

'With the young man with whom I saw her?' The sunken eyes glinted. 'Ah, even in this country romance still flowers. He has no doubt taken her as his mistress since their social positions do not match. If he settles her in a pleasant little house and takes care of her then her brother must regard himself as fortunate. You know, dearest, I am more eager to hear about your affairs. Are you still studying French? You know at the Court only French is considered to be the polite language.'

She meant the Russian Court, Tansy knew, and lacking the courage at this moment to explain who she really was she took refuge in a cordial, 'Yes indeed I study French. It is a beautiful language.'

'And you grow to match it.' The old lady was speaking fondly, her gaze on Tansy's face. Something in her expression broke and quivered.

'I pass muster in the twilight,' Tansy said. 'Tell me more about your neighbours. You said that in bad weather your shopping is sometimes done.'

'The sisters of St Winifred's come by now and then and are most obliging about getting me anything I require,' the old lady said, 'and Mr Goldman sends over smoked salmon when he has some over at the end of the day. But it would never do to become too intimate with such people. One day the Tsar will relent and we will return home. I await the royal command.' She sounded triumphantly, pathetically certain.

'I have to go now,' Tansy said. 'Next time I visit I'll bring you something. What would you like?'

'I need very little these days.' The thin, beringed fingers folded themselves about the teacup as if to capture the last warmth of the tea. 'A little caviare perhaps. I do not stipulate beluga but a small pot of some good-quality caviare, but you must not spend too much on me, dearest.'

'You shall have the best caviare I can buy,' Tansy said, rising.

'You are very good.' The old lady also rose, her gown whispering across the floor as she moved to the door. 'You must not talk to any strange gentlemen on your way, mind. One cannot be too circumspect.'

'I'll take care,' Tansy said.

The thin fingers gripped her own and the old lady said, her voice trembling a little, 'You are not Tatiana, are you, my dear?'

The eyes that had fed on dreams were sad and sane.

'My name is Tansy,' she said gently.

'We were separated on our way out of Russia,' the old lady said. 'She will come one day. She will find her babushka.'

'I'm sure she will. Goodbye.'

Going down the spiral staircase she felt a tiny chill as if in some part of herself she had glimpsed a possible future. Would she too end up alone, with her father gone and Mrs Timothy gone, and Frank Cartwright married to someone else? And would she wait for someone who never came?

Dusk was blurring the edges of the buildings. A bare-legged boy, carrying a loaf of bread under his arm, darted past her and ducked into a nearby entrance.

She walked slowly, turning over in her mind the little she had learned. It did begin increasingly to look as if Mary Denny had taken advantage of her brother's absence to set herself up as the mistress of an elegant young man whose position would make marriage with her impossible.

As she rounded the corner a footfall behind her caused her to turn round abruptly. Nobody was there, but the footfall had been real enough. Someone had presumably stepped back into the darker shadows and stood there.

She frowned and hurried on, into the brighter street where people were on their way home or setting out for some night duty. The few cabs that bowled past were already occupied.

The newspaper offices were still open and more crowded than earlier in the afternoon as print-boys scurried with freshly folded broadsheets under their arms and piled them onto the covered carts that would take the evening editions to outlying parts of the city.

Tansy looked in at the relevant office where Valentine had placed his advertisement and saw at once that behind the glass the two letters still remained unclaimed.

She came out again onto the pavement and scanned the road for a cab. The hair at the back of her neck prickled slightly and she turned swiftly but saw only the figures and faces of those hurrying about their own business. Nobody appeared to be paying her any attention at all but the sense of unease persisted.

It was a relief when a vacant cab was drawn up in response to her raised hand and she climbed in, giving her father's address.

It would be interesting to hear her father's views on what had transpired. Laurence had a knack of putting his finger on the salient points of a case, a talent that had earned him a reputation as a formidable investigator.

She leaned back in the privacy of the cab and tried to imagine what Frank had made of the story that Patrick Denny had to tell. Frank too was shrewd and intelligent, a friend whose opinion she valued.

They had reached the far side of the park. Tansy lowered the window and called up to the driver to stop.

'I shall walk from here. How much do I owe you?'

'You all right by yourself, Miss?' He had a round, red face with a beaming, almost paternal smile.

'Perfectly. Thank you.'

Paying, adding a handsome tip – it was rare and pleasant to be regarded as if she was a helpless type of female who couldn't find her way home by herself! – she entered the side-gates and slackened her pace, aware of the soft, scented breeze that blew from the surrounding bushes and ruffled the surface of the pond.

There had been a small boy sailing a little boat on the calm water on the day before Geoffrey had set sail for Jamaica. They had sat together on the bench nearby, the bench on which she had first seen the weeping, crumpled little figure of Tilde. It had been a summer afternoon and the sunlight had glinted on the water and struck fire from her emerald ring.

'I wish you were coming with me,' Geoffrey said.

'It wouldn't do at all.' She had smiled tenderly at him, loving the quiet, grave lines of his countenance. 'Pa is unconventional but not as unconventional as all that.'

'Six months is a deuced long time. But I have so much business to settle there that my time will be fully occupied.'

'There, you see. You won't have time in which to miss me,' she had teased.

'I shall miss you from the moment I board the ship to the moment that I step off the gangplank when the ship docks in London again.'

It was on the tip of her tongue to suggest that they marry before he sailed, that there was no need for a big wedding with neither of them having hordes of relations, that she had no desire to wear a ruched and frilled white dress and stick orange-blossoms in her hair. But there were certain things a young lady couldn't say, and she was already conscious of the fact that he had a strong sense of what was fitting.

'I shall occupy myself in choosing furniture and drapes for our home,' she had promised him. 'Only think! In five years time our own child may be sailing a boat on the pond here.'

'Tansy, hush.' He had smiled at her but he looked round and she saw him relax as he realized that the nearest adult, a nurse-maid hovering near the toddler, was too far off to hear the remark.

He had sailed the next day and she had waved as he went down the steps, for he had no wish that she should see him off at the dockside, and as his cab bowled away from the crescent she had felt no touch of fate, no stirring of premonition.

She sighed and went on past the bench and the overhanging willow. In her mind Geoffrey's face wasn't as clear nor his voice as plain as in the years before. Middle age was nearer than she liked to think, she mused, and jumped as the bushes behind her rustled suddenly as if some wind had overtaken the gentle, early-evening breeze.

'Who is it?' Her own voice sounded more confident than she felt. 'Who's there?'

There was no answer. The bushes were still again.

An animal of some kind probably. Tansy reminded herself that it was not yet full dark, that there were people in other areas of the park. She could hear voices chatting and laughing. There was no need in the world to wish suddenly that she'd taken the cab all the way to Laurence's door.

She turned and walked on just as something struck her on the back of the head. The blow was a hard one but not apparently with a heavy instrument for it caused her to stagger only for a moment before she recovered her balance and swung about.

At her feet lay the missile that had struck her. Tansy stooped, her fingers curling back in pitying disgust. A small kitten, one of many which played about in the park, lay limply on the path. A black kitten with a bright pink ribbon tied stranglingly about its neck.

She forced herself to pick up the limp little body and push it under a hydrangea that sprayed itself over the border and then she walked on swiftly towards the laughing voices.

FIVE

Finn had excelled himself, providing a delicate soup, a jellied salmon and lamb chops that partnered redcurrant sauce.

'I cannot understand why you never took up the profession of chef in a Parisian restaurant,' Tansy remarked when the lemon sorbet was reached.

'Never 'ad a cookery lesson in me life, Miss Tansy,' Finn said, looking as flattered as his lugubrious features would allow. 'And French ain't a language I got round to talking, though I can *parlez-vous* a bit when it's called for. Mind you, nobody ever thought I were French.'

'One wonders why,' Laurence said *sotto voce* with a glance of amusement towards his daughter.

'And crime paid better,' Finn added. 'There's no denying that crime pays better'n any other job you care to mention.'

'If that is a hint for higher wages . . .' Laurence began.

'Since I seed the light,' Finn said, 'I wouldn't leave if you was to offer me fifty pounds a month.'

'Good heavens, Finn! Have you got religion?' Tansy enquired.

'Worse,' said Finn gloomily. 'I got religion, Miss Tansy, when I were last doing porridge but it wore off very quick. Then I got loyalty and that don't wear off. It sticks to a fellow.'

'Serve the coffee and stay and have some with us,' Laurence ordered.

'Time to talk about the case, Pa?'

Tansy, who had been glad of the unwritten rule that good food should be enjoyed with no more than an occasional triviality expressed felt her spirits rising.

The incident in the park had shaken her more than she cared to admit. Someone knew that she was interested in the murders. Someone had given her an unmistakable warning. That meant that someone had been following her. Either in the newspaper office, which seemed the most likely place, or someone had seen her in the mews and if the latter was correct then Mary Denny's disappearance was connected to the case in some way.

'Well?' Laurence was looking at her.

'Well what, Pa?' She roused herself with an effort.

'You are the one who went off to share surveillance time with Frank. Or did you decide it would be a waste of time?'

'Not entirely. I took Frank's place in the newspaper office – there are two letters in the pigeon-hole for Valentine which haven't been collected. A young man came in, looked at the letters through the glass without opening the box and went away again.'

'You followed him I trust?'

'To a mews not far off Fleet Street.'

'And?'

Laurence might worry if she related the full story. She said, 'His name is Patrick Denny from County Wicklow. He's an artist, not yet well known but he was fortunate enough to obtain a commission from the War Office to go out to India and make a series of sketches depicting life on the frontier. He left his younger sister in their rented accommodation in London. When he returned to England three weeks ago she had disappeared.'

'How long had he been away?'

'Since last October.'

'How old was this sister?' Finn asked, having poured the coffee and installed himself in a chair.

'Seventeen. She is near eighteen now. Her name is Mary. I have a sketch of her.'

She reached for her bag, took out the sketch and unrolled it. The pretty, heart-shaped face smiled up at her.

'He left the girl alone in lodgings?'

'Apparently she's very self-reliant and the brother is – somewhat Bohemian in his thinking.'

'Somewhat daft if you was to ask me,' Finn said. 'Fancy walking off and leaving that piece of flotsam floating about.'

'I thought the same myself,' Tansy agreed, 'but he kept on telling me how quiet and sensible she was. He had left money for her and he wrote to her.'

'But did she write back?' Finn enquired.

'Once or twice I believe. The last letter he received in February. He showed it to me. She'd written in December to tell him that she had a new gentleman friend who was going to escort her to the Valentine Ball. After that he heard nothing and when he arrived back in London he found their lodging locked and empty and some of her things gone.'

'Did he report the matter to the police?' Laurence asked.

'Not yet. He seems to feel that she would be shamed in some way if he were to report her missing.'

'More likely he has a shrewd idea where she's ended up,' Laurence said.

'He was adamant she had no need of money.'

'Call me stupid,' Finn broke in, 'but I can't see where this Valentine comes in.'

'Mary Denny left a cutting from the newspaper in her drawer. When Patrick Denny brought himself finally to make a real search he found the cutting.'

'The Valentine advertisement!'

'It was in the drawer with a length of bright pink ribbon. Her brother hadn't realized the significance of that but he had gone down to the newspaper office to see if anyone came in to collect any replies.'

'The ribbon might not be significant at all,' Laurence said. 'We know that Ellie Watson had ginger hair and would've been unlikely to wear that particular shade and that Fanny Jones was a Methodist and wouldn't have worn such a bright colour, but this Mary Denny – is she dark as she appears in the sketch?'

'Her brother says so, but she generally wears green.'

'She might still have worn a pink ribbon. It's worth bearing in mind but certainly not conclusive. When was she last seen by other people?'

'The people who live in the mews are a fairly transient group,' Tansy said. 'Immigrants, respectable people down on their luck, newcomers to the city waiting to establish themselves. People tend to keep themselves to themselves.'

'No old lady who has nothing to do but sit at her window?' Laurence asked.

'One. An elderly Russian lady. She seems a trifle confused in the head but she does remember seeing Mary Denny going past and on one occasion she saw her with a young gentleman, formally dressed. It was evening so she didn't get a clear look at him.'

'And where is the brother now?'

'We went back to the newspaper office to meet up with Frank. To introduce them. They went off together and I went back to the mews to make a few enquiries for myself.'

'And met the Russian lady.'

'Yes.'

'What was your view of this Patrick Denny?' Laurence asked.

'Twenty-seven – twenty-eight, slim and dark, middle height, rather fine features, clothes shabby but not badly cut, long eyelashes.'

'Noticed his eyelashes, did you?' Laurence looked amused.

'You taught me to notice details,' Tansy said, blushing faintly. 'He is certainly very attractive, with a slight Irish accent. He said his parents had owned a small farm but when they died there wasn't any money so they, his sister and himself, sold at a loss and came to London.'

'Micks on the make,' Finn said dismissively.

'His sketch is very good,' Tansy defended.

'It's a charming portrait but we cannot tell if it's a good likeness or even if it is of his sister at all,' her father said.

'He seemed most concerned about her absence.'

'But not concerned enough to go to the police.'

'Perhaps you were right, Pa, when you hinted he might suspect she had eloped with her new friend.'

'Leave a pretty girl alone and the worst always 'appens,' Finn said.

'In this case one hopes not. However, if she was actually seen with a young man – how recently?'

'The old lady thought in January, but she is a mite confused.'

'Suppose that the young man had earmarked this Mary Denny as a mistress, and her brother came home, had a furious quarrel with her and killed her?'

'And then killed two other girls to cover his tracks? You don't really think that, do you, Pa?'

'I don't as yet think anything,' he returned. 'I'm turning over all kinds of possibilities. But he might be playing a double game.'

'Well, he certainly isn't Valentine.'

'How d'ye know?'

'He didn't have a key for the pigeon-hole so he couldn't read the letters.

'He told you that,' Laurence pointed out. 'He might have realized that you were watching and invented the story – my dear, I'm not saying that he did but it's possible, you must admit.'

'Not if he was still sailing home from India after Ellie Watson was killed, Pa. He only landed three weeks ago,' Tansy reminded him.

'That's not been checked out, has it?' Laurence looked at her.

'Not yet,' she admitted.

'Finn? You can check on passenger-lists over the next few months?'

'I thought they were confidential,' Tansy said.

'Finn has friends in low places,' her father said.

'Better take a look at the ferry-boat sailings while I'm at it,' Finn put in.

'He said they'd lived here for almost a year before he obtained the War Office commission.'

'I've no friends there,' Finn remarked to nobody in particular.

'You may take round a note from me requesting the confirmation.'

'Have you had any word from the police yet?' Accepting more coffee, Tansy glanced at her father. 'You are still in an advisory capacity after all.'

'Jarrold chooses to forget that,' Laurence said, with a touch of bitterness, 'and I certainly don't have the right to push myself into the forefront of any investigation. In fact I'm surprised that I have not yet been asked why I am taking an interest in these murders.'

'But if they haven't connected Valentine—' Tansy began.

'There's no proof that this Valentine fellow is connected at all.'

'Pa, how can you say that?' she exclaimed. 'The advertisement was on the same page as the report of Ellie Watson's death, and the same cutting was found in Fanny Jones's and Mary Denny's rooms.'

'Do you have a portrait of Her Majesty in your house?'

'A small one over the sofa. Why?'

'Many people have portraits of the Queen in their dwellings. Does it then follow that if two girls are murdered who possess such a portrait that we must suspect Her Majesty of sneaking out of Balmoral and killing them?'

'No, of course not – but an advertisement is hardly a portrait of the Queen.'

'Many young ladies with personal problems may have snipped out the cutting, put it at one side meaning to answer it later and not plucked up the courage to do so. We can't take anything for granted, Tansy.'

'I suppose not, but I can't picture Mr Denny as a violent criminal,' she said obstinately.

'This Valentine Ball – public or private?' Having made his point he was too wise to pursue it.

'I've no idea. A private ball would have invitations and for a public one tickets would be sold?'

'You never went to balls.' Laurence gave a regretful little shake of the head. 'Had your mother lived she would have chaperoned you about.'

'She had as little taste for society as I have,' Tansy said. 'Valentine balls, public or private, were never in my line. And I met Geoffrey despite my lamentable lack of social graces.'

'There might be lists of names if tickets were sold to rather more classy public balls,' Laurence said. 'If this gentleman friend of Mary Denny's is a gentleman he'll not have invited her to anything too raffish. Finn?'

'I know,' said Finn with resignation. 'Go round and find out what balls were 'eld on – what night?'

'February the fourteenth. It's a long shot but we may find something out.'

'Check the Irish ferries, check the Indian clippers, check the balls for that geezer Valentine – it's a good job my feet are flat already,' Finn said gloomily.

'You know you love every moment of it,' Tansy laughed as she rose.

'Going already?' Laurence indicated the still half-full coffee-pot.

'Pa, you always say that!' Tansy bent to kiss his cheek. 'I have a house of my own and Mrs Timothy won't stir to bed until I'm home. Oh, by the by, I've invited Frank and Patrick Denny to dinner tomorrow evening. We can discuss the progress of our investigations.'

'Always assuming that Mr Denny isn't Valentine. I'll have Finn come round and let you know if he really was on that ship from India when he said he was.'

'Begging your pardon,' Finn said promptly, 'but I've not yet put myself in the way of meeting that 'ousekeeper and I don't figure on starting now.'

'Finn is terrified of being trapped into matrimony,' Laurence said, recovering his good humour somewhat. 'Can you call round again tomorrow, Tansy? Late afternoon?'

'Yes of course. Do you want to come to dinner too?'

She had often asked the question before and as usual Laurence shook his head.

'I'm perfectly content here. I'll not be wheeled through streets where I once strode. Go carefully, my dear. Don't make assumptions about guilt or innocence without proof.'

'I won't, Pa.'

Straightening her hat, she waved her hand and was escorted down the stairs to the front door by the ubiquitous Finn.

'Walking through the park tonight?' he enquired.

'It's about due to close I imagine.' She kept her tone casual, refusing to permit the tremor of uneasiness to sweep through her.

'It's nowhere near midnight yet.' Finn consulted his watch. 'Pretty dark though. I'll 'ail you a cab, Miss, when you tell me what's bothered you.'

'Two murdered girls and a third missing would bother anybody,' Tansy said.

'Don't come the old soldier with me, Miss Tansy,' Finn said

severely. 'I've known you since you was fifteen, remember. I can read you like a racing column. You've been 'olding something back all evening.'

'When I walked through the park earlier this evening someone hidden in the bushes threw a dead cat at me,' Tansy confided. 'It had a bright pink ribbon tied round its neck. I didn't say anything to Pa because I didn't want to worry him, but it was a bit of a shock.'

'Someone knows you're taking an interest in this Valentine cove,' Finn said.

'Which means I've been followed.'

'Best I get you a cab,' Finn said sensibly. 'I won't say nothing to your pa. And you ought to 'ave a weapon, Miss Tansy. Now I'm the soul of lawful living these days but I could lay me 'ands on a nice knuckleduster you could 'ide in your muff. Or a sword-stick now, 'idden in a parasol? Very quick and clean if you was to be menaced.'

'Just call the cab, Finn,' Tansy said firmly. 'I shall keep a sharp look-out now you may be sure.'

Finn sent her a disappointed look and loped off along the crescent.

'I do wish that Jarrold'd ask your pa to 'elp out on the case,' he said, returning with a cab trailing behind. 'Your pa 'as more sense in one little finger than Jarrold 'as in a whole brain!'

'I'll see what I can do.'

As the cab turned the corner she rapped on the trap-door and altered the destination that Finn had given.

Twenty minutes later she alighted at the door of an exclusive gentlemen's club where her father, in common with other police-officers, had often met with his colleagues in the old days to enjoy a whisky and talk over the progress or lack of progress in a current case.

The doorman at the discreetly narrow entrance gave her a bow that was icy rather than frosty.

'Good-evening, madam.' His tone contrived to suggest that she had no business even to stand outside the premises, being a female and therefore inferior.

'If Inspector Jarrold is within be so good as to inform him that

Miss Clark is here to speak to him on a matter of police business,' Tansy said.

'I really could not presume to say whether the officer in question is here or not,' the door-keeper said loftily.

'If he is then kindly mention the name of Inspector Laurence Clark.'

She had drawn herself up to her full height and fixed him with an unwavering green stare.

'If you'd care to wait in here, Miss Clark?'

While not completely cowed, his voice held a tinge more respect as he ushered her into a small, sparsely furnished room where those few members of the inferior sex admitted within the sacred portals were evidently expected to wait.

Tansy looked at the hard, slippery-seated chairs and elected to remain standing. Bearding Jarrold in his club was unconventional and not likely to put him in a good humour but she had no intention of going to the Yard and risking her errand being relayed back to Laurence.

'Miss Clark, this is an unexpected honour.'

The portly frame of Inspector Jarrold took up most of the remaining space in the room. His bow, like his complexion, was florid, his eyes full of curiosity.

'I apologize for calling upon you here, Inspector Jarrold.' She shook hands with more cordiality than she felt. 'I trust Mrs Jarrold is well.'

'Very well, thank you, Miss Clark. Your father keeps in good health too?'

'On the whole, yes.' Tansy plunged in. 'He does get very bored sometimes, naturally. After an active life—'

'In many ways your father is fortunate,' Jarrold broke in heartily. 'I sometimes envy a man who has leisure to enjoy great literature, perhaps to consider writing his memoirs.'

'It doesn't entirely compensate for the loss of physical mobility,' Tansy said coldly.

'Of course not,' he agreed hastily, 'but who of us leads the perfect life? I myself have great difficulty in devoting sufficient attention to Mrs Jarrold while maintaining a watchful presence at headquarters.'

'So you must find my father's occasional advice most stimulating?'

Tansy saw with a mixture of annoyance and amusement that Jarrold seemed almost literally to withdraw without actually moving.

'Naturally,' he said stiffly, 'I make a point of consulting your father when necessary.'

'And it is not necessary now?' Tansy said. 'I understand that a second girl has been murdered.'

'Ah, your father takes an academic interest?'

'He does read the newspapers,' Tansy said sharply.

'We are progressing at a slow but steady rate.'

'You have linked the crimes together then. Both girls were killed in the same manner? Both wore bright pink ribbons in their hats?'

'Those two details are possibly significant,' he said cautiously. 'Of course three months separate the two deaths, so one must keep an open mind.'

'My father—'

'Oh, I don't think we require his expertise at this juncture.'

'My father doesn't know that I'm here,' Tansy said, tiring of fencing and coming to the point. 'He would be most annoyed if it became known to him, but the truth is that he suffers to some extent from depression at times and it would be a kindness to him if you were to call and discuss the case.' Her voice trailed away uncertainly. Inspector Jarrold's eyes were cold and blank.

'If we need to consult your father rest assured that we shall have no hesitation in doing so,' he said stiffly. 'However, perhaps the time has come for him to accept the fact – sad but inescapable – that he is retired and has been for some time. Certainly I doubt if he would approve of your coming here in this fashion.'

'He'd be furious,' she admitted. 'I hoped, however, that if the investigation was not progressing quickly enough then you would call upon him for advice?'

She had used the wrong word again. Inspector Jarrold took nobody's advice. Coming here like this she had merely made it look as if she were touting for business on Laurence's behalf.

'If advice is required,' Jarrold said, 'your esteemed father will be the first person I shall consult.'

'Then I apologize for wasting your time. I'll bid you good-night.'

'A dutiful daughter is one of nature's glories,' he said.

'And a man who recognizes his limitations is another!' Tansy retorted as she swept out.

Inspector Jarrold wasn't, according to Laurence, a fool. No complete fool could have attained his position in the force. But he was plodding when he should have been quick-witted; unimaginative when he would have done well to employ his instincts, and above all, jealous of the reputation of a man into whose shoes he had stepped.

Outside the cab was still waiting. She paid the driver and dismissed it, preferring to walk for a while and cool her temper.

Jarrold had at least recognized that the *modus operandi* in both murders had been the same and had noted the pink ribbon motif, but he hadn't spoken of Valentine, though that didn't mean he wasn't on the same track as herself and her father. What was clearer than anything was that he had very little liking for any consultation whatsoever and her visit had been ill-advised.

A cab had drawn up just ahead of her and a plumed hat on a familiar head was thrust out.

'Miss Clark? Surely it's Miss Clark!'

'Mrs Mainwaring, good-evening.' Tansy took the few steps forward that brought her level with the milliner.

'I thought it was you.' Mrs Mainwaring gave several little nods. 'Are you going anywhere near me? I'd be happy to offer you a lift.'

'I'm on my way towards Chelsea,' Tansy said.

'And I can perfectly well take a longer route home. Do please join me, Miss Clark. Is your gentlemen friend not with you?'

'My – Oh, you mean Frank.' Tansy stepped up into the cab. 'No, he really is just a friend. I've been on business.'

'On your father's behalf? Yes, of course. It's fortunate that neither you nor I are a very young woman, Miss Clark, else we wouldn't risk walking unaccompanied after dark. Of course I always carry a small bag of pepper myself. Do you?'

'No,' said Tansy somewhat shortly, not at all sure she relished being classed along with Mrs Mainwaring as middle-aged.

'Have there been any developments?' her companion asked. 'Concerning my late unfortunate employee?'

'Inquiries are still going on,' Tansy said, quoting a phrase she had heard her father employ on countless occasions.

Mrs Mainwaring nodded, the black plume on her hat waving in time with her head.

'This must be extremely upsetting for you,' Tansy said.

'Beyond what I can express, Miss Clark. Beyond what I can express! You know I made quite a favourite of Miss Jones. She was such a gentle, ladylike little creature, with that singsong Welsh accent which, of course, I was constrained to urge her to moderate, and I must confess that she did her best.'

'And you can't think of any reason why she should have gone to Kew Gardens in the evening without telling anyone else?'

'Fanny never went anywhere,' Mrs Mainwaring said. 'Only to chapel in Wellinburgh Street on Sunday mornings, and occasionally I allowed her a couple of hours off in the late afternoons on Wednesday so that she could attend meetings of the Band of Hope. She had quite a pretty singing voice, you know.'

'No, I didn't know,' Tansy said sombrely.

'Poor girl.' Mrs Mainwaring heaved a noisy sigh.

The faint but unmistakable odour of gin drifted to Tansy's nostrils.

'There's nothing more you can remember about her then?' she asked.

'I make a point,' the other said, 'of leaving my young ladies as much freedom as is possible without the sacrifice of respectability. Each has her own key to the room where she sleeps. I am not against them having gentlemen friends provided that the young man is made known to me and there is no covert carryings on, for hanky-panky, Miss Clark, I will not have!'

'No, of course not,' Tansy agreed. 'And Fanny didn't. . . ?'

'She was such a pale, plain little soul, Miss Clark. She had left a violent father you know. Found the courage to run away. I often marvelled at her actually having come to London for she was in all degrees very timid. Is this where you wish to be set down? I can go further if you so desire.'

'This will do splendidly, Mrs Mainwaring.'

In fact it fell well short of where Tansy lived but she judged it prudent not to allow the other too much into her confidence.

There was probably no harm in the milliner at all but the prospect of her turning up on the doorstep, claiming close friendship and smelling ever so faintly of gin, wasn't one that gladdened her heart. Mrs Timothy for one, she thought with a *frisson* of amusement, would be scandalized.

'I do hope the villain is speedily apprehended, Miss Clark,' Miss Mainwaring hissed as Tansy climbed down into the road. 'She was such a harmless kind of girl.'

The long plume nodded again several times as the cab drove off.

That was a sad epitaph, Tansy reflected. A harmless kind of girl. Yet someone had wanted her dead, had struck her so violently as to kill her outright and then, like some macabre jester, remained only long enough to tie a bright pink ribbon round her sober, navy hat.

'If you want to discover a murderer, my dear, first look very closely at the victim.'

Laurence's voice echoed in her memory. She even recalled the occasion, with her father giving a riveting account of a case he had managed to solve at the start of his career and herself listening avidly with Geoffrey – yes, Geoffrey had been there too, sipping an after-dinner brandy and with a faint smile on the face that was no longer so clear in her mind. Geoffrey, she thought suddenly, had secretly been rather shocked by her unconventional upbringing, had found it hard to understand why a young lady should have such a deep interest in the sordid subject of murder and its unravelling.

She had dimly sensed it at the time, and pushed the realization away from her.

'Cab for hire!' The familiar cry jerked her back to the present.

She gave her address and climbed inside, aware as she leaned back in the darkness that she had been on the verge of wondering if she and Geoffrey had been so well suited to each other as she had believed.

'You didn't ought to be rambling round by yourself, Miss, in the dark,' the driver said, paternally scolding when she paid the fare. 'The streets ain't safe these days. Not even in Chelsea, if you was to ask me. Why, a girl could just up and vanish and be found in the river next day with no one able to tell 'ow she got there!'

'I shall take great care,' Tansy assured him solemnly.

It was rather flattering after Mrs Mainwaring's comments to be regarded as a vulnerable girl. She added an extra large tip to the payment and waved as he bowled off down the quiet street.

Tilde had been contemplating drowning herself in the park pond when Tansy had come across her. Pausing by the gate, Tansy leaned against the bars and contemplated the road with its few, equally spaced lamps as a new idea struck her.

Mary Denny, according to her sketch and her brother's description, was small, dark and pretty with a cloud of curly hair. That same description applied equally to Tilde Miles. Was it possible the two were the same?

Tilde had no Irish accent but it was possible that Mary Denny had succeeded in losing her brogue since her arrival in England. According to her she had lost her mother, failed to make a living trimming hats for Mrs Mainwaring and had found work in the match factory too hard. So she had become a tweeny in an upper-class household and been unjustly dismissed, though the butler had given her a good character reference.

Tansy's well-shaped brows drew together in a slight frown. She had neglected to check on that reference, which was careless of her, though the murders had occupied her thoughts.

If Mary Denny had been seduced away from her lodging by a smooth-spoken charmer it was possible she'd gone with him expecting marriage. It would have come as a dreadful shock had she been seduced and abandoned. It was certainly unlikely that she would have returned to her brother and also unlikely that she would have gone on the streets.

Perhaps she had invented a new identity for herself in an attempt to make an honest living.

Tansy bit her lip. It was too neat, too coincidental, she mused. Life and death were seldom so tidy. Anyway, with Patrick Denny expected for dinner along with Frank the following evening she would soon find out if Tilde Miles was really Mary Denny.

She unlatched the gate and went up the short path, breathing in the night-scented stock with pleasure as she always did.

Mrs Timothy must be in her room at the back, Tansy thought, or occupied somewhere since she obviously hadn't heard the cab arrive and depart. Tansy took out her key and fitted it into the lock. The door swung open into the warm, lamplit hall just as the housekeeper made a stately entrance from the kitchen.

'I was becoming quite fretted about you, Miss Tansy!' she exclaimed. 'I sent Tilde off to her bed and was having a little nap before the range when I heard your key.'

Tansy made some indeterminate reply. Her eyes were riveted to the door-knocker, gleaming brightly in the lamplight, with a bright pink ribbon tied in a jaunty bow around it.

SIX

'Will you be going out this morning, Miss Tansy?'

Mrs Timothy, bringing extra toast, folded her hands on her apron and waited for an answer with the air of someone who wouldn't have been surprised had her employer announced she was calling in at Buckingham Palace.

'Yes. Do you need anything from the shops? I can call in to order the meat.'

'The meat is already ordered,' Mrs Timothy said. 'A nice piece of brisket.'

'Ah! As to that,' Tansy said, remembering, 'I've invited two gentlemen to dinner this evening.'

'Two gentlemen?' Mrs Timothy looked hopeful.

'Mr Frank Cartwright whom you know and a – an acquaintance of his, a Mr Denny. I should've mentioned it last night but I was tired.'

She had also been at pains to get the pink ribbon off the door-knocker before Mrs Timothy noticed it.

'I'm very glad to hear it,' the housekeeper said. 'If I may make so bold, a young lady ought to have more social life. All this musing on murders is not healthy, Miss Tansy, and that's my sworn opinion.'

'Well, what do you advise for the menu?'

Tansy, who had no intention of discussing her social life or lack of it with Mrs Timothy, gave her an enquiring look.

'A nice cold soup, a piece of salmon – poached with a lemon sauce – a crown of roast-lamb with new potatoes and peas and a bit of fresh mint, a trifle and an apple-charlotte – gentlemen always love the desserts – then some nice cheese with fruit and angels on horseback to finish.'

'Mrs Timothy! This is a simple dinner not a Lord Mayor's banquet,' Tansy protested laughingly.

'I'll leave out the trifle,' Mrs Timothy yielded. 'The meat I can get for myself. Tilde can come with me and learn how to choose a good cut.'

'You are finding her satisfactory?' Tansy asked.

'She shows promise,' Mrs Timothy said. 'It's too soon to render a more definite opinion. She has very pretty manners I do admit, and she is a kind little soul too. She makes a very drinkable cup of tea when my back gets chronic and forces me to sit down for a spell.'

This, from Mrs Timothy, was praise of the highest order.

'I'll leave you to deal with it then,' she said. 'Oh, I will stop at the wine-merchant's and ask them to send round some good – what do you recommend?'

'Six of red and six of white and some brandy, port and sherry,' the other instructed.

'You're evidently anticipating an orgy,' Tansy said drily. 'Very well. I hope the housekeeping bill won't bankrupt me this month.'

'We shall make economies in other directions,' Mrs Timothy said, sweeping grandly from the room.

Tansy finished her breakfast, put on her hat and bolero jacket and went out.

Wellinburgh Street where the Sion Chapel was situated wasn't far from the British Museum, she mused, an old and favourite haunt for herself and Geoffrey. He had taken particular delight in lingering over the Etruscan pottery with its curving lines, the Egyptian frescos with their still, stylized figures of birds and animals.

'Had I followed my natural bent I would have specialized in archaeology,' he had told her once. 'The past fascinates me.'

Because the past was dead, Tansy thought now. Geoffrey had not been a man who gripped life with both hands. Perhaps that had been why he had fallen in love with her, because she herself was more decided, more practical. Yet, in time, had they married, might he not have found her too vivid, too full of energetic plans?

She frowned slightly, not liking the direction of her thoughts, and walked more briskly towards the few local shops that occupied an inconspicuous corner of the small square beyond the crescent.

Giving her order for wine she was somewhat taken aback by the wine-merchant's breezy, 'Having some company, Miss Clark? Do you good! Get you out of yourself. I'll have it sent round directly. Give it time to breathe.'

Evidently she was regarded locally as something of a recluse. Tansy hid a wry smile, thanked him, and went on to the cab-stand.

When she alighted at the British Museum the temptation to go inside, to spend a pleasant hour wandering among the exhibits about which Geoffrey had been so knowledgeable, was almost overwhelming. After all, she had no real business to go poking her nose into a couple of murders which even her father hadn't been consulted about. Nor was he likely to be, she mused, as she recalled her brief, abortive meeting with Inspector Jarrold.

Two faces she had never seen swam into her imagination. One was pale and plain with ginger hair and the other was a thinner face with fair hair drawn severely back. Ellie Watson and Fanny Jones. Two young, respectable working girls both killed suddenly and brutally in the middle of the night, neither of them, apparently, with family or close friends. A third girl missing. Tenuous connections which might or might not mean anything.

She turned away from the enticing entrance and walked firmly towards Wellinburgh Street.

It was a narrow road, tucked away parallel to another narrow road. On both sides small, mean houses were held apart by narrower alleys. The gutters were choked with refuse.

In the mews the buildings had held traces of past grandeur. Here each building seemed to apologize for having ever been erected.

At the end of the street a structure that looked as grim as all the other buildings stood in a patch of waste-ground where someone had made a half-hearted effort to clear away the nettles and plant some roses. The result made the surroundings even more unprepossessing. The flowers were dry and dusty, their stems spindly. The chapel itself was brick-built, its roof of dark slates, a gold-lettered board outside proclaiming it to be Sion Chapel. Beneath in small letters were the words 'Wesleyan Methodist'.

Fanny Jones had left her home in order to escape a drunken father but she had clung to the faith she knew, Tansy thought, reading the words before she went across the uneven ground and pushed open the chapel door.

Neither of her parents had been regular worshippers at any place of worship, though they had followed convention in so far as to have their only child baptized and confirmed. Tansy went to services on special occasions but privately preferred to sit quietly in one of the great London cathedrals when she was troubled, and soak up the silence.

The large, echoing space within the chapel door struck her as less than inspiring. An expanse of clean but unpolished floor was occupied by rows of wooden benches and chairs with a broad aisle running between them. At the far end was a carved lectern and a pianoforte with a stack of hymn-books on its lid. Someone had arranged some flowers in a tall vase, but they too had an air of being dusty and tired and the two inches of water in the vase was, she saw as she moved nearer, brackish.

A side-door opened and a tall man emerged, with more hymnals balanced on the crook of his arm.

'Good-morning! May I help you?'

He had stopped abruptly and was staring at her as if a well-dressed young woman was the last person he expected to find here.

'Are you the minister here?' Tansy asked.

He loped over to the piano, deposited the books there in an untidy heap, and shook his head.

'I'm very sorry, madam, but since the Reverend Elias Hatch died last year we have no regular incumbent,' he said.

'And you are?'

'Wesley Brown. I am a deacon here. If you require a minister we have a list of visiting clergy who generally come and take the Sunday service. We also have several lay preachers upon whom we can call. I have the list somewhere. Now where did. . . ?' He looked around vaguely.

'I don't need a minister,' Tansy said. 'I merely came to enquire about the funeral arrangements for one of the members of your congregation. A Miss Frances Jones?'

'Are you a relative?'

'No, I – I am by way of being an acquaintance of Miss Jones's employer, but I was never personally. . . .'

She should have had some feasible explanation ready instead of flushing and stammering, she thought crossly. Mr Wesley Brown, however, seemed not to notice.

'Ah, Mrs Mainwaring,' he nodded. 'A most worthy woman. Not a member of our little congregation but a good Christian soul for all that. She has offered to defray the expenses of the interment. And you are – forgive me but I didn't quite catch. . . .'

'Miss Clark. Fanny Jones worshipped here regularly, I believe?'

'She was a most devoted member of our congregation. Welsh, you see. The fervour of the Wesleys lit fires in Wales that will not soon be extinguished.'

'No indeed,' Tansy said politely. 'It must have been a great shock when you heard of her death.'

'A great grief for us all, Miss Clark. A police-officer came by, during a meeting of our Band of Hope. Perhaps you have heard of our Band of Hope?'

'Yes indeed,' Tansy said and saw that what she said made no difference. She was going to be told all about it anyway.

'There are so many distractions that take our young people away from the Path of Righteousness.' He capitalized the words impressively. 'Drink, Miss Clark! The music-halls! Finery and frippery and other attributes of Mammon. Poor young women are beset with the wiles of the Great Deceiver.'

'Fanny Jones would not, of course, have earned a large salary,' Tansy managed to insert.

'I believe the girls receive a modest stipend and a room of their own. She was not a person who complained of her lot. Prior to her employment at the millinery establishment she had worked briefly at the match factory where, as I understand it, her position was far less comfortable. A very quiet, shy girl. I often regretted that she did not persuade some of her co-workers to join us here.'

'She always came alone then?'

'Quite alone. Like a solitary grey bird,' Wesley Brown said, impelled suddenly to poetic flight. 'Every Sunday morning and when she obtained leave late on Wednesday afternoons for our Band—'

'Of Hope. Yes. She probably preferred to keep her friends at work apart from the friends she made here.'

'She made no friends here,' he said. 'You must understand that particular friendships can lead to petty jealousies in a community. Our young people are encouraged to be polite and kindly to all, but not to have favourites. Miss Jones was most scrupulous in that respect.'

'She had a pretty singing voice.'

'She did, I believe, sing in the choir. Many of our young people like to offer melody to the Lord.'

'And the great Charles Wesley enjoyed a good, rousing hymn,' Tansy agreed. 'She sang solo perhaps?'

'Oh no, Miss Clark! Female solos are not a feature – no, she sat there, on the end of the row, always modestly clad with her eyes cast down. Quite unnoticed.'

'You seem to have noticed her, Mr Brown,' Tansy said.

'Because she embodied those qualities of virtue and purity we seek to instil into all our young people. We seek out the white lambs that they may serve as examples to the rest.'

He spoke calmly but she noticed with interest that his high forehead was beaded with sweat.

'And Frances Jones was a white lamb?' she queried.

'She was of the Elect.' He was twisting his large, white, flaccid-looking hands together. 'Yes, from the very beginning she was a chosen vessel of the Lord.'

'About the funeral?'

Tansy averted her eyes from those twisting hands.

'I understand it will be held next Monday at ten in the morning – a very quiet and modest affair but she was—'

'A very quiet and modest girl,' Tansy said. 'Thank you, Mr Brown.'

'You yourself are not. . . ?' He paused.

'Church of England,' Tansy said briskly. 'Thank you again, Mr. . . .'

The side-door was pushed open again and a smaller man stepped into the large room, his expression one of mild annoyance, his tone querulous.

'There are the flowers to be changed and the brasses polished and not one sniff of Mrs Dixon! Are you sure she left no message with you – Oh, I beg your pardon!'

He had caught sight of Tansy and stopped, giving her a hasty little bow.

'Mrs Dixon did mention that she might be a few minutes late,' Wesley Brown said. 'Miss Clark, may I present my fellow-deacon, John Mason? Miss Clark very kindly came to ask if she might contribute to the funeral expenses for Miss Jones but I explained that it was all taken care of – we have not, of course, chosen the hymns yet. Are we to use the first or second edition of—'

'You seem to have thoroughly mixed them up already, Mr Brown,' John Mason observed with an impatient glance towards the piano. 'Mr Brown, since Mrs Dixon is already more than a few minutes late perhaps you'd be kind enough to step round and see what is delaying her?'

'I'll do it directly, Mr Mason.'

Wesley Brown looked as if he were about to shake hands. Tansy hastily put her hands behind her back and bowed.

'Yes, well. . . .' He twisted his hands together in a final wrenching motion and sidled through the door.

'Miss Clark?' John Mason shook hands briskly. 'Forgive my impatient manner but Mr Brown is so busy gathering souls for the Lord that he sometimes forgets more practical matters. You're here about the late Miss Jones?'

'I wondered if her family had been informed,' Tansy said.

'As far as I know nobody has come forward. I always had the impression that her background had been rather unhappy – the father drank I believe. She did not mention. . . ?'

'She mentioned nothing to me,' Tansy said truthfully.

'You offered to contribute to the funeral expenses? Most kind, but Mrs Mainwaring, who employed the young lady, has kindly offered to bear the whole of the expenses. We have space in a small cemetery just five minutes' walk away and the occasion itself will be a simple one. In such tragic circumstances – there is a great deal of wickedness in the world, Miss Clark.'

'Yes,' Tansy said. 'Yes there is. Fanny joined your congregation about two years ago, I understand?'

'Yes. We have been established here for nearly forty years, Miss Clark. Originally this was a temperance hall but a wealthy family bought it and most generously donated it to us though they were not themselves of our religious persuasion. Miss Jones came very regularly up to a couple of weeks ago. A very nice, respectable girl.'

'She stopped coming?'

Tansy looked at him alertly.

'About a fortnight since. She didn't come to the Band of Hope meetings either but there were weeks when she had work to do that prevented her attendance.'

'Did anyone make any enquiries?'

John Mason looked slightly disapproving.

'Attendance isn't compulsory, Miss Clark,' he said. 'We seek to persuade, never to compel people to attend our meetings. However Miss Jones did seem to be worried about something.'

'Oh?'

'I have worried about it myself.' He frowned slightly as if he was chiding himself. 'In fact I have wondered whether or not I ought to have said something to the police constable when he came to ask questions.'

'The police did come here then?'

Jarrold was at least doing something!

'Only to ask if anyone knew Miss Jones's address in Wales or whether she had any gentlemen friends. Nobody knew the address and we knew of no male admirers. She was a very plain girl I'm afraid. Not much personality.'

She had had sufficient to escape from an unhappy home and earn an honest living, Tansy reflected. Aloud she said, 'You thought she was worried about something? Why?'

'About three weeks ago – it was before the customary Wednesday meeting.'

'Yes?' Tansy controlled her impatience with an effort.

'I came here about an hour before the meeting was due to

start. We take turns in conducting proceedings – Mr Brown and myself, and usually one or two of the ladies provides some light refreshments – lemonade, tea, buns, that kind of thing. A little social gaiety.'

'And?'

'We have a small library of books suitable for young people, tales that are guaranteed to instil a sense of virtue to be attained and sin to be resisted. Pleasant little tales of two young people coming together to serve the Lord.'

'They sound thrilling," Tansy said, straight-faced.

'Anyway, I came early, as I said, to check over our modest stock. Also to indulge in a little quiet reading myself. My dear wife becomes quite agitated if I neglect her conversation for a book. When I arrived Miss Jones was already seated over there, in her usual place.'

'How did she get in?'

'Oh, we leave the door unlocked most of the day so that people may slip in for a period of quiet reflection.'

'What was Fanny Jones doing?' Tansy enquired.

'Merely sitting there, looking at her hands. Then as I bade her good-afternoon she lifted her head and I saw she had been crying.'

'Did she tell you why?'

'I took the liberty of asking her if I could be of help in any way,' he said, looking distressed. 'Of course, though I am a deacon here, that gives me no right to interfere in the private concerns of our members, but one doesn't like to see a young creature in trouble of any kind. So I did ask her but she shook her head. I then enquired whether she would prefer to speak to Mr Brown. He takes a great interest in the welfare of our young people and he has considerable experience in the counselling of troubled souls. She looked at me and – she laughed, Miss Clark. She laughed.'

'Hysteria?' Tansy guessed.

'That was what I feared, Miss Clark, so I went out to the back to get her a glass of water, but when I returned she'd left.'

'Did you see her again?'

'Not at the Band of Hope. She didn't return for that. She was at the Sunday service as usual though. She arrived shortly before we began and she slipped out just before the final hymn was sung, so I didn't get the chance to have a word with her.'

'And after that?' Tansy asked.

'That was the last time I saw her.' John Mason shook his head again. 'I do wish that I had persuaded her to confide in me what was troubling her. I cannot help feeling – perhaps I ought to have mentioned it to the police constable when he came but he merely asked the whole congregation if they had any information, and to reveal that she had sat here in tears all alone – it seemed like an invasion of her privacy somehow.'

'The dead have no privacy,' Tansy said soberly.

The picture of Fanny Jones was becoming clearer in her mind. She felt a stab of pity for the plain young woman who had come to this cheerless place to cry her heart out.

'Ought I to go to the police?' John Mason said nervously.

'My father is a retired police-officer,' Tansy said. 'He is taking a keen interest in the case. I can pass on the information to him.'

'That would be very kind of you,' he said gratefully. 'One wishes to do one's duty but one doesn't wish to bring any taint of scandal. Our patrons, the Edges—'

'Who?' Tansy jumped slightly.

'Sir Joshua Edge, the present Sir James Edge's father, was a great philanthropist,' he explained. 'When our little congregation was seeking a place in which to hold services he bought the land and the old hall and most generously presented it to us – to our predecessors I ought to say. It was particularly kind of him because he was not of our persuasion, and he also left when he died a small sum of money to help defray running costs, which is paid annually out of a separate trust fund. Of course I never met Sir Joshua myself but he was, from all accounts, a gentleman of the old school. So you can understand. . . .'

'One wouldn't wish to offend the Edges,' Tansy said. 'You've been very helpful, Mr Mason. Thank you.'

'I'd better get on. Mr Brown will hardly appreciate being left to deal with everything while I stand talking. Goodbye, Miss Clark.'

Shaking hands, retracing her steps to the museum, Tansy was lost in thought.

Connections between the girls were becoming more frequent, even reaching out to include Tilde. She needed a little time in which to compose her ideas into some kind of coherence.

In the reading-room she showed her ticket and was greeted by one of the curators whom she knew slightly.

'Miss Clark, it's been a while since we had the pleasure of seeing you here! Is there any particular collection that interests you? We have—'

'I need a quiet corner where I can make some notes,' Tansy said.

'As you know, Miss Clark, ink and pencils are not permitted in the reading-room,' the curator said in the breathless whisper reserved for that hallowed ground. 'Not that you would – but it would astonish you to know how many perfectly respectable scholars, professors some of them, are given to scribbling in the margins of illuminated manuscripts. So the rule must apply to all. If you'll come with me. . . ?'

Five minutes later she was seated in a small, somewhat airless cubicle with paper and pencil before her and a cup of coffee at her elbow.

Four girls, she thought, tapping her teeth with the indiarubber end of the pencil. All aged seventeen and largely without any connections or close friends in the city. Two plain and shy. Two pretty and lively. Two dead, one missing, one in her own house working with Mrs Timothy.

She wrote down 'Ellie Watson' and stared at it. Ellie had worked in a match factory, had had ginger hair and apparently no family who had come forward to claim her body. Fanny Jones had worked in a match factory too, as had Tilde. Could it be the same factory?

Fanny Jones had worked for Mrs Mainwaring, earning promotion because of her cleverness at trimming hats. She had attended Sion Chapel and a couple of week's before her death she had been upset about something, yet when John Mason had suggested she seek advice from Wesley Brown she had laughed. And Fanny had cut out the Valentine clipping and inserted it in her Bible so almost certainly she had considered asking for advice from him. She had gone out, leaving her door unlocked, which argued that she'd been excited about an appointment she intended to keep. Or had she run away not meaning to return? No. She was a devout Methodist and would never have left her Bible behind.

Tilde had worked very briefly at the match factory, had tried and failed to get work at Mrs Mainwaring's shop, had worked as a tweeny in the Edge household – the same family that had funded the chapel?

Mary Denny had written to her brother telling him about a Valentine Ball and had been seen with an elegantly clad young man.

She had covered the paper with scribbled notes, some underlined, had written the names with lines connecting them to the Edges, to the chapel and the match factory and to Valentine. Leaning her chin on her hand she gazed in bemusement at the results of half an hour's concentrated thinking.

'Did you get your writing finished, Miss Clark?'

The curator came softly to her side as she emerged from the cubicle.

'Not finished, no. Thank you anyway.'

She had opened her purse but the man shook his head.

'It was my pleasure, Miss Clark,' he whispered earnestly. 'I well recall the days when you and your young gentleman used to wander round the exhibits here. Such a cordial gentleman. His death was a great loss I'm sure.'

'Yes. Yes it was.'

She had been crushed by it like a flower after a storm – or so Finn had picturesquely phrased it. But she was a human being not a flower, and humans were resilient, not content to spend the rest of their lives in mourning. Geoffrey, she thought, would not have wanted that.

'If there's anything else—' The curator was hesitating.

'Would you know anything about matches?' she asked abruptly.

'Cricket matches, Miss Clark?'

'The kind you strike to produce a flame. There are factories where they are made, are there not?'

'At least half a dozen in the city, Miss Clark. Possibly more. The work is very ill-paid and of course the saltpetre ruins the skin and eventually the health of those employed there.'

'Have you heard of a match factory owned by the Edges?'

It was a shot in the dark but it hit its mark.

'Yes indeed, Miss Clark. It's no more than a short cab-ride from here. Of course I've never been there myself but the Edges are reasonably well known in the district. If you were contemplating some charity-work. . . ?'

'Something like that. Could you write down the address for me?'

'Certainly!'

Emerging with the address tucked away in her bag, her purse somewhat lighter since she had insisted on his accepting a remittance, Tansy hailed a cab and found herself ten minutes later in a crowded street lined with warehouses and offices with a goodly variety of humanity jostling and bustling along the cobbles.

She stood for a moment, getting her bearings, then beckoned to a lad who was hovering hopefully at a few yards' distance, clearly expecting a hand-out.

'Can you tell me where the Edge factory is?' Tansy asked as he came over.

The boy looked blankly at her.

'They make matches there,' she elucidated.

'Over there.' He jerked his head, disappointment in his sharp little face.

'Thank you.' Tansy tossed him a threepenny-bit and, wishing she had not worn a dress that required looping-up when the ground was muddy, went on towards the building he had indicated.

It was quieter within than she had anticipated. Somehow she had expected the clatter of machinery, the hum of voices – not this heavy silence that seemed to be poised over the brick structure.

The entrance, a narrow doorway with 'J. Edge & Son' scrolled above it brought her into an outer office where a clerk sat at a high desk, writing.

'Yes, madam?'

An older man had appeared, limping towards her, his swollen joints indicative of some long standing complaint.

'My name is Miss Clark.' Tansy put on her most elegant

manner. 'Would it be possible to speak to Sir James Edge?'

'Sir James Edge isn't in London at the moment, madam.' The voice was as creaky as the joints, the eyes suspicious.

'It concerns the girls who work here,' Tansy began.

'You from the League for Fallen Women?' the other demanded.

'I'm not from the league for anyone,' Tansy said. 'I'm here on – official business.'

It was, if not exactly true, not an outright falsehood.

'Oh?' The unwavering stare didn't falter.

'I believe that one of your employees was murdered three months go,' Tansy said.

If she had hoped to shock some response out of him she was destined to be disappointed.

'Ellie Watson, yes,' said the man.

'And you are?'

'Tobias Simpson, madam. I am manager for the firm.'

'In what capacity?'

'I hire and fire,' he said.

'You hired Ellie Watson?'

'About eighteen months ago. Her parents had died and left nothing but debts and she needed a respectable job. Are you connected in some manner with the authorities?'

'My father is Chief Inspector Laurence Clark. I don't know whether. . . ?'

'I read the newspapers,' he said stiffly. 'Some years ago he was involved in a heinous incident, I believe?'

'He was shot.'

'Most regrettable. So, Miss Clark, you're making enquiries on his behalf?'

The eyes were still hard and probing. Tansy said meekly, 'Yes, but he is not yet officially involved with the case. There are those who are of the opinion that a bullet in the back damages one's thinking processes.'

She hadn't meant to sound bitter but unwittingly she had struck the right note. Mr Simpson visibly relaxed, a wintry smile creasing his features.

'I can sympathize with the inspector,' he said. 'Until Sir James took me on I found great difficulty in obtaining employment commensurate with my qualifications. Rheumatism, Miss Clark, is no respecter of persons. How may I help you?'

'I wished to find out more about Ellie Watson,' Tansy said frankly.

'As I said – Mr Thomas, you may take fifteen minutes' break.' He had interrupted himself to address the clerk who silently slid from his stool and vanished through a door in the rear.

'Would you like to take a seat, Miss Clark?' He had opened a door and was ushering her into a larger room which seemed to be furnished entirely with cane chairs and tables and palms.

'Sir Joshua made his money in India,' Tobias Simpson said. 'Very fond of Indian styles he was. Now what can I tell you about Ellie Watson? Came to us for a job and I hired her.'

'Without references?' Tansy took a fragile-looking chair and sat cautiously on the edge.

'Match girls don't usually need references, Miss Clark.' He had remained standing. 'It's hard to get girls for the job as it is. Most are dead by the time they're in their late twenties. The phosphorus they dip the match-heads into, you see, and the saltpetre – both corrosive. Sad, but there's no other way to make matches.'

'It sounds appalling!'

'It's honest labour,' he said somewhat defensively.

'And the hours are long?'

'Ten hours a day six days a week. Some of our girls have homes; others sleep on the premises. I'll show you.'

He limped to a further door and opened it. Beyond, stone stairs wound down.

'This way, Miss.'

He went limpingly ahead of her down the stairs. Tansy following, was aware of gloom and cold.

Ahead of them a long chamber stretched, lit by tiny lamps set high in the walls. Four rows of girls, heads bent, sat down both sides of two long tables, their hands moving in a curious, mechanical rhythm.

'The slivers of wood are brought round in boxes,' Mr Simpson said, pausing to point to the nearest girl. 'Each one must be dipped in phosphorus and stuck upright to dry. The phosphorus sometimes drips so the trick's to twist the match quickly before setting it to dry.'

The fumes were so bad that she instinctively drew back, drawing her thin scarf across her mouth. Some of the workers had scarves wound about the lower parts of their faces. Others had not. In the lack-lustre light from the walls she glimpsed scarred and blistered faces, ungloved hands with burns scored deeply into the fingers, heard more than one rasping cough.

'Sylvie! Here, if you please!'

He had summoned a girl from halfway along one row who rose at once and came docilely to stand before them.

'This lady wishes to know about Ellie Watson,' Mr Simpson said. 'You sat next to her.'

'Yes, sir. Miss.'

Sylvie's face was as yet half-scarred. Her voice, however, had an ominous huskiness.

'Do you sleep here, Sylvie?' Tansy asked.

'Yes, Miss. Two to a bed. Through there.'

'The place is absolutely dry. Damp would render the phosphorus both dangerous and useless,' Mr Simpson said.

'So you knew her well?' Tansy said.

'Sort of,' Sylvie admitted.

'You were good friends?'

'We was on speaking terms,' Sylvie said in a pathetically proud tone.

'You can't tell me anything about her private life?'

Even as she spoke Tansy felt a fool for asking the question when it was very clear that these young women, working and sleeping below ground at a job that would eventually mar their looks and might well kill them had very little time to enjoy any private lives.

'We went to the music 'all now and then. Liked a good laugh Ellie did,' Sylvie volunteered.

'They occasionally went as a group, Miss Clark,' Mr Simpson said in an anxious tone. 'All quite respectable. They need a little pleasure now and then.'

'On the night that Ellie Watson died—'

'She went out,' Sylvie said. 'I already told the copper. Went out for a bit of a walk she said. She never come back.'

'She went to Kensington. Did she know anybody in that district?'

'Not that I know, Miss.' Sylvie shrugged.

'Is there anything at all you can tell me?' Tansy asked in some desperation.

'I told the copper I don't know nothing about Ellie,' Sylvie said.

Her face had an obstinate set. In the gloomy light her eyes flickered away.

'Well, thank you anyway. Oh, do you know Tilde Miles?'

'Tilde Miles worked here for only a short while I'm afraid,' Mr Simpson said. 'We engaged her to replace Ellie Watson, but she worked very slowly and insisted on wearing gloves which slowed her up still further. A most unsatisfactory young woman. If that's all, Miss Clark?'

'Yes. Thank you.'

Nodding at Sylvie who immediately resumed her seat again, Tansy felt a chill as she cast a last glance over the silently toiling girls.

'If there is anything else you wish to know?' Mr Simpson had steered her back to the stairs.

'I don't think so,' Tansy said. 'I'm grateful for your attention.'

'I hope they find out who killed Ellie Watson,' he said. 'She was quite a harmless kind of girl. Unfortunate hair.'

'I beg your pardon?'

'Ginger. Judas colour. Very unlucky, Miss Clark.'

He had evidently not noticed her own dark red chignon, she reflected, as she took her leave, or perhaps only ginger was unfortunate.

Outside the noise and dust hadn't been mitigated by any midday lull. In this world only the rich stopped work to eat. Tansy walked on, turning over the few facts she had learned in her mind.

Behind her footsteps came running and a voice hissed hoarsely, 'Miss? Miss!'

In the daylight the way in which the phosphorus had eaten into Sylvie's skin was cruelly plain. The girl seized Tansy's arm and pulled her into the shadow of a warehouse.

'I 'opped up the back stairs,' she said breathlessly. 'I daren't say anything down there, but Ellie went to meet someone.'

'Then why not say?'

'Can't afford to lose me place, can I?' Sylvie said. 'Slimy Simpson'd 'ave me out in one second if I let on I was talking to you private like.'

'Slimy?' Tansy questioned in surprise.

'Likes to get 'is 'ands up a girl's skirt,' Sylvie said. 'Lord God Almighty that one thinks 'e is! Ellie 'ated 'im, simply 'ated 'im.'

'Mr Simpson harassed Ellie Watson?'

'Ever since she come. Month after month, Miss. . . ?'

'Clark.'

'Miss Clark. In the end she just couldn't take it any more. She was going to get 'elp from someone.'

'Who?'

'Someone called Valentine,' Sylvie said. 'She'd gone to meet 'im on 'er afternoon off. She liked to go walking in one of the parks or sit down near the river. Dead dull if you was to ask me! But she was to meet this Valentine and 'e was going to 'elp 'er. She said she'd tell me all about it when she come back but she never did come back.'

She turned abruptly and scuttled away, pulling her scarf over her half-ruined face and was lost in the noisy crowd.

SEVEN

Tansy felt sick and shaken, more by what she had seen than by anything she had heard. She had done her share of helping out at various charity functions, of occasionally taking her turn at serving in the soup-kitchens and had accustomed herself to the smells and the raucous comments of the poor who were expected to be grateful and not make mock of the ladies who were trying so earnestly to do their Christian duty. In the East End life pulsated with a raw vitality that amused and stimulated her. But the long rows of silent, neatly clad girls who dipped the slivers of wood in the phosphorus, whose ungloved fingers were blistered and whose faces were in many cases already eaten into by the corrosive elements had had about them a terrible resignation.

Ellie Watson had endured it for nearly two years without getting her fingers or face corroded. Perhaps she had been neater and quicker in her movements. Tansy could almost imagine that she'd seen her, face pale under the ginger hair, fingers moving swiftly and surely. And under her quiet face buzzed the need to escape from this respectable slavery, from the detested attentions of Tobias Simpson, until she had been driven to seek help from the man who called himself Valentine.

She had completely forgotten to ask about Fanny Jones who had also worked in the match factory for a time! Tansy bit her lip in vexation. Pa would tell her that one ought not to begin asking questions until one knew what and about whom to ask. Pa would remind her that getting personally involved in a situation solved nothing.

She debated whether or not to return and repair the omission, but that might bring suspicion upon Sylvie. The sensible thing to do was to buy herself some luncheon in a respectable place where a solitary female might lunch alone and then take up Tilde's reference with the Edges.

She found a pleasant little restaurant already occupied by several ladies, one or two of whom, judging by the circulating novels propped up beside them, were not expecting any companion, settled herself at a corner table for one and ordered trout and salad with a glass of wine.

All around her conversation was being carried on in low, well-bred voices. She suspected that few, if any, of these prettily clad ladies with their frilled and ruched bustles, their winged lace-collars and bolero jackets, their elaborately flowered and beribboned hats perched on their well-groomed heads, knew or suspected that within a couple of streets, in the part of the city where respectability ruled, girls about whom nobody cared sat hour after hour dipping slivers of wood into death-dealing chemicals.

She herself had never given it a moment's thought until now. Ellie Watson and Fanny Jones had both been seventeen, both respectable girls trying to cling to their small stock of self-worth. Their deaths had hurt only themselves, meriting no more than a few short paragraphs in the newspaper once the first excited discovery of their murders had been cried in the streets.

What had begun for her as an academic exercise, something to assuage both her father's boredom and her own, had become important. Too important, she decided grimly, to be left to the careless methods of Inspector Jarrold.

'Was the trout not to your liking, madam?' the waiter asked coming with the bill.

'It was very good but I wasn't as hungry as I thought. Will you hail a cab for me, please?'

'I'll have the door-keeper do it, madam.'

His little sniff reminded her what his position entailed. Tansy flushed slightly at her own absent-mindedness and increased the tip.

She needed to find out more about the Edges who seemed to

have a finger in every pie, owning as they did the match factory and having donated the chapel to the Methodists. She wondered as she stepped into the cab if an Edge could be found among Mrs Mainwaring's gentlemen friends.

She had, perhaps half-unconsciously, imagined the Edge house to be over-grand, vulgarly opulent. The kind of house in which a nabob, having ground the faces of the poor in two continents, would dwell in selfish splendour, but the broad avenue near Grosvenor Square where the cab set her down was the epitome of understated good taste, the extravagances of the nineteenth century retreating before the Palladian elegance of the Regency.

She stood for a moment looking at the high façade with the exquisite fanlight over the door. Nets covered the tall windows, shielding what was behind the glass from the sunlight and the curiosity of passers-by. The front steps were sparkling white and the iron railings that separated the basement quarters from above-stairs glittered like raised black spears.

It was a house where order and beauty were synonymous, she decided, and tried unsuccessfully to picture a weeping Tilde being thrust out after dark. On the other hand appearances were deceptive. The Edges didn't spend much time fretting about the girls in the match factory they owned.

She went up the steps and rang the bell firmly.

A few moments elapsed before the door was opened by a footman in livery, his hair so shiny that it looked wet, his nose carried rather too high so that in looking at her he gave the impression of squinting slightly.

'Yes?'

A jumped up pot-boy, Tansy judged, assuming an expression of the utmost hauteur as she said, 'Miss Clark to see Mr Hawkins.'

'To see Mr 'Aw – Hawkins?'

The nose had been slightly lowered.

'If you please,' Tansy said sweetly.

It was clear from the uncertainty in the other's face that Mr Hawkins was not in the habit of being visited by well-dressed young ladies.

'Come in, Miss.'

The door was held wide and she stepped into a long, narrow

hall, its floor covered with a carpet patterned with golden horses on a crimson background, the panelled walls covered with a collection of ivories, which were so finely carved and so translucent that it was obvious they were very valuable.

'Will you wait in here?'

Aspirating the 'h' just in time the footman ushered her into an ante-room furnished with several pieces of elaborately carved furniture and with a small model of an elephant, fashioned in ebony and silver mounted, on a plinth by the window.

The footman withdrew, unable to resist a last curious look, and Tansy occupied herself in walking up and down, pausing now and then to look at the elephant from a different angle. Looked at from one direction it had a cheerful, almost roguish air; looked at from another its sharp tusks, again of ivory, menaced.

'You wished to see me, Miss. . . ?'

The man who had quietly entered was tall, spare and greying with an air of dignity that the footman would never quite manage to attain, sound his 'hs' as hissingly as he might.

'Miss Tansy Clark.'

'Yes, Miss Clark?'

'You provided Mathilde Miles with a character reference when she left her post here,' Tansy said.

'I did indeed. May I ask – Oh, please won't you sit down?'

'Thank you.'

Tansy took the nearest chair and gestured to him to follow suit, which, after a momentary hesitation he did, drawing up an adjacent chair and seating himself neatly upon it, coat tails flipped back.

'I have engaged Miss Miles as housemaid,' Tansy said, 'so naturally I wish to check up on her former job and the reference she received.'

'She was employed here as a between-maid, Miss Clark.'

'A tweeny. Yes, so she said. The reference that you provided was excellent and expressed most warmly.'

'I wished her to obtain a good place,' he nodded. 'You may rest assured that what I wrote is no less than the truth.'

'She is honest, polite, hard-working and loyal?'

'Indeed.' He bowed his head gravely.

'Apart from her habit of tasting the soup before it's taken to table?'

He pressed his lips together, glanced at the floor, then said, 'I believe there was something of that nature, yes.'

'Did the family complain of the habit?' Tansy pressed.

'The family is away from home at present, Miss Clark. They have been abroad since February. Sir James suffers from rheumatics during the winter and Lady Cecily suffers from hay fever in the spring. They usually spend at least half the year on the Continent.'

'Tilde came to work here from the match factory, I believe.'

He nodded.

'Which is owned by the Edges.'

'The family is concerned with several manufacturing and mercantile outfits, Miss Clark.'

'So Tilde was taken out of the match factory and brought here to work as a tweeny? Who recommended her?'

'She came on her own initiative, in hopes of bettering herself. I took the precaution of asking for information from Mr Simpson who manages the factory and he informed me that Mathilde Miles had worked there for only a week or so. He had considered her unsuitable for the job and suggested she look elsewhere. She had chosen to come here having heard the name of the factory owners.'

'And you hired her?'

'Yes. Yes, I did.' He was silent for a moment before continuing, 'She did strike me as a girl who might have done better for herself than as a between-maid but here she could have progressed to lady's maid had she applied herself properly.'

'But she dipped into the soup, according to the cook?'

'Yes. Mrs Bradshaw came to me in some distress complaining that Mathilde had sluttish habits and refused to be corrected. Left to myself I might have given her another chance but Mrs Bradshaw is of a somewhat fiery nature and—'

'Good cooks being hard to find.'

'Exactly!'

'Yet you turned her off at a moment's notice after dark.' Tansy gave him a long, puzzled look. 'Mr Hawkins, you strike me as a very sensible and humane man, so how could you simply turf a friendless young girl into the night when she had nowhere to go?'

'Miss Clark, it didn't happen precisely like that,' he said defensively. 'I gave the girl the reference she showed to you and the wages due to her and I offered to furnish her with the address of a respectable and inexpensive lodging but she said she didn't need a lodging because she had a friend who was going to look after her. She picked up her bag and walked out, throwing back some quotation from *Hamlet* on the way. "The slings and arrows of outrageous fortune". Perhaps you are familiar with it?'

Tansy nodded, the corners of her mouth quirking with amusement.

'She simply marched off and got into a cab. May I enquire how you came to engage her?'

'She was seated on a bench in a small park near my father's residence,' Tansy said slowly. 'It was past nine and getting quite dark. She was evidently in some distress and as I could hardly leave her alone there at that hour – anyway, she provided a reference and as I needed a housemaid I engaged her.'

'Probably the friend she'd arranged to meet hadn't turned up,' Mr Hawkins said.

'Probably.'

But Tilde hadn't mentioned any friend. She had given the information that she was completely friendless and alone.

'I mustn't take up any more of your time,' she said aloud, rising. 'I simply wished to check up on the character you gave her. Would it be possible for me to have a word with Mrs Bradshaw?'

'I'm afraid it's Mrs Bradshaw's afternoon off,' he regretted.

'Oh well, never mind. Thank you for your time.'

Mr Hawkins had also risen and now bowed slightly.

'Forgive me but I neglected to offer you any refreshment, Miss Clark,' he said. 'A cup of tea, perhaps?'

'Thank you but I'm due at my father's.'

'Is your father acquainted with the Edges by any chance?' he asked.

'No, not at all. My father is something of an invalid and no longer finds society entertaining. Are they a large family?'

'At one period they were a considerable family, I believe, but

Sir Joshua went out to India at the end of the last century and made his fortune there. Unfortunately, of his children only Sir James survived the heat and the various diseases endemic on the subcontinent, and Sir James and Lady Cecily had only one living child – Leslie.'

There was a perceptible hesitation before he uttered the name.

'And I suppose there is some friction between father and son?' Tansy said lightly.

'Oh no, Miss Clark. Nothing like that. The family is, as I've said, away at present.'

'Thank you again, Mr Hawkins.'

Tansy preceded him into the hallway where the supercilious young footman hovered by the door.

'Mathilde does suit you, I trust?' The butler gave her an anxious look.

'She hasn't started sampling the soup yet,' Tansy said.

Mr Hawkins gave an uncertain little smile and went along the passage through a baize-covered door at the far end.

'Will you hail me a cab please?' Tansy requested the footman.

'Yes, Miss.'

He sounded marginally more respectful so she was startled as he turned to run down the front steps to hear him say, 'Tilde never took any soup, Miss. And Cook never told Mr Hawkins that she took any soup. He made up the whole thing himself.'

'Surely you must be mistaken?'

Tansy joined him on the pavement, taking a few coins from her purse.

'No, Miss, I'm not.' He spoke rapidly, keeping his voice low and an eye on the half-open door. 'She was only here a few days and Cook got on very well with her, honest! Then Cook went off to see her sister who wasn't very well on account of the influenza, and Mr Hawkins sent for Tilde and told her that Cook wanted her gone on account of her tasting the soup, but that was Mr Hawkins's story, not Cook's, and when she came back the next day and wanted to know where Tilde was Mr Hawkins said that Tilde had left of her own accord.'

'How do you know all this?' Tansy demanded.

'Being a footman I get to waiting about a lot outside doors and in passages and hearing things,' he said ingenuously. 'And Tilde was settled nicely here though she wasn't much for the rough work, but Cook liked her and she had real nice manners.'

'Have you told Cook the real reason for Tilde's leaving?'

'Not likely! Mr Hawkins rules the house all right and he'd fire me if I started talking out of turn,' the footman said. 'Mind you, he's not a bad old buffer. Very fair and he seemed to like Tilde too.'

'Perhaps he liked her a little too well?'

It was dreadful of her to stoop to gossiping with a servant but investigating involved being unconventional she had discovered.

'Mr Hawkins? No, Miss, he's a widower with a grown-up daughter,' the youth said earnestly. 'He never gets up to any funny business.'

'So he lied about what Mrs Bradshaw had said and dismissed Tilde while she was away visiting a sister? And then told her when she came back that Tilde had left of her own accord?'

'And that's not true, Miss. Tilde was upset when she left. She asked me to call her a cab, said she was going to get advice from a friend of hers and went off.'

'Do you remember the address she gave you?'

'Some park in the West End.' He wrinkled up his forehead. 'Adelaide Park. That was it.'

'I see. Thank you.'

'Thank you, Miss.' He pocketed the coins and waved down a passing cab.

Tansy gave her father's address and sat hunched in thought during the journey.

So nice, decent Mr Hawkins had dismissed Tilde for a spurious reason that had nothing to do with any complaint from the cook, and Tilde had taken a cab to the park opposite Laurence's house where she had sat on a bench waiting for an unnamed friend. Like Ellie Watson and Fanny Jones. Tansy shivered, thinking of Patrick Denny's sister who presumably was still missing and might also have set out to get advice from an unnamed friend.

'You look tired, my dear,' Laurence greeted her when she entered the large, comfortable room filled now with mellow sunshine that glinted on the teacups and warmed the spines of the old books lining the walls into amber and coppery gold.

'I've had a busy day, Pa.'

She hastened to remove her hat and jacket, sensing boredom in his tapping fingers. Finn brought in the tea-tray and, at a nod from Laurence, poured three cups.

'Doing what?' Laurence asked.

'You first, Pa. Has Inspector Jarrold – he's not called?'

The faint possibility that he might just have been moved by her pleas to come round and consult his predecessor dwindled into nothing as her father shook his head.

'He will only condescend to visit me and pick my brains when the newspapers are calling for his resignation because he has failed to make an arrest in the cases of Ellie Watson and Fanny Jones,' he said.

'Finn?' Tansy glanced at the man-servant.

'Your Mr Denny was telling the truth,' Finn said. 'Sailed to India last October, sailed back three weeks ago. Your pa sent me to the War Office with a note and the feller there sent me back with a note.'

'Patrick Denny certainly had a commission and came back with an excellent series of sketches which apparently will prove invaluable for information about life on the frontier. Said he was an artist with a promising future.'

'I thought he was honest,' Tansy said, feeling unwonted pleasure.

'I didn't 'ave no luck with the Valentine balls,' Finn said. 'The private ones 'ad private guest-lists and the public ones was for anybody and didn't 'ave no guest-lists at all. Beats me why they want to 'old balls for the feller.'

'Saint Valentine is the patron saint of lovers, Finn,' Tansy said, amused.

'When I was in a courting mood I didn't reckon to no saint patronizing me,' he retorted.

'Why, Finn, you never mentioned you were romantic!' Tansy teased.

'I ain't romantic but I've 'ad me moments,' Finn said.

'So our tale is soon told,' Laurence said. 'What have you been busy doing all day?'

'I went to the chapel where Fanny Jones had worshipped regularly,' Tansy said. 'Apparently it was donated to the Methodists by Sir Joshua Edge, who made his fortune in the India trade and became something of a philanthropist. The Edges are not Methodists but he bought the land and left a small annuity to the congregation in his will. They don't have a regular incumbent but there are two deacons there who seem to run the place.'

'So they knew Fanny Jones?'

Laurence leaned forward, the last vestiges of ennui wiped from his face.

Tansy recounted in as much detail as she could recall the conversations she had held with Wesley Brown and John Mason.

'Looks as if Fanny was in some kind of trouble and had written and made an appointment to meet Valentine,' Laurence said thoughtfully.

'If she had she didn't mention it to John Mason,' Tansy said. 'I think that at the time she turned up in the chapel so upset she didn't know what to do. It was later that the advertisement appeared again and she hadn't been to chapel in the mean time.'

'So where did you go then?' Finn enquired.

'To the match factory. Pa, the Edges own it! I doubt if they ever go near the place but the family owns the factory and has other businesses around the city. The factory isn't far from the British Museum. Would you believe that a place where young girls work with dangerous chemicals and spend nearly all their time below ground is so close to a building where works of great antiquity and beauty are gathered for people to marvel at and for scholars to study?'

'The pyramids were built by slaves, weren't they?' Laurence said mildly.

'I'd've hoped that we'd evolved a bit since then,' Tansy retorted. 'Anyway, I spoke to the manager – a rather creepy individual called Tobias Simpson. I wanted to find out everything I could about Ellie Watson.'

'And did you?'

'She had no parents and she'd worked in the factory since she was fifteen. One of the girls – women, told me that she was quick-fingered and didn't get the phosphorus on her hands or her face – Pa, if you'd seen some of those poor girls!'

'You're an investigator, albeit on an unofficial basis, not a charity-worker,' Laurence reminded her.

'Anyway, after I left, this woman – her name's Sylvie – sneaked up the backstairs and told me that Ellie Watson had been harassed by Tobias Simpson and had confided that she had a new friend called Valentine who was going to help her deal with it.'

'So it was a Valentine killing.' Finn whistled.

'It seems fairly conclusive,' Laurence agreed. 'Did she say anything to the police?'

'No. She was scared of losing her job if she talked about the manager.'

'And the police didn't ferret too deeply into that first killing. What about your Tilde Miles?'

'I forgot to ask about her,' Tansy confessed. 'There really wasn't much time. Tobias Simpson was there at the factory and afterwards Sylvie just gabbled out what she had to say and ran off.'

'And then?'

'Then I had some lunch and then I went to the Edge's residence to check up on the reference that Tilde gave me.'

'And?'

Tansy took another swallow of her tea and launched into her account of her interview with Mr Hawkins and the words spoken by the footman.

'Cor! Seems to me the Edges is in it up to their necks,' Finn said.

'There's no proof of that,' Tansy said. 'They own other businesses and other houses too, I dare say, and we haven't heard of girls from them getting murdered, have we?'

'There's no proof there haven't been more killings either,' her father said, 'that haven't yet come to light.'

'So what do we know?' Tansy asked.

'We have a lot of circumstantial stuff which any self-respecting barrister could demolish in five minutes flat,' Laurence said. 'The Edges own the match factory and donated the chapel and your new protégée, Tilde Miles, who is neither dead nor disappeared worked for them briefly, first in the match factory and then as tweeny before being unjustly dismissed. She never mentioned her friend to you?'

'I assumed she was destitute.'

'And Ellie Watson told her friend Sylvie that she was going to talk to her friend Valentine because of some problem she had.'

'The manager was harassing her.'

'So she goes to meet this Valentine and is found dead. Did you discuss Fanny Jones? She spent a short time at the match factory before she got a more congenial job with Mrs Mainwaring, didn't she?'

'She was only there a few days before she found herself a better post.'

'And Sylvie was in a hurry. Never mind, you did well to get as far as you did, especially when we consider that Jarrold would burst a blood-vessel if he knew you were going round asking questions.'

'We will be turning over what we've learnt to the police, won't we?' Tansy said.

'Yes, but we'll know more soon, I hope,' her father said. 'I don't mean to present Jarrold with a load of unrelated facts that actually lead nowhere. Tansy, aren't you expecting two gentlemen to dinner?'

'To a banquet if Mrs Timothy has her way.'

'Then you must hurry home and make yourself beautiful.'

'There are only about four hours before they arrive,' she said with self-deprecating humour. 'Not long enough for a miracle.'

'Nonsense.' Laurence scowled at her affectionately.

'If anybody was to ask my opinion,' Finn said, 'I'd say that no miracle was wanted to turn Miss Tansy into a stunner, but a bit of a dust-down never did no 'arm.'

'Well said, Finn!' Laurence approved. 'Enjoy your evening, my dear, and don't lose your heart to the Irishman.'

'I am not likely to lose my heart to anyone,' Tansy said, putting on her hat and jacket and giving her father the airy wave that he preferred to a more sentimental embrace.

'I'll step across the park with you,' Finn said when they reached the front steps.

'You'll do no such thing!' Tansy retorted. 'I'll not be nursemaided.'

'I've run out of baccy so I can pick some up in the shop by the cab-stand,' Finn said innocently. 'You ain't ashamed at being seen with an old lag, are you?'

'Of course not. Anyway you've gone straight for so long that I reckon everybody looks upon you as a responsible citizen now.'

'There was a time when Fingers Finn was known all over town,' he said sadly. 'Respectability is somewhat lowering to the reputation.'

'You've not mentioned the kitten that was thrown at me to Pa?'

'Not a word, Miss Tansy.'

Loping at her side as they crossed the road and entered the park he added, with an obstinate look, 'If anyone else starts giving you grief or if you find any more pink ribbon I can't keep my promise. I'll feel obliged to split to your pa.'

Which meant she couldn't tell him, as she had planned, about the bright pink ribbon tied round her door-knocker. Laurence would certainly insist that either she backed off completely or that she went back to his house to sleep under male protection.

Instead she said thoughtfully, 'You know this is the first time that Pa and I have really worked together on a case. And we're not even doing it officially. It's as if all the games we used to play suddenly became serious.'

'Your pa liked playing at detectives when you were a bit of a thing,' Finn agreed. 'Remember when I first came to work for 'im. You was about fifteen and thin as prison gruel and nearly as tall as you are now.'

'With a face that hadn't grown to match my nose and hair so thick that it wouldn't let a comb near it. Hardly a bit of a thing.'

'A brave bit of a thing,' he insisted. 'Your ma was mortal sick by that time, but there was still a lot of spirit in 'er. It's a crying shame she never saw you all growed up and solving murders.'

'All growed up and running round chasing my own tail,' Tansy said with a grin. 'Finn, I went to see Inspector Jarrold at his club.'

Finn stopped dead and stared at her.

'You what?' he said.

'Pa gets so bored,' she pleaded. 'Having me asking questions, Frank and you going here and there for snippets of information – that's all very well as far as it goes, but there's no satisfaction in it for Pa when he's not been asked for his advice. I hoped Inspector Jarrold would understand that.'

'You went to his club? They never let you in!'

'With great reluctance, into an antechamber. Inspector Jarrold was polite – just, and patronizing. I hoped he might have changed his mind and gone round to see Pa. Evidently he hasn't. Maybe I shouldn't have gone to the club.'

'Women ain't generally welcome in gentlemen's clubs,' Finn agreed.

'But I didn't get the usual kind of education that a girl gets,' Tansy said. 'You know when other girls were going to their first balls and trying to paint charming water-colours, I was studying back-copies of the *Police Gazette* and working out solutions to unsolved crimes instead of doing my embroidery. Finn, d'ye think Pa wanted a boy and has always been a mite disappointed that all Ma managed to produce was a female?'

'I wasn't around when you was born,' Finn said, 'so I can't go evidencing myself about the way 'e acted then, but I reckon he was pleased enough. 'Oping for a son later. But I guarantee you, Miss Tansy, your pa never wastes time thinking of sons now. Proud as a peacock of you 'e is, so it's your duty to take good care of yourself and don't go looking for any trouble.'

'And perhaps Inspector Jarrold will come and see Pa after all. Thank you, Finn.'

They had almost reached the other side of the park and she looked back towards the pond and the bench by the willow tree, not with nostalgia for the marriage that had never been but with puzzlement.

'When I found Tilde here,' she said, 'she was in great distress. Genuine distress. About being dismissed from her place at the Edges naturally, but she'd come here to meet her friend.'

'Valentine,' Finn said.

'She had written to him before and obviously received an answer telling her where to come. She never mentioned that to me.'

'Probably reckoned you might not employ 'er if she let on she was waiting for a gentleman.'

'Who obviously hadn't turned up. I wonder why. Of course the park was due to close for the night.'

The moment she had uttered the words she knew she had said something significant. She knew also that it tied up with some casual remark of Finn's made quite recently. Something about. . . ?

'The park don't get locked until midnight,' Finn said in a puzzled tone. 'You left your pa's around 'alf past eight.'

'And came across Tilde a few minutes later. But the park-keeper warned me as I entered that the park was due to close.'

'Did you see 'im plain?' Finn demanded.

'He was just a vague shape in the gathering dark. I heard his voice, thanked him and walked on. It never crossed my mind to look at him. One doesn't often look at park-keepers and – why would he tell me. . . ? Oh, my God!'

She put her hands to her mouth and stopped still.

'Looks like you got to that young girl just before Valentine arrived,' Finn said soberly.

EIGHT

Tilde opened the front door before Tansy had taken out her key. She was clad in a black silk dress with lace collar and cuffs and looked very pretty with her dark curls held back by a stiff lace bow.

'Have you been promoted to parlour-maid already?' Tansy asked as she stepped inside.

'Mrs Timothy said you were having two gentlemen to dinner this evening,' Tilde said. 'This is my Sunday dress which I made just before Mamma died.'

'It looks very becoming,' Tansy approved.

'Is that you, Miss Tansy?' A flushed Mrs Timothy put her head out of the kitchen door, the cap on her head slightly askew. 'The wine and spirits were delivered in good time and everything is in order. How is your revered pa?'

'In good spirits, Mrs Timothy.'

'And young Tilde here has been a big help to me which you'll know is true for I never praise lightly,' the other said. 'However, when the cooking rises to a crescendo, so to speak, I like my premises to myself, so if Tilde could help you dress?'

'I can dress hair,' Tilde said eagerly.

'Come up in fifteen minutes and you can dress mine then.'

Tansy went on up the stairs to her bedroom with its attendant bathroom and spare room where she had lodged boxes of old papers and dog-eared books from which she didn't wish to be parted though it was years since she'd read them.

Her bedroom had been decorated in the pale cream and

buttercup yellow that intensified the sunlight and made her feel cheerful on those occasions, carefully hidden from others, when a sick loneliness overcame her, and the years since Geoffrey's death seemed pointless and empty, despite the various activities in which she had immersed herself.

This evening she felt a mixture of emotions. She had, she felt, found out many more links among the four girls but the most recent revelation had chilled her to the bone. She must have passed the killer on her way into the park, even spoken, albeit very briefly, to him and gone serenely on her way. He had wanted to ensure that the park was as deserted as possible so that he could kill the girl waiting unsuspectingly by the pond without interruption. By inviting Tilde to accompany her home she had foiled his purpose. No wonder he had twice tried to frighten her off by the throwing of a dead kitten and the tying of a bright pink ribbon on her door-knocker.

She had just finished washing her face and changing her undergarments when a knock on her bedroom door announced Tilde.

'Mrs Timothy says that I'm to help you lace up, Miss Tansy,' she said.

Tansy, who had a healthy appetite and the good fortune to remain slim despite that, grimaced.

'Mrs Timothy would be very happy if I was laced so tightly that I fainted into the arms of the nearest eligible gentleman,' she said. 'You may pull the laces one inch tighter but no more. I intend to enjoy my dinner.'

'Mrs Timothy is a wonderful cook, isn't she?' Tilde put her foot in the small of Tansy's back as she clung to the bedpost, and yanked the laces more tightly. 'There! won't it be lovely when the day comes that ladies don't have to wear corsets at all?'

'You're a girl after my own heart,' Tansy said, straightening up. 'Pass me the amber dress.'

It was of thin velvet, its neckline scooped low, its elbow-sleeves threaded with chocolate-brown ribbons, its long skirt swept back into a bustle ruched with brown silk.

'Oh, you look so elegant!' Tilde stepped back, clasping her hands to admire the results. 'Now if I can plait your hair into a coronet and leave some little curls just on your temples – rather like an Alexandra fringe – both the gentlemen will fall in love with you.'

'That would be like eating two dinners at once,' Tansy observed, seating herself obediently at the dressing-table. 'And these gentlemen are not prospective suitors.'

'I never had a suitor of any kind,' Tilde said wistfully.

Tansy saw the opening and seized it.

'But you were meeting a gentleman in the park on the evening I first saw you,' she said.

The face behind her reflected in the mirror showed faint surprise and a certain embarrassment.

'However did you find that out, Miss Tansy?' she asked.

'Never mind how I found out,' Tansy said severely. 'Why didn't you mention you were there to meet someone?'

'Because he hadn't come,' Tilde said simply.

'You told me that you had no friends.'

'I haven't! Hadn't then anyway. I'd never actually met the gentleman for whom I was waiting,' Tilde said in something of a fluster. 'I couldn't tell you about it, Miss Tansy, because you would have thought I was a girl without virtue and without honour and that would have mortified me, for Mamma brought me up to be very virtuous and honourable.'

'I think,' said Tansy, 'that you had better tell me the full story.'

'I needed some advice.' Tilde's fingers were steadily plaiting.

'About what?' Tansy enquired.

'About whether or not to have my fortune told,' Tilde said.

'Your fortune?'

Of all possible answers this was the one least expected.

'It is possible for some people to pierce through the veil and see what the future holds,' Tilde said earnestly. 'I was so tired of lugging pails of water upstairs and peeling vegetables for Mrs Bradshaw. Oh, they were very nice to me, until Mr Hawkins told me that Mrs Bradshaw had complained, and I couldn't tackle her about it because she'd gone off to see her sister and Mr Hawkins said I had to leave at once. The only comfort I had was that I was going to meet Mr Valentine and—'

'Mr?' Tansy picked up the word.

'Mamma often consulted him when she was alive,' Tilde said. 'He used to look at the lines in her hand and tell her what was going to happen – and sometimes it did! So naturally when I saw the advertisement – there was one in the newspaper—'

'But not offering to tell fortunes.'

'That's against the law, isn't it?' Tilde looked puzzled. 'I remember Mamma saying that he only ever admitted to giving ladies advice otherwise the police might arrest him.'

'Yes, of course. It comes under the Act against Witchcraft.'

'I don't think that Mr Valentine is a witch,' Tilde said. 'Mamma used to go occasionally to see him and she told me he was very spiritual.'

'Did you go with her?'

Tilde shook her head and carefully adjusted one of Tansy's braids.

'Mamma said that I was too young to have problems and it wasn't necessary.'

'So when you saw the advertisement you thought the Valentine was the Mr Valentine whom your mother consulted?'

'I answered the advertisement,' Tilde said. 'There was a box number to answer so I sent it there.'

'And received a reply?' It was hard to keep the excitement in her voice within bounds.

'Only a slip of paper giving me the time and day and the park where I was to meet him.'

'Not at his house?'

'No. Maybe the police were watching his house because of the fortune-telling,' Tilde suggested.

'Do you still have the slip of paper?' Tansy asked.

'No. It said "destroy this" on it so I put it in the kitchen fire.'

'And it was in this Mr Valentine's handwriting?' Tansy pressed.

'I don't know. I never saw any letter from him before,' Tilde said.

'But he knew where you lived?'

'I put the address of the Edge house on my letter,' Tilde said. 'If I hadn't he wouldn't've known where to send his reply would he? He sent me an answer by return of post. It was very quick.'

'And when did his answer arrive?'

'On the very day I was dismissed. That made having to leave less of an upset, though it was still pretty upsetting. I mean – I didn't much like being a tweeny but I did try and I would have bettered my position only I never got the chance.'

'So that was why you were sitting in the park?' Tansy said.

'And Mr Valentine never came,' Tilde said mournfully. 'I'd been waiting and waiting and it was getting darker and darker and all at once I felt so – hopeless! I suppose Mr Valentine must've been arrested for fortune-telling because he didn't turn up.'

But he had turned up, Tansy thought. He'd been hanging around waiting for the park to empty itself of visitors before he went softly along the twisting path to where another girl innocently waited.

Carefully she said, 'Did your mother ever tell you where Mr Valentine lived?'

'Fenter Lane. Near St Martin-in-the-Fields. He has two rooms there above a shop where you can hire dominoes and masks. I've not been there myself but Mamma told me about it.'

'Tilde, I want you to keep what you've told me strictly to yourself,' Tansy said. 'You are to tell me immediately if you hear from this Mr Valentine and you are not to meet him without my express permission.'

'How would he know where to write to me when he doesn't know where I am?' Tilde said.

But he knew, Tansy reflected. When he'd sent the note to Tilde he'd already killed twice, possibly three times. Had he in each case sent a brief note, stipulating the time and place of meeting and ordering the recipient to burn it? Outside Kensington Library, outside Kew Gardens, in Adelaide Park – why Adelaide Park?

Because it was opposite Laurence Clark's house, she thought suddenly. That wasn't a coincidence. Valentine needed someone to know what he was doing, needed someone to realize how clever and cunning he was. Who better than a retired police inspector to tease by committing another murder under his nose?

The doorbell rang. Outside a cab drove off.

'That will be one or both of my guests,' she said, wrenching her mind from the possibilities teeming there. 'Go down and answer the door and show the visitors into the drawing-room.'

'Your hair looks lovely, Miss Tansy,' Tilde said, vanishing stairwards.

Tansy cast a quick and pleased glance in the mirror and followed the girl's trim little figure onto the landing. From here she could see the expression on Patrick Denny's face as he saw Tilde. She considered it very doubtful that Tilde could possibly be Mary Denny but it did no harm to make certain.

Both Frank and Patrick had arrived together, the former breezing in, the latter following with a spray of carnations in his hand.

'Good-evening, Tansy! You look very fetching up there,' Frank called cheerfully, thereby ruining any chance she might have had of making a dignified descent.

Behind him Patrick Denny had handed his hat and cape to Tilde with a pleasant smile that revealed no recognition at all.

'Good-evening, Frank, Mr Denny. The flowers are lovely. Thank you.'

The delicate spray was by chance the soft, pale yellow that glowed against the amber of her skirt.

They went into the drawing-room. A fire had been lit to counter the chill of the evening and Mrs Timothy had arranged a selection of bottles and glasses on the sideboard.

Not until they were seated about the fire, Tansy on the sofa and her guests on adjoining chairs, drinks in their hands did she look expectantly at Frank.

'Mr Denny told you about his sister?' she said.

'Yes indeed. I took him off to my club last night and we talked until past midnight,' Frank said. 'Is there any further news?'

'A little.' Tansy hesitated, decided to keep back Tilde's latest revelation and spoke briefly instead about her visit to Sion Chapel and to the Edge residence.

'I went round to see Pa,' she concluded. 'Inspector Jarrold hasn't visited him yet but Pa is convinced that eventually he will. Meanwhile we must continue in a strictly unofficial way. And of course any definite proofs we find must be communicated to the authorities.'

'Are there any?' Frank enquired with a note of scepticism in his voice.

'Nothing that would stand up in any court of law,' she admitted.

'You're not suggesting that my sister was – Mary has too much sense to allow herself to be enticed away by some man.' Patrick's face had flushed slightly.

'If she answered the Valentine advertisement,' Frank said, 'that is hardly the same as allowing herself to be enticed away. She needed advice—'

'You can't know that!' Patrick said sharply.

'We can't know for certain that she wrote to the fellow anyway,' Frank allowed, 'but if she did it would have been for advice.'

'If Mary wanted advice she could have asked me.'

'Mr Denny, you were in India!' Tansy exclaimed. 'It takes weeks for a letter to get there. You said so yourself.'

'If you please, Miss, Mrs Timothy says dinner is served,' Tilde announced brightly, appearing in the doorway.

'Thank you, Tilde. Shall we go in, gentlemen?'

Somewhat relieved at the interruption, since she had felt her own temper beginning to kindle, Tansy rose and led the way into the small dining-room where the table had been laid with such an abundance of white linen, the best monogrammed cutlery, the Crown Derby service and as many dishes of silver and copper as could be crammed on to the side-table that she rapidly concluded that Mrs Timothy, at least, demanded great results from the event.

'Let me put these flowers in a vase. Tilde, fill the glass vase with water and then bring in the first course, please.'

Seating herself, arranging the carnations in the vase and putting them on the side-table where they could be admired without interrupting conversation, she was amused to hear her guests exchange a few stilted words of conversation. No doubt they had been close enough in the club, but the presence of a woman seemed to bring out the sulky boy in both of them.

'Shall we enjoy the meal and get down to discussion later?' she suggested tactfully when the soup had been served. 'Mr Denny, tell us something of County Wicklow. I've never been to Ireland.'

'It would provide a fitting setting for you, Miss Clark,' Patrick said.

'Surely you'd die of boredom in a week there,' Frank said.

'It's one of the grandest places on God's earth,' Patrick said. 'From our farm you could look over the fields to where the mountains swept down to the rocks that bordered the sea.'

'So you and your sister came to London,' Frank said.

'To advance yourselves,' Tansy said somewhat hastily. 'That seems to me to be entirely praiseworthy. Your sister liked London?'

'Very much. Mary enjoys visiting museums and art galleries as do I.'

'But once you had left the city she must have felt somewhat lonely?'

'Mary has resources within herself,' Patrick said. 'Of course she looked forward to my coming home but she was contriving to occupy herself.'

'And a gentleman friend had invited her to a Valentine ball, Tansy said.

'So it seems she could be enticed to a ball,' Frank said, gently sardonic.

'Then it would've been with a respectable man whom she met in a museum or was introduced to somewhere or other,' Patrick insisted.

'Was your sister—? Thank you, Tilde. We can serve ourselves now. Was Mary – you said she had no suitors. That seems unlikely if she looks anything like the sketch you drew of her,' Tansy said, watching the door close behind Tilde.

'Of course she had men eyeing her.' Patrick sounded proud. 'Tossed her head and went on her way did Mary.'

'She was seen with a young man sometime in January,' Tansy said.

'What!' Patrick stared at her. 'How do you know? I beg your pardon, Miss Clark, I didn't mean to sound too abrupt.'

'There is a witness,' Tansy said cautiously. 'I'm not at liberty to disclose—'

'My sister has been missing for – Lord knows how long, and you're not at liberty to disclose. . . ?'

'The witness saw her with him once and from a distance,' Tansy said. 'She wasn't able to give a very clear description. I'm sorry.'

'Then it could've been Valentine.' Frank looked at her.

'It could've been anybody,' Tansy said. 'Finn made enquiries but it's quite impossible to get hold of any guest-lists for the balls whether public or private. I take it the letters for Valentine haven't been collected yet?'

'I hung around the office most of the morning and Patrick here sat there all afternoon,' Frank told her. 'The two letters are still there.'

'And the other connections. . . ?' Patrick broke off, looking from one to the other. 'Look, forgive me, but I can't get fretted about girls I never met. I'm sorry about what happened to them but surely the city has its dark side. Mary'd not be linked with that.'

'Your sister can do needlework?' Tansy asked.

'Mary can make lace,' he said. 'Real Irish lace with the odd Celtic knot pattern incorporated in it. She's talented in that.'

'Could she have sold her lace in order to make a living?' Tansy wondered.

'She has no need to earn her own living! Hasn't it been made clear to you that I'm able to keep us both in modest comfort? Mary has only to keep house and do a little domestic sewing and amuse herself.'

'Perhaps she got tired of keeping house and amusing herself and decided to put her talents to good use. Women aren't always content to stay at home and amuse themselves,' Tansy said.

'There are those who must work to support themselves,' he conceded, 'but they have no husbands earning sufficient to take care of them. Mary has a brother.'

'Some women may choose to work in order to enrich their own lives,' Frank said mildly.

Tansy beamed upon him.

'Possibly,' Patrick Denny said unwillingly.

A tap on the door brought Mrs Timothy, in a splendidly ruffled black silk dress, her manner maternal as she set down the main course.

'Good-evening, gentlemen.' Her voice reeked of gentility. 'Mr Cartwright, you don't require a welcome from me being such an old friend as you are. Mr Denny, I hope you're enjoying some nourishing food here now that you're settled in London? I hope that Tilde is giving satisfaction in her table duties?'

'Everything is perfect, Mrs Timothy,' Tansy said. 'Tilde is shaping very nicely and the meal is splendid.'

'Then I'll leave you to enjoy it.' Mrs Timothy withdrew with great dignity.

'Your housekeeper caught the Irish in my accent,' Patrick said with a rueful look.

'Very little escapes Mrs Timothy,' Tansy told him with a grin. 'She has an insatiable curiosity about everything that comes within her sphere. Tell me, what do you think of my new maidservant?'

'The girl you met in the park. Mr Cartwright told me about her. She's a pretty girl. Why?'

'I wondered if she resembled your sister.'

'The same colouring,' he said with a faintly dismissive note in his voice, 'but not so much character there. Mary is a strong-willed, independent girl.'

'Who doesn't want to earn her own living?'

'Independent within her proper sphere,' Patrick said with the pomposity of a very young man. 'Certainly she isn't the kind of girl who would be tempted away by a handsome face or a smooth tongue.'

'But she was seen with a gentleman.' Frank helped himself to vegetables.

'I'll not deny that she wrote to me about having a splendid new friend,' Patrick said reluctantly. 'But had she met someone, which seems likely, surely he'd be a gentleman and not a man who murdered women.'

'So only the lower classes commit murder?' Tansy said playfully. 'What a snob you are, Patrick Denny.'

'This isn't getting us very far,' Frank pointed out. 'Let's relish the wonderful cooking and then make a list of suspects over our coffee.'

Tilde brought in the pudding, the cheese and fruit while the conversation limped along on more general topics.

When they were seated in the drawing-room again, brandy and coffee at their elbows, Tansy handed out cigars and, partly to tease Patrick Denny, partly because she enjoyed the occasional habit, lit up a small cheroot for herself, aware of the young Irishman's slightly disapproving look.

'What suspects do we have?' she asked. 'Obviously Valentine tops the list.'

'The point is,' Frank said, 'who is Valentine? Any ideas?' He looked questioningly from one to the other.

Tansy remained silent. She had no intention of telling anyone about the Mr Valentine who told fortunes until she had checked him out for herself. Neither did she intend mentioning the dead kitten or the ribbon tied to the door-knocker. Frank gave lip-service to the notion of female independence but he might suddenly become protective if she confided in him fully.

'He is a man who preys on poor working girls?' Patrick said.

'One of the Edges?' Frank glanced at her.

'The Edges have been abroad with their son since – for months now. I can't recall exactly what Mr Hawkins the butler told me but they always winter abroad.'

'What about Mr Hawkins?' Frank said.

'He seemed a thoroughly respectable, decent man. A widower.'

'But he dismissed Tilde on the word of the cook,' Frank reminded her.

'Actually he didn't.'

Tansy swiftly recounted her brief conversation with the footman.

'So Mr Hawkins waited until this Mrs Bradshaw was out of the way and then proceeded to dismiss Tilde Miles on the basis of a tale concocted by himself. Why not simply dismiss her for the right reason?'

'Perhaps there wasn't a reason,' Patrick suggested. 'Perhaps she really was doing well as she claims but for some reason – another reason – he wanted her out of the house?'

'You just said there might not have been a reason and then you give us one,' Tansy said.

'As an Irishman,' said Patrick with unexpected humour, 'I claim the right to express myself in a roundabout way.'

'If Hawkins goes round killing young women he might have sent Tilde away because he liked her and didn't want to kill her as well.'

'That sounds a mite far-fetched, Frank,' Tansy objected.

'It's a possibility. I'd not cross the respectable Mr Hawkins off the list just yet,' Patrick said. 'As the butler, left in charge while the family is away, he might be entrusted with certain matters of business connected with the match factory where Ellie Watson, Fanny Jones and Tilde worked for varying periods of time.'

'I almost forgot!' Frank brought out a paper from his inside pocket. 'I've a summary of the inquest on Ellie Watson. Not much was reported in the papers. I had a look through the back-numbers but the case didn't attract much attention. I was in Scotland at the time and it certainly wasn't reported there.'

'What happened at the inquest?' Tansy asked.

'The victim was identified by a Mr Tobias Simpson as being the body of Ellie Watson, aged seventeen, orphan, who had worked at the match factory for two years.' He ran his eye over the paper he held. 'She was a plain girl with ginger hair, described as quiet and shy. No particular religious affiliations but she did knit and donate the finished articles to the Society for the Conversion of the Jews. She had no known gentlemen friends and no police record.'

'A thoroughly decent girl in fact. Go on.' Tansy stubbed out her cheroot and leaned forward eagerly.

'She went out one late afternoon and didn't return that night. Apparently the girls who work in the match factory also sleep there.'

'I know,' she said sombrely.

'She was found the next morning lying on the pavement near a bench outside Kensington Public Library. She had been killed by a blow to the back of the head, almost certainly with a heavy instrument. Her hat, which was still on her head, being securely pinned to her hair, had a bright pink ribbon tied round it.'

'Tied there before or after death?' Tansy asked.

'Doesn't say. No attempt had been made to further damage the body, and forensic examination revealed that Ellie Watson had been virgo intacta.'

'So that hadn't been the reason for a frenzied attack?' Patrick said.

'Hardly frenzied!' Tansy objected. 'One blow on the back of

the head? That's the way you'd kill a fish you'd just caught, or a rabbit you wanted for the stock-pot.'

'You met the manager – what's his name? Simpson – could he. . . ?'

Tansy considered. 'He has a stick,' she said slowly, 'on account of his rheumatism, and Sylvie told me that he was always trying to put his hand up the girls' skirts. But he limps quite badly. Would he have been able to move so softly that Ellie Watson and later on Fanny Jones still had their backs to him when he struck them?'

'Your pa trained you well,' Frank said with an approving nod.

'When is the inquest on Fanny Jones?' Tansy asked.

'Tomorrow afternoon. Are you going? I mean to be there myself.'

'Yes. Yes, I'll probably be there.'

She would visit Mr Valentine in the morning, she decided.

'What about the chapel? That seems to figure somewhat,' Patrick asked.

'The Edges donated it and Fanny Jones went there and was very upset about two weeks before she was killed. The deacon, John Mason, mentioned it to me,' Tansy recapitulated.

And Fanny laughed when it was suggested she consult Mr Brown, didn't you say?' Frank remembered. 'You met him, didn't you?'

'Wesley Brown, yes. Large, flabby, unhealthily pale. He kept on rubbing his hands together and talking about lost lambs. I didn't care for him.'

'But Fanny Jones was the only Methodist, wasn't she?' Frank said. 'You and your sister aren't. . . ?'

'We're Catholics, though we have fallen away a bit since we came into this country,' Patrick supplied.

'That report you just read out!' Tansy exclaimed suddenly. 'Something about the conversion of the Jews?'

'Ellie Watson contributed knitted articles to the Society.'

'There might be some link there with Sion Chapel? The Methodists are forever trying to convert people.'

'It's a possibility,' he agreed.

'So putting our heads together hasn't been entirely useless,' Frank said.

'That sounds as if you're about to take your leave,' Tansy said lightly.

'Not unless you're giving me a hint.'

He raised an eyebrow almost imperceptibly in Patrick Denny's direction.

'I intend to bid good-night to both of you,' she said firmly, 'when we've had another coffee. I have a busy day tomorrow.'

'I doubt if anybody will come up with anything very interesting at the inquest,' Frank said. 'It will be murder by a person or persons unknown. Unless Inspector Jarrold has got on to Valentine's track by now?'

'I doubt that.' Tansy curled her lip loyally. 'Inspector Jarrold plods to what is frequently the right solution but Pa has that extra dimension that enables him to think his way to the end of a problem more quickly.'

'Your father sounds like a man worth meeting,' Patrick said.

'Oh, I'm sure that you'll meet him in due course,' Tansy said. Laurence, she knew, would be anxious to form his own opinion of the young Irishman.

'I still feel we ought to keep an eye on the newspaper office,' Frank said. 'I've a feeling that Valentine will take the risk of picking up his correspondence before too long.'

'I can take the morning shift,' Patrick offered.

'Better if you can manage the afternoon one,' Frank said. 'I'm usually down at the office in the morning anyway and I want to go to the inquest.'

'The afternoon then.' Patrick nodded amiably.

The dinner and the wine had ameliorated the slight antagonism between the two men, Tansy thought.

'What about you, Miss Clark?' Patrick looked at her.

'Please call me Tansy. Miss Clark sounds very formal, or as if I'm a rather stern schoolmistress into my forties,' Tansy begged.

'Surely nobody would mistake you for a day over twenty-five and very far from being a schoolmistress?' he protested. 'I was going to ask if your own plans. . . .'

'I shall attend the inquest on Fanny Jones,' Tansy said. 'In the morning I – have some social calls to make.'

'Damn it, Tansy, but you can't go flouncing off to make social calls in the middle of a murder investigation!' Frank said vigorously.

'We're not, officially speaking, in the middle of any kind of investigation,' she pointed out. 'We've no authority to go asking questions at all and if we do find any solid evidence we must hand it to the police. It will be easier if and when Inspector Jarrold brings Pa in for consultation, but even if he doesn't we can't keep what we might discover to ourselves. This man has to be found and arrested before he kills again.'

'You think he will?' Patrick frowned slightly.

'I'm sure he will,' Tansy said soberly. 'Frank?'

'I agree,' Frank said. 'I wish we knew why he started killing. And when?'

'Earlier than three months ago?' Tansy felt a small shiver ripple over her despite the warmth of the room.

'While I'm down at the office tomorrow morning I'll take a look through the files,' Frank said, rising. 'There are unsolved cases that might fit the pattern. Tansy, I shall take my leave before you put your threat into execution and fling us out. That was a marvellous meal. Coming, Denny? We can share a cab.'

Patrick Denny, who looked as if he would have chosen to stay a little longer, rose with evident reluctance.

'May I join my thanks to my new friend's sentiments?' he said. 'However I would add that far superior to the food, perfect though that was, has been the charm of our hostess. Good-night, Miss Tansy.'

He kissed her hand and went into the hall where she heard him thanking Tilde for the good care she had taken of them.

'Smooth-talking broth of a boy, isn't he?' Frank murmured. 'Let's not forget that we still haven't found his sister.'

'But he was still in India when—'

'We've only his word that she'd already disappeared when he arrived back in England,' Frank said. 'Don't cross him off the list just yet – and have a care for your own safety, Tansy.'

'I'm hardly a poor but respectable working girl,' Tansy said.

'No, but you're a striking young woman of obvious breeding and intelligence, who is going hither and thither asking questions. Be careful, my dear.'

For an instant his blue eyes were unsmiling. Then he kissed her cheek lightly and went out into the hall.

'What a lovely young gentleman!' As the front door closed Tilde came back into the drawing-room.

'Which one?' Tansy enquired.

'Well, I'm sure both of them are very handsome,' Tilde said politely, 'but Mr Denny now! Did you ever hear such a beautiful voice! And those dark eyes. Quite soulful, don't you think so, Miss? And both of them fathoms deep in love with you.'

'Tilde, you're a romantic little fool,' Tansy said, laughing. 'They are not in the least interested in me save as a friend who can provide them with a very good dinner courtesy of Mrs Timothy. Mr Denny I scarcely know and Mr Cartwright is an old friend, almost like a brother to me.'

'Yes, Miss Tansy.'

Tilde looked as if she thought the lady was protesting too much.

'Clear away the cups and glasses,' Tansy said briskly, deciding it was time to check her maid-servant's headlong rush along the road of romantic fantasy. 'Oh, and Tilde, you will not now go and see Mr Valentine. I am very much opposed to fortune-telling.'

'Oh, I don't need to go now,' Tilde said. 'My fortunes changed for the better when we met in the park, Miss Tansy – and Mr Valentine never turned up anyway. Will there be anything else?'

'I took up the reference you gave me,' Tansy informed her. 'I spoke to Mr Hawkins, the butler.'

'He's a nice gentleman, isn't he?' Tilde said.

'He seemed very nice and he spoke highly of you,' Tansy said. 'I did wonder – he did not, perhaps, think rather too highly of you?'

'Oh no, Miss,' Tilde said promptly. 'There was nothing like that in the Edge household. Of course I never met the family because they were all still abroad but I did get the impression they were very strict in their morals. And Mr Hawkins never said or did anything out of place. Nobody did. Even Alfred – that's the footman, Miss Tansy, he behaved very respectfully indeed once I'd slapped him.'

'I'm glad to hear it,' Tansy said gravely.

'Mind you,' Tilde said confidingly, 'I was only there for a week but I did feel they started as they meant to go on. I believe I would have settled there and worked my way up, but the work was very hard.'

'But you didn't grumble about it?'

'No, Miss, not even when Mrs Bradshaw told me that in the early evenings when the family was away she expected me to knit things for the Jews' basket.'

'The Society for the Conversion. . . ?'

Tilde nodded vigorously.

'I didn't see what use they'd have for woollen garments out in the Holy Land, but Mrs Bradshaw told me the various items were collected and sold. A whole pile of things were collected while I was there.'

'By whom?'

'A tall gentleman with a big moon face,' Tilde said with a giggle. 'He had an oily kind of voice and he kept asking me if I was saved. I was quite relieved when Mr Hawkins came into the kitchen and told me to be about my work. He came back the next day and left a notice about Band of Hope meetings but Mrs Bradshaw said we weren't interested. The day after that I was dismissed so I never saw him again.'

'Was his name Wesley Brown?' Tansy asked.

'I don't know, Miss. If he gave his name I never heard it because I never listen to people who keep asking me if I'm saved,' Tilde said.

'Very wise of you, Tilde,' Tansy approved. 'Clear away now, there's a good girl.'

In the hall she hesitated, wondering whether or not to call a cab and inform her father of the latest developments but a moment's thought told her the hour was late and the information would keep.

Her next task was to call upon Mr Valentine. The possibility of coming face to face with Mr Wesley Brown again wasn't a pleasant one, and for an instant she wavered in her determination. It would be more sensible to take an escort in the shape of Frank Cartwright. On the other hand she was no unsuspecting young girl meeting a person she thought of as a friend after dark in some deserted place.

Having reaffirmed her own private decision she went into the kitchen to congratulate Mrs Timothy on the splendid repast they had been served.

NINE

That night, for the first time in many months, she found it difficult to sleep. The bedroom felt too warm though the fire had burned down to a faint red glow and when she opened the window the breeze was clammy on her skin. In the glass her eyes were emeralds and her hair glowed like the outer edge of a flame. If entertaining two gentlemen acquaintances to dinner stimulated her to this extent, she thought wryly, then it was high time she entertained a few more!

But of course it wasn't either Patrick Denny or Frank Cartwright who had imparted the sparkle to her eyes or the spring to her step. The truth was that the murders, greatly as she deplored them, had brought a new interest into her life, given her a puzzle to solve. In that she was like Laurence, she decided, for he was never happier than when wrestling with a case.

Yet that conclusion didn't bring peaceful slumber. It was past two before she slept and when she did so she was conscious that she had left the window open and that it would be wiser to shut it, a resolve that was very clear in her mind though her sleeping body refused to obey.

'Miss Tansy, you've let in all the night air!'

Mrs Timothy's scandalized tones woke her into full morning. She sat up, pushing her hair out of her eyes.

'Night air's the same as day air,' she said mildly.

'Not to mention the possibility of burglars,' Mrs Timothy continued, clearly regarding Tansy's remark as too silly to comment on. 'We might have lost the silver or been murdered in our beds.'

She did not, Tansy noticed, mention the two recent murders. Mrs Timothy wouldn't connect the killings of two lower-class girls with the middle-class household over which she reigned supreme.

'Well, we haven't been,' Tansy said sensibly. 'However you're probably right. I meant to close the window but I forgot. And it was very warm.'

'Young Tilde cleared everything away beautifully last night,' Mrs Timothy said, putting down the tea-tray. 'I will admit to you, Miss Tansy, that she's shaping better than I might have hoped.'

'I think that it would still be wise to keep her under your eye for a while longer,' Tansy said.

'Oh, I shall keep a sharp eye, never you fear!' Mrs Timothy assured her. 'She's still very young, Miss Tansy, and missing a mother's protection, so I shall regard it as my duty to keep a very sharp eye until she has proved herself absolutely. Will either of the young gentlemen be coming for dinner this evening?'

'I shall probably go over to see Pa.'

'They did seem to enjoy themselves,' Mrs Timothy said with a glance.

'That,' said Tansy firmly, discouraging any possible romantic speculations on the part of her housekeeper, 'was due to the excellent dinner.'

'If you say so, Miss Tansy.'

Mrs Timothy withdrew.

Today was a day for quiet, sustained investigation, Tansy decided. Her grey and white striped dress had a small bustle and only a narrow frill of lace at the high neck and elbow-length sleeves. It would be practical, with her hair coiled under a small, forward-tilting hat of burnt straw which matched the parasol she had chosen to carry, partly because it matched the hat, partly because it had a wickedly sharp tip which might serve as a weapon of self-defence should the situation turn nasty.

Before going out, however, she wanted to jot down further notes on events so far, and accordingly after breakfast had been cleared away she went to her desk and settled herself to some serious thinking.

Two victims and two potential victims. She wrote their names neatly. 'Ellie Watson, Fanny Jones, Mary Denny, Tilde Miles.' Possibly Mary Denny was already a victim. Tansy hoped not. Up to now no attempt had been made to conceal the bodies. They had simply been struck down from behind and left on the ground.

All four girls were or had been around seventeen years old – the two dead ones plain with ginger and fair hair and pale complexions, the other two darkly pretty. All were either orphans or separated from their family. Ellie had been employed at the match factory owned by the Edges. Fanny had been employed at the match factory and then bettered herself by getting a position at Mrs Mainwaring's millinery establishment. Tilde had worked very briefly at both the match factory and the Edge house and had failed to obtain a job with the milliner. Fanny had attended Sion Chapel and Tilde had been requested to donate knitted objects to the Jews' basket which had been brought round by Wesley Brown, the deacon at Sion Chapel.

The advertisement placed in the newspaper by Valentine had been cut out and kept by both Fanny Jones and Mary Denny, and Ellie Watson had confided to Sylvie that she had a special friend just as Mary had confided to her brother that she had a splendid new friend who was taking her to a Valentine ball. And Tilde's mother had regularly consulted a fortune-teller called Mr Valentine.

It was time to list the suspects, she decided, hesitating before she put Patrick Denny down, after which she stared at it doubtfully.

Patrick had been in India when Ellie Watson had died. He had landed back in England less than a month before and according to his own account had found his sister gone. He might have disapproved of her new friend and lost his temper sufficiently badly to harm her. It was a faint possibility but needed to be kept in mind.

The Edges? They had been abroad all winter. There was the possibility that either father or son might have briefly returned. Again she thought it unlikely but she wrote down Sir James Edge and Leslie Edge.

Mr Hawkins, the butler? Again it was possible since during the absence of his employers there was nobody to question his comings and goings, and his reason for dismissing Tilde was still by no means clear.

Wesley Brown? She thought again of the large, white hands with their thick fingers constantly twisting, the heavy, pasty face, the oily voice. And Fanny Jones had laughed hysterically when John Mason suggested she confide her troubles to his fellow-deacon. Tansy reminded herself that she had no proof of what Fanny had said or done beyond John Mason's word and jotted his name down too.

Tobias Simpson, the manager at the match factory, had a heavy stick and harassed the girls in his charge. Was he also a member of Sion Chapel?

There remained the infamous Valentine who, at infrequent intervals, put an advertisement in the evening newspaper inviting people to tell him their troubles. Valentine, she thought soberly, had to be the main suspect.

It was time, then, to sally forth and meet him. She locked her notes in her desk and rose to put on her hat as Mrs Timothy came across from the kitchen.

'Will you be in for lunch, Miss Tansy? It's mainly left-overs,' she added.

'Left-overs will be fine,' Tansy said, deciding that it might be as well if someone expected her at a particular time when she was moving into a situation which might be perilous. 'One o'clock?'

'Very good, Miss Tansy.'

Mrs Timothy looked as if she would've liked to enquire if any gentlemen were going to be present but didn't quite dare.

Tansy hired a cab and directed the driver to St Martin-in-the-Fields. There was no sense in giving away her direct destination even to a cabbie, she reflected. If Tilde's Mr Valentine wasn't the murderer then it might be almost any man.

Cab-drivers, she thought uneasily, were abroad at all hours. Nobody ever thought of questioning them. Most of the time one scarcely glanced at them. After dark they were cloaked bundles with shadowed faces.

'Here we are, Miss Clark.'

The present cabbie's cheerful tones startled her from her reverie.

'How do you know my name?' she asked sharply as she alighted with the fare in her hand.

'I knowed your pa since I was first started in this business,' he said. 'Used to be a bit of a wild one in my younger days but your pa, he set me straight early on – even gave me a character when I began with this company. Got shot, didn't he? Bad affair all round. He's a real gentleman is your pa.'

'Yes,' said Tansy, feeling suddenly relieved. 'Yes he is.'

'Next time you see him then tell him that Archie Benning was asking after him,' he instructed.

'I'll do that. Thank you, Mr Benning.'

Tansy waved her hand as he drove off in search of more passengers.

She entered a tiny church and knelt down, striving to control a sudden fit of trembling that had unaccountably gripped her. This, she told herself crossly, was ridiculous. What possible harm could come to her in the middle of a warm, sunny morning in one of the busiest parts of the city? On the other hand nobody knew where she had come and if by chance she didn't return for lunch Mrs Timothy would merely assume that she'd gone to see Laurence.

The unaccustomed nervousness ebbed away. Her father had paid her the compliment of rearing her to be independent, to think for herself as if she had been the son that nature had denied him. It would be a poor return if she couldn't carry out one part of the investigation entirely under her own initiative.

By the time she rose she was in command of herself again. She came out of the church and headed towards the winding, cobbled lane.

The costume shop was half-way along it, its windows bulging slightly, the glass in their tiny panes darkened by the years. The words 'Theatrical Costumiers' had once blazed in gold across the façade but now the gold was tarnished and some of the letters faded almost to invisibility. The bell on the door tinkled as she went in.

She had stepped into gloom. A counter ran down one side at a right angle to the window where a few hats and a feathered head-dress were perched on stands, looking as if they had forgotten what it was like to perch on a real head. The air was musty and she suspected that the whole place required a good cleaning.

'Yes? May I help you?'

The man who came forward from the back of the shop wore slippers that made softly slithering sounds over the dusty floor, and a velvet smoking jacket that had once been trimmed with gold braid but was now decorated with stains of mysterious origin. His trousers were tight knee-breeches of the previous century and his hair, white and abundant, reached his shoulders. Wide shoulders, she registered, and the man himself was tall, well over six feet though the height of the ceiling caused him to stoop a little.

'Mr Valentine?'

Instinctively she clutched her parasol more securely.

'William Valentine, yes. You wish to hire a costume?'

'I . . .' Tansy looked round at the dingy, half-empty shelves. 'I wondered what you might have in stock for a costume ball?'

'My best stock is in the next room,' he said. 'This way.'

Said the spider to the fly, Tansy thought and allowed him to precede her through a curtain composed of long strings of tiny coloured beads that parted and fell closed again behind her with a series of tiny clicking sounds.

The back room, unexpectedly, was both larger and better lit, with a large french window beyond which she could see a small yard in which a few tubs were planted with surprisingly cheerful geraniums.

'What costume did you have in mind?'

In the better illumination she could see that his complexion was olive and his eyes keen though he was obviously well into his fifties.

Tansy looked round at the long rails on which garments hung limply, the shabby, velvet-seated chairs, the little dais on which a headless lady wore a robe of black and scarlet.

'Lady Macbeth,' Mr Valentine said. 'I saw the great Mrs Siddons wear that robe when she played the part. It chilled the blood. Chilled the blood and froze the heart.'

'I thought – something more cheerful?' Tansy said.

'Of course, of course.' He took a couple of small, skipping steps backward and narrowed his eyes at her consideringly. 'You would make a magnificent Boudicca. She too was flame-haired you know, or Cleopatra, that serpent of old Nile, or Helen of Troy? '. . . The face that launch'd a thousand ships, and. . . .'

'You used to be an actor?'

'A thespian, my dear lady! Not, alas, successful in the financial sense nor acknowledged by the public in general, but within the profession – my Shylock was approved by – name-dropping is a reprehensible habit. Now tell me whether Boudicca or Cleopatra appeals to your sense of history and drama or – you may perhaps have come for another purpose?'

'What other purpose?' Tansy asked.

'Sometimes ladies wish to lift the veil of the future and. . . .'

'Mrs Miles came sometimes to consult you I believe?' Tansy said.

'The late Mrs Miles. She passed away, poor lady, some time since.'

'Did you prophesy that?' Tansy asked drily.

'There was no need. Consumption sends a clear message without the need for an intermediary. She was a very sweet lady. Naïve and trusting and yet with some inner strength. So you knew her? She never mentioned. . . .'

'I never met her,' Tansy said. 'Her daughter Tilde works for me.'

There was little harm in telling him that since if he was the real killer he would know it already and if not no harm was likely to result.

'And I never met her daughter,' he said. 'Mrs Miles spoke of her often. She wished her to get on in society.'

'She never came here?'

'The young don't consult us,' he said softly and sadly. 'It is the middle-aged and the dispossessed who wish to arm themselves against the future. But I worried about the daughter when I heard the mother had died.'

'How did you hear?' Tansy asked curiously.

'Mrs Mainwaring came – that was an unfortunate slip on my part, and I beg you to overlook it,' he interrupted himself. 'There must be confidentiality between my clients and myself. In the present climate of the law. . . .'

'I'll not say anything to Mrs Mainwaring,' Tansy said. 'I take it that she's been a – a client for some time?'

'You heard it not from me,' he said, laying a finger alongside his nose.

'Perhaps I came in reply to your advertisement,' Tansy said.

'I don't advertise, dear lady. To peer into the future is against the law. An antiquated law, but still operative.'

'You've never placed an advertisement in the newspaper? Surely you've seen the one in question?'

'I read Shakespeare, Congreve, Sheridan – never the ephemeras of modern life.'

Tansy stared at him with deep distrust.

'You don't believe me,' he said. 'Yet I tell the simple truth, Miss – you see I haven't even enquired your name.'

'Clark. Tansy Clark.'

'Well, Miss Clark, I assure you that I do not obtain my clientele through the medium of the popular press,' he said with great dignity.

'Then you have not heard of the murders?'

'One hears news called out in the streets,' he said indifferently. 'Since it is nearly always bad news it does not encourage one to buy the paper on which it is printed. A young woman was found dead recently in – was it Kensington?'

'She worked for Mrs Mainwaring,' Tansy said. I'm surprised that she hasn't been here.'

'Not yet.' He shook his head. 'She came to inform me of the death of Mrs Miles from whom she bought scarves and other trivia of feminine apparel from time to time. She informed me that Tilde Miles had gone to her to ask for a position and she wanted my advice. Mrs Mainwaring had a feeling that she ought not to employ the girl.'

'Mrs Mainwaring is psychic too, is she?' Tansy said drily.

'We all have intuition, Miss Clark. Some of us develop it more than our neighbours.'

'And?' Tansy brushed aside the implied rebuke.

'I told her that it would be a bad move to employ the girl.'

'You didn't tell her that Fanny Jones was also in danger?'

'I never heard of her until her death was cried in the street.'

'And Mrs Mainwaring hasn't consulted you since?'

'Neither officially nor unofficially. Miss Clark, why do you ask me all these questions?'

His eyes suddenly pierced her. Tansy swallowed convulsively and took a step backwards, aware in that moment that the room was so quiet that scarcely a breath disturbed the dust and that no sounds penetrated from the lane.

'Three months ago – a little more now – a girl called Ellie Watson was found dead outside the library in Kensington,' she said.

'I thought – wasn't someone called Frances. . . ?'

'Frances Jones was found dead just outside Kew Gardens. You heard both deaths announced and muddled them slightly.'

'I believe you are right.' He frowned. 'I try to wipe bad news out of my mind. Two girls dead? You knew the girls?'

'No. I never met either of them,' Tansy said. 'My father is interested in the case. He is a retired police-officer.'

'Oh dear!'

'Mr Valentine, my father has no interest in bringing the occasional fortune-teller to court,' she said quickly. 'He's interested in the man who killed these two young women. He's not even officially on the case as yet and the police certainly haven't picked up the connections that exist between the girls – and there were several links. Now another young woman has—'

'If you wish to consult me,' he broke in, 'then it's best you say nothing further. Do you wish it?'

'Yes,' Tansy said, and wondered if she had made the gravest mistake of her life.

He regarded her thoughtfully for a moment, then, as if making up his mind to trust her, moved to the french windows and opened them.

'A little sunshine clears the brain. Please sit down.'

His manner was that of a man accustomed to wielding authority. He must have had a considerable stage-presence, Tansy thought, taking the thronelike chair from which he swept a heap of discarded costumes, and noting with some relief that it stood close to the wall.

'What do I have to do?' she asked, concealing her nervousness.

'Don't you use a crystal or something?'

'Crystals, cards – they are merely the props of the trade,' he said impatiently. 'Murder is a serious affair. Let me think.'

Thinking also involved pacing. Up and down, up and down, passing in and out of the sunlight that slanted through the window, now pausing briefly, now turning on his heel and continuing his perambulations.

Tansy began to feel slightly dizzy and sleepy as if she was enveloped in a waking dream.

'You came not to be told the future but the past,' he said, stopping abruptly, startling her into wakefulness again. 'There are three Valentines. One is myself – William Herbert Valentine. In a past life I was, of course, that same Mr W.H. to whom Shakespeare dedicated his work. That is not to our present purpose. Two Valentines left – one false, one true. I speak of name not nature. The false one lures. I cannot see why. He has killed three.'

'Oh no,' Tansy heard herself whisper.

'He will kill a fourth,' Mr Valentine said.

'The two Valentines – one bears the name and one has assumed the name. Is that what you mean?' Tansy asked.

'I am sure.'

'The third killing,' Tansy said, holding her parasol so tightly that the handle bit into her palms, 'Was it a girl called Mary Denny?'

'Mary? No, not Mary. Not Mary,' he said in a muttering tone.

'Then who?'

'I cannot tell.'

He sat down in a chair opposite the one she occupied and brought out a large, red, spotted handkerchief with which he mopped his brow in a gesture Tansy would have dismissed as theatrical had she not seen the shine of sweat.

'My apologies, Miss Clark. I can see nothing more,' he said. 'Let us have some refreshment.'

He rose and opened a tall, narrow cupboard, took out a bottle and two glasses.

'Thank you but no,' Tansy said, holding on to the remnants of her caution. 'I have to go. Thank you.'

'You thought that perhaps. . . ?' He poured himself a generous measure of the liquid in the bottle and tilted his head to receive the libation.

'There was that possibility,' she said.

'Violence is not in my nature, Miss Clark. Passion for me has always been contained within the pages of a play, trapped in the acts of a play. And you. . . ?' He hesitated, took another draught of the drink and then bowed.

'Mr Valentine?' Puzzled, Tansy also rose.

'I was going to say that you, like myself, divert your passions into other channels,' he said. 'However, as you didn't come here to seek advice for yourself then it's not my place to say so. I'll see you out.'

He closed the windows and led the way through to the front part of the shop.

'Thank you, Mr Valentine.'

She took some silver from her purse and laid it on the counter.

'Not at all, Miss Clark. Thank you.'

He bowed again with a little flourish.

'Good-day to you.'

As she opened the door she heard above the tinkling of the bell his grave and measured tones.

'Miss Clark, take care. You swim in untested depths.'

The bell tinkled again as she closed the door and walked rapidly away.

She needed time to make some sense of what she had been told so changed her mind about going to Laurence's and instead caught a cab home.

'Did you buy yourself something pretty?' Mrs Timothy wanted to know as she served the cold cuts.

'Buy? No, I ended up not buying anything. Where's Tilde?'

'She went to the wine shop with some empty bottles.'

'I think it best you find plenty for her to do around the house over the next few days,' Tansy said.

'You think. . . ?' Mrs Timothy set down the water-jug, folded her hands across her apron and said, 'Miss Tansy, it's not my place to enquire and I scorn listening at doors but one cannot avoid overhearing a word dropped here, a word dropped there. Are you and your revered father assisting the police in some capacity?'

'We are garnering evidence which will be handed to the police.'

'Concerning the murders of those two unfortunate girls?'

'I'm sorry, Mrs Timothy. I ought to have said something.'

'Not at all, Miss Tansy. Your business is your business,' Mrs Timothy said. 'However, one feels impelled to enquire – is there any chance of our being murdered in our beds? Forewarned is forearmed as the saying goes.'

'I think it hardly likely,' Tansy said, amused despite herself. 'I do think that as Tilde is in our charge so to speak—'

'And two poor girls have met their Maker too soon. Say no more, Miss Tansy! I will guard Tilde like a mother, you may be sure.'

'Thank you, Mrs Timothy.'

Tansy continued with her luncheon, thinking wryly that she had better get on with the quasi-investigations as quickly as possible since Tilde for the immediate future was destined to feel the housekeeper's breath on the back of her neck.

Laurence would be looking forward to a visit but since she had undertaken to attend the inquest she decided to go there first.

'Inquests are generally dull affairs with interesting details often kept from the general public,' Laurence had lectured during one of their long discussions on legal procedure. 'Evidence is sometimes withheld because it may form part of a prosecution case later or may be judged unsuitable for public knowledge.'

She wondered what evidence would be made public at the inquest on Fanny Jones. Probably very little but it would be interesting to see who attended.

The report of the inquest on Ellie Watson returned to her mind. Ellie had been a virgin, struck violently on the back of the head and left where she had fallen. No attempt had been made to molest her further save that a bright pink ribbon had been tied round her hat. Nobody had come forward to say anything more though Sylvie had been aware that Ellie had been going to see a friend. Valentine?

She donned her hat again and went out, pausing at the kitchen door to catch a conspiratorial nod from Mrs Timothy who had put out every piece of silver she could lay her hands on, obviously with the intention of keeping Tilde under her eye for the rest of the day. Tilde herself, a large apron covering her from neck to toe, her curls demurely confined, had a polishing-cloth in her hand and seemed not too unhappy with her task, since her chatter never ceased.

'Of course Lady Caroline Lamb was so madly in love with Lord Byron that she once dressed herself as a page-boy and flung herself at his feet.'

'Very foolish,' was Mrs Timothy's rejoinder. 'She would almost certainly have got dust on her breeches.'

Tansy smothered a chuckle and went on into the street where a dawdling cab waited conveniently.

This was not the first inquest she had attended. Now and then her father, during his days of active policing, had encouraged her to attend some inquest connected with a case in which he was interested.

'Look at those who are there,' he had advised. 'Many people lead lives of unremitting dullness and an inquest becomes a chance for them to touch the fringe of something more dramatic.'

He had been training her to estimate human character, she reflected. It was part of Laurence's creed that an ability to sum up a person stood one in good stead.

Had she summed up Mr Valentine correctly? He had seemed to her to be a curious mixture of charlatan and genuine sensitive. She couldn't really imagine him sneaking up behind a young woman with the intention of dealing a deathly blow. On the other hand he had been an actor and her interview with him might have been an interview with the character he chose to assume.

Frank was waiting outside the court, hat tilted rakishly, pad and pencil in hand. We all play our several parts, Tansy thought, greeting him. This afternoon Frank is the hard-bitten reporter, possibly a future Dickens. And I? I am the single lady with nothing much to occupy her time who comes to inquests so that she may have the illusion of sharing in a little left-over life.

'The letters are still there,' he said. 'I hung around most of the morning but not a sniff.'

'What happens if nobody picks them up?' Tansy enquired. 'They can't be left there for ever.'

'Eventually they'll be collected and kept somewhere or other. Denny's there now so he may get a result. Thank you again for last night by the way. I enjoyed it.'

'The meal or the company?' she teased.

'The whole meal and half the company. Patrick Denny is a pretty selfish sort of fellow in my opinion.'

'Why?'

'Leaving his seventeen-year-old sister alone and friendless in a strange city. While he was travelling around the North-West Frontier soaking up the native atmosphere, Mary Denny was apparently expected to entertain herself with housework and trips to the local museum. Charming he might be but reliable he isn't!'

'You thought him charming, did you?' Tansy said.

'I thought women would probably find him charming. He obviously liked you.'

'I rather liked myself last night,' Tansy said. 'Frank, I've got something to – Oh, here comes Inspector Jarrold.'

The inspector had seen them and came over, his manner over-cordial in contrast to Tansy's frosty bow.

'How are you, Miss Clark? And your father? Still soldiering on, I trust?'

'As he was when I spoke to you in your club,' Tansy said pointedly. 'You ought to go and see him for yourself, Inspector. He'd appreciate a good long talk with you – unless of course an arrest is imminent?'

'Investigations,' said Inspector Jarrold quellingly, 'are progressing. If you will excuse me?'

He processed past with almost as much dignity as Mrs Timothy.

'Are you going in?' Frank looked at her. 'I shall be in the press seats.'

'I'll speak to you later then.'

She joined the people filing into the courtroom, her smart clothes gaining her a good seat as a court usher shooed aside several women to point her to a seat. Tansy, who didn't much enjoy preferential treatment, consoled herself with the reflection that she was interested in solving the case while the others seemed to be merely spectators. She was glad of her comfortable seat by the time the coroner entered because the room grew progressively stuffier and warmer.

Mrs Mainwaring, wearing a black hat that was obviously the most fetching in her collection, entered the witness-box to give evidence of identification and to give a commendably concise account of her late employee.

Yes, she had taken Frances Jones into her employment two years before, after the girl had left the match factory. Yes, she had quickly promoted her, Frances being very clever with her fingers. No, she knew nothing of any young man who might have struck up a relationship with the girl.

The next witness, Mrs Mainwaring having been duly thanked and invited to step down, was the police surgeon.

A younger man than her father's former compatriot, he gave his evidence in a bored monotone as if he was used to examining the bodies of murdered girls.

'Seventeen or eighteen years old. Slim but well nourished, pale complexion, light yellow hair, teeth sound save for two decayed molars, wound on the back of the head caused by some heavy object probably of steel or brass, death instantaneous. Face slightly marked where it had hit the pavement as she fell.'

'And your conclusion?' The coroner looked expectant.

'The blow shattered her skull,' the police surgeon said. 'Pieces of bone were embedded in her brain and the brain itself was leaking. She would have died instantly. She would have died almost without feeling anything. The child too.'

'Child?'

This was clearly unexpected. The coroner looked up sharply.

'Frances Jones was in the early stages of pregnancy,' the surgeon said. 'About two months. The child, of course, would die with the mother.'

Fanny Jones weeping in Sion Chapel and telling John Mason that she had a grave problem. Mr Valentine in the dusty, sun-streaked back room as he paced slowly, his voice grave and weighted with meaning.

'He has killed three times.'

Ellie Watson, Frances Jones – and the child she carried.

Tansy felt hastily in her bag for a note-pad, scribbled a brief message for Frank which she handed to the usher as she slipped out.

In the street she hailed a cab and instructed him to drive her to Fenter Lane.

TEN

Frances Jones had been pregnant at the time of her death. So John Mason had been telling the truth when he had informed her of having seen the girl in great distress a couple of weeks before her murder. And Mr Valentine had been right when he declared there had been three murders. Which meant, Tansy reflected, nibbling the curved handle of her parasol and wishing vaguely that it was a piece of candy, that either Mr Valentine had a real psychic gift or he had known of Fanny's condition and committed the murder himself.

She paid off the driver and hurried down the narrow lane. The bell on the shop-door tinkled loudly as she entered. Closing it behind her she stood for a moment looking round the dim and dusty interior with the few hats and head-dresses ranged along the counter.

'Mr Valentine?'

The room in a curious way echoed her words, faint and indistinct – . . .tine . . .tine . . .ine. . . .

If he was in then he must have heard the bell and since the door had been unlocked then he was definitely in.

Tansy stepped to the beaded curtain and cautiously lifted it.

'Mr Valentine, are you there? It's Tansy Clark!'

The beads clicked into place behind her and broad shafts of sunlight fell through the windows on to the floor, sending dust motes swirling. The rubbed velvet of the two thronelike chairs had once been crimson, faded now to greyish pink; the various costumes hung limply on their rails. In the yard she could see the gaudy geraniums in their earthenware tubs.

'Mr Valentine!'

In the corner of the room a spiral staircase twisted upwards. Tansy went to the foot of the staircase and put her hand on the twist of iron that formed the newel post. Looking up she could see a square landing and two doors, both slightly ajar.

'Mr Valentine, are you in?'

Something was wrong. She felt it in her bones. Something was very wrong. She set her foot on the lowest step, hesitated, biting her lip, and then went swiftly up them.

The left-hand door, thrust wider open by her parasol, revealed a room which obviously ran over the front of the shop. There was a bed, the covers tumbled, against one wall, a small, unexpectedly shining stove in one corner, a couple of suits hung on pegs, a round coffee-table with some plates and mugs set on it, a three-cornered stool, a wash-stand under the small-paned, slightly bulging window. On a shelf a couple of saucepans kept company with a tin of sprats, a loaf of sugar, and a jar of coffee.

Mr Valentine cooked, washed himself and slept in the one small, crowded room.

Tansy turned to the right-hand door, pushing it wider, saying again in a tone which she recognized as tremulous, 'Mr Valentine?'

Faces stared at her from the walls. Men with white wigs and cocked hats, a bareheaded man holding a skull, women in towering feather head-dresses, women with impossibly long hair and little juliet caps. Pencil-sketches, coloured posters, stiffly posed photographs. Playbills, their edges tattered, were pinned among the faces. Cast lists with 'Mr W.H. Valentine' near the foot were pasted with loving care to thin cardboard boards round which faded and lovingly clipped reviews were tacked.

On a table in the centre a few objects lay – a leather glove, a dagger, a carefully polished skull, a necklace of amber and cornelians.

The entire life of a man who had loved the theatre even though he hadn't prospered in it was spread before her, but of the man who had lived that life there was no sign.

Turning, holding the steeply curving iron rail she went down the stairs again. Mr Valentine wasn't here.

Perhaps, on an impulse, he had gone out somewhere, decided for once in his life to buy a newspaper. Perhaps in this small house-cum-shop there were other rooms, tiny chambers from which a man might watch as someone trespassed.

She reached the ground floor with undisguised relief. Now where? Since she had left a note for Frank she might as well wait here until he arrived or Mr Valentine returned. Walking through into the front of the shop she paused suddenly, noticing for the first time that the small till at one end of the counter was not quite closed. She could see the edge of the drawer protruding slightly.

'At some point in the investigation,' Laurence had said, 'one small point will force itself upon your attention. Don't rush. Stand very still and feel what is there before you look.'

Tansy stood still, trying to feel what was as yet not apparent. Under the soles of her feet the dust stirred and settled. She wasn't alone in the place. Like someone in a coal-cellar who knows a black cat is by she sensed the presence of someone else.

She could leave at once and walk along the lane and wait for Frank to arrive. She could look a little further.

She moved to the counter and leaned over, stretching out her hand to push the till-drawer back into place.

Mr Valentine lay on the floor behind the counter, staring up at her. His dark eyes were intact, filmed over, the rest of his face a bloodied mass of bone, skin and tissue. Mr Valentine, she thought in sick horror, had never been away, and never would return.

From the doorway Frank said, 'What the devil are you doing here?'

'Frank! Oh, I'm so glad you're here!'

Tansy still clung to the edge of the counter, her eyes dilated as she stared at him.

The jaunty expression on his face altered to one of concern. He took a couple of long strides towards her, put one arm about her in a tight and comforting clasp and looked over the counter.

'Who's that?'

'Mr Valentine. W.H. Valentine, as in Shakespeare's dedication.'

'Tansy, you're babbling.' He gave her a little shake. 'Now, are you going to faint or are you going to tell me what all this is about? I take it you didn't kill him?'

'No, of course not! Don't be ridiculous!'

Irritated, she pushed him away slightly, a touch of colour returning to her face.

'And he didn't commit suicide. Did you see. . . ?'

'He was dead when I got here but I didn't see him until I was on the way out,' Tansy said, sinking down onto a stool. 'I went over the rest of the house looking for him.'

'With a search-warrant?'

'What? No, of course not! I came back to see him and tell him that he'd been right about there having been three murders – the unborn child was the third victim but Mr Valentine didn't see that clearly. He—'

'Came back!' Frank stared at her. 'You've been here before then? When?'

'This morning,' she said shiveringly.

'Alone? Tansy, you're not making sense.'

'Tilde told me that her late mother sometimes consulted a fortune-teller called Mr Valentine. She'd never met him herself though she knew where he lived. She was working as a tweeny for the Edges and wondering how she could get a better place and when she saw the Valentine advertisement she wrote to the box number and received a note back telling her to meet him in the park opposite Pa's house – in Queen Adelaide Park. That's what she was doing when I found her waiting on the bench by the pond for him to arrive.'

'But you got there first.'

'I think Valentine was already there waiting for the park to be quieter. As I went in a keeper told me the gates were due to be locked soon. It was only later that I remembered the park doesn't close until midnight and it was only just getting dark. So he can't have been a genuine keeper, but at the time I didn't even trouble to look at him and it was getting dusky and he only spoke one sentence and—'

'Whoa!' Frank said, checking her. 'Take it slowly.'

'But we have to tell the police now,' Tansy said.

'That can wait a few moments.' There was a grim edge to Frank's tone. 'Mr Valentine, whoever he is, isn't going anywhere. One second.'

He went to the front door, lifted the 'Closed' notice from its hook, hung it up and slid the bolt on the door.

'Come through to the back. Is this the private living-room?' Lifting the bead curtain he looked at her. 'Tansy, wake up!'

'I'm sorry. I've never seen a murdered person before,' she said. 'My mother – the end came very peacefully, and Geoffrey died out in Jamaica. I hadn't realized – he was a nice gentleman, Frank. Yes, a gentleman. You should see all the portraits of famous actors and actresses in the room upstairs, and the souvenirs – stage props from various productions.'

'You said he was a fortune-teller,' Frank said, shepherding her into the back room.

'He hired out costumes for fancy dress balls and told fortunes for a few ladies – Mrs Mainwaring was one of them – but in his younger days he was an actor. Not a very good one, I suspect, but he loved the profession and he was proud of having appeared with them.'

'You searched the entire house?'

'I was looking for Mr Valentine. I came here this morning to see him and—'

'You came here alone without telling anybody, knowing he might be the man who had killed two girls? Tansy, what possessed you?'

'I wanted to do something on my own, to get some evidence that I could show to Pa,' she said wearily. 'Ever since I was a little girl, Frank, he's talked about his work as a policeman. Other children were feeding the ducks in the park when he was showing me how to track for footprints. I loved every moment of it and yet we both knew that I couldn't ever follow in his footsteps. I was a daughter, not a son. He has never once hinted that he would have preferred a boy, but deep down – and then I was pleased when Geoffrey and I planned to marry, because, well, I would've made a good marriage and just maybe in time – a grandson? And then Geoffrey died out in Jamaica and left me the house and an income and Pa insisted that I lead an independent life. And now for the first time I might be able to help him out in a real case.'

'Which isn't his.'

'Sooner or later Inspector Jarrold will ask his advice. I wanted to use my training, Frank. Is that so wrong?'

'No, of course not, but putting yourself at risk surely wasn't part of what Laurence taught you, was it?' Frank said.

'No, of course not. I was just being stupid. Frank, Mr Valentine told my – well not my fortune exactly. I mean he didn't use cards or a crystal ball, but he had some kind of gift. He really did!'

'Did he tell you that you were going to meet a tall, dark stranger?'

'He told me there were three Valentines. Himself who knew nothing of the murders, a true Valentine who caused but didn't commit them, and a false Valentine who lured and killed. And he said the false Valentine had killed three people.'

'Mary Denny?'

'A nameless person. Frank, don't you see? Fanny Jones was with child when she was killed. As soon as I heard that I came back here, to see if he could tell me more. The shop was open but there was no sign of him so I came through here and went upstairs – I didn't touch anything. I was puzzled. I kept thinking of Mary Denny who wasn't at home when her brother came back. On the way out I noticed that the till-drawer was slightly open so I leaned across to. . . .'

'If the drawer was open then he was killed by someone who probably went behind the counter with something heavy – a brick, a weighted walking-stick, whatever, and Mr Valentine heard him and turned and—'

'Don't!' Tansy put up her hand instinctively. 'Poor Mr Valentine. How dreadful that he had to die in order to be proved innocent.'

'We can't say that. He might've been killed by a robber. Did you check the contents of the till?'

'No, of course I didn't! I'd only just seen him when you walked in.'

'Having received an execrably scribbled note from the court usher. The verdict was murder by a person or persons unknown by the way. The usual verdict. We'd better look in the till.'

'You look,' Tansy said shudderingly.

'Not that it will do very much good,' Frank said, exiting through the bead curtains again. 'After all we have no idea how much money was in the till before he was killed.'

'Probably not very much,' Tansy said, following reluctantly. 'I doubt if hiring out costumes brought in much income.'

'Let's have a look anyway.' Frank had stepped round to the other side of the counter and was sliding out the drawer again.

'Yes?' Tansy said.

'A few coppers. No silver. A couple of cheques. Not cashed yet. One from a Caroline Gordon and – well, well!'

'Well, well what?'

'A cheque signed by Leslie Edge,' Frank said. 'Dated back in February.'

'And not cashed?'

'It's possible that Mr Valentine didn't have a bank account, or kept the cheques as security for the costumes he hired,' Frank said. 'It's for eight pounds, the one from Caroline Gordon for four.'

'Then Leslie Edge hired two costumes for the Valentine Ball?' The sick feeling inside her was diminishing now. Tansy avoided looking over at the figure still staring up from the floor but her tone was eager.

'For himself and Mary Denny?' Frank said.

'I wonder if Mr Valentine kept any records of who hired the costumes. No.' She answered her own question. 'I don't think he hired out many of the costumes at all, and he wasn't the sort to keep records except of the theatre. Frank, we have to tell the police. We can't just leave the poor man lying here.'

'I'll go and report it to the first constable I see,' Frank said. 'Did anyone see you coming here this morning? The cab-driver?'

'I asked him to set me down near St Martin-in-the-Fields. I'm positive that nobody – why? Does it matter?'

'The police don't appreciate the bungling attempts of amateurs,' Frank said drily. 'I'll tell them that you and I came to check up on the name Valentine, to find out if it was the same Valentine who advertises in the newspapers. We found him like this and we haven't touched anything. You came over faint—'

'I did not!'

'For the purposes of the local constable's information you did. I sent you home in a cab and stayed to inform the police.'

'But why were we checking up on Mr Valentine in the first place?'

'Human interest story? Don't fret. I'll think of something.'

'Will I see you later?'

'I'll call round this evening to see your father. Come on.'

There was little point in arguing. Tansy allowed herself to be escorted to the end of the lane where the bustle of ordinary life sounded unusually loud after the deathly quietness of the little shop.

Mr Valentine had been murdered which, as Frank had pointed out, didn't exactly prove that he hadn't killed Ellie Watson and Fanny Jones. It was possible that he had disturbed a sneak-thief rifling the till and been struck down. Possible but not really likely. Sneak-thieves knew where the richest pickings were and Mr Valentine's modest little business wasn't exactly lucrative, a fact almost any thief would've known. Neither did she think that petty criminals went round during the early afternoon with weapons in their hands.

But why had Mr Valentine been killed? Seated in the cab as it slowed at a crossroads Tansy knew the answer. Valentine had seen her going into the shop, had gone in later and, fearful of what Mr Valentine knew or had told her, struck him down. But Mr Valentine had told her very little because his life was lived still in a glorious past when he had strutted the boards.

She was being followed. Wherever she went someone followed close behind. Someone knew that having a dead kitten thrown at her and a pink ribbon tied to her door-knocker hadn't deterred her. Someone had been at the inquest and seen her there, or followed her earlier that morning, but for the life of her she couldn't remember being aware of anyone watching her.

If she hadn't gone to see Mr Valentine he might still be alive. That conclusion, though deeply disturbing, seemed inevitable.

She rapped sharply on the roof of the cab and gave instructions to the driver to take her to Fleet Street instead.

There was no sign of Patrick Denny when she walked into the newspaper office. The two letters were still in the pigeon-hole.

Tansy sat down, picked up a magazine and read it doggedly from cover to cover, without taking in the sense of a single word.

No back-of-the-neck prickle alerted her to some covert watcher. Those coming in and out seemed intent on the gathering, reporting and filing of news, and spared her scarcely a glance. It was perhaps a hopeful sign that the sight of a female in such surroundings no longer excited the indignant and chauvinistic regard of the men working there.

Nobody had followed her here. Of that she was sure. She put the magazine back into the rack and stood up.

Outside it would have been almost impossible to tell whether anyone was following her or not. Tansy strolled on, pausing to examine the various goods in the windows, seeing no familiar face reflected in the glass. At a corner-shop she went in and purchased a jar of caviare.

Making her way to the mews entailed taking several twists and turns until she stood finally below the window with the lace curtains from which the old Russian lady had seen Mary Denny pass by with her male companion.

She looked back along the cobbled mews but no other trod the stones or lurked in a doorway.

'I remember you!'

The still pretty voice fluted down the stairs that rose up out of the far corner of the empty stable.

'I am not Tatiana,' Tansy said.

'Of course you are not Tatiana! Hair too red. Your name is Tansy. Have you come to visit me, my dear?'

'To make certain you are all right. Coming here I picked up a trifle.'

She held up the pot of caviare.

'I have biscuits,' the old lady said. 'Please come up!'

Nothing had changed in the overfurnished, elaborate room. Looking round as she took the proffered chair and handed over the jar, Tansy thought that Mr Valentine and this old lady in her lost grandeur would have had a great deal in common.

'You have the advantage of me,' she said aloud. 'You know my name but I don't know yours.'

'It is better not to give one's name.' The other laid a finger along her nose. It is not that I mistrust you, boobla, but the Tsar's spies are everywhere. Call me Babushka. That would please me and remind me of the old days. It is seldom that I have visitors these days.'

'You haven't noticed any strangers in the mews?'

'None, but then I am not always looking out of the window. Here you are! We shall have some vodka with it. One must always have a soupçon of vodka with caviare.'

At least her visit here didn't seem to have put the old lady in any danger, Tansy thought, accepting the biscuits and the generous spoonful of caviare on a cracked but exquisitely patterned saucer. The old lady measured the dregs of her vodka into two tiny glasses and lifted her own with a sudden beaming smile that stripped away her years.

'*Prosit*!' she said.

'*Prosit*!' Tansy echoed obediently.

'So! Tell me about yourself, my dear. Why do you come and visit an old woman whom the world forgot?' the other enquired.

'I came to ask about Mary Denny,' Tansy reminded her.

'The little girl with the dark curly hair. Ah yes. You have found her?'

'Not yet,' Tansy said soberly. 'Her brother is very anxious for her safety.'

'For her safety or her reputation? Did I tell you that I saw her one late evening with a young man? I have been thinking about that. The young man reminded me of someone but I cannot tell who.'

'You're sure he was a young man? You didn't see his face.'

'I saw how he moved – easily, without stiffness, back straight, head high. The old move differently, my dear – you are not Tatiana?'

'Tansy. My name is Tansy.'

'The yellow flower that grows in the hedgerows. Very pretty. Yes, we must wait longer yet to see Tatiana again.'

'Babushka, you don't let in everybody who visits you, do you?' Tansy asked.

'No indeed! I am not so foolish!' Babushka looked at her haughtily.

'And you do have a strong lock on your door?'

'Indeed I do. Why do you ask? Are there agents of the Tsar about?'

'One hears things,' Tansy said vaguely.

'Then I will take extra care. Eat your caviare!'

Obediently Tansy nibbled the biscuit with its glistening black beads piled high.

'Something troubles you, child?' Babushka had leaned forward slightly.

'I was thinking,' Tansy said slowly, 'how one can do something in itself quite innocent which leads to ill-fortune for someone else.'

'We are all bound together, linked without knowing it,' the old lady nodded gravely. 'Often I have asked myself if the dear general would have spoken so frankly had he known what the results would be for others, for others who loved him and were part of him and suffered after he had spoken. I know that it would have altered nothing. We each of us must act as we see right.'

'Yes. Yes, I think you're right,' Tansy said.

'We all have our fate to face.' Babushka spoke as if to herself. 'The Creator uses the actions of other people to bring it about. To feel guilty over a good deed that ends badly is arrogant, my dear. We are only pawns after all.'

'And this pawn must leave. Lock your door,' Tansy said, rising. 'I'll visit you again soon.'

Babushka rose, her long skirts hissing across the rugs as she moved to the door. As she opened it wide for Tansy to step through, she said in a bewildered way, 'What exactly have we been talking about?'

'I'm not certain but you've been a great help,' Tansy said, and on impulse bent her head and kissed the cool, papery cheek.

'*Au revoir, ma chérie*! Continue to study your French. It is the language of courts,' the old lady said and had closed her door before Tansy had reached the bottom of the spiral stair.

She waited until she had heard the shooting of a bolt into its socket and then turned in the direction of the Dennys' lodgings.

Patrick, for whatever reason, had abandoned his post at the newspaper office. She wondered suddenly if the errant Mary had surfaced unharmed, and reached the wide entrance to the ground-floor stable where the pony, hearing her approach, put his head over his stall and whickered.

'I wondered who it was.' A well-knit figure rose from a stooping position within the stall, the sudden shock of his appearance driving the breath from her as effectively as if she had been winded.

'Mr Hawkins?' She found her voice with an effort.

'Good-afternoon, Miss Clark.' He reached to wipe his hands on a towel that hung against the post. 'I was not aware you had acquaintance in this area.'

'I know Mr Denny slightly,' Tansy said.

Had he watched her mount the stairs to the old lady's lodging? Possibly not, since he looked as if he had been here for some considerable time, in his shirt-sleeves with a bottle of strongly smelling medication in his hand.

'I suspected a spavined foreleg but it is only a bruise,' he said, as he unlatched the lower half of the door and came out.

Tansy instantly, instinctively took a step backwards.

'Are you turned groom, Mr Hawkins?' she asked.

'Saffy is a particular charge of mine. The Edges stable a few of their horses in the mews when they are in town. The stables behind the house have been undergoing extensive repairs so another arrangement had to be made.'

'But the Edges are abroad,' Tansy said. 'So what are their horses doing in town?'

'Just Saffy at the moment,' he corrected. 'She has stayed a little longer than was envisaged and as I promised. . . .'

'Mr Leslie Edge to look after her?'

'A promise must be kept though it is sometimes inconvenient. She needs a good gallop but since – you say you know Mr Denny?'

He was rolling down his sleeves and assuming his coat again.

'Slightly. He has recently returned from India. Do you know him?'

'No, Miss Clark. The young gentleman and I have never met.'

'But you know he's a young gentleman.'

'I assumed – from what his sister said that—'

'You know Mary Denny! When did you last see her?'

'I had occasion to speak with her once. She came to the house to try to sell some embroidered cushion-covers she had made. Mrs Bradshaw was not in need of any cushion-covers but the girl spoke very nicely so she offered her a cup of tea.'

'But nothing was bought?'

'No, Miss Clark. Had the girl appeared destitute then Mrs Bradshaw, out of the kindness of her heart, might have bought from her anyway but the girl was well dressed and nicely spoken. She mentioned that her brother had recently gone to India and that she hoped to surprise him by earning some money by her own efforts before he returned.'

'When was this?' Tansy asked sharply.

'I believe last November – early December. I really cannot say.'

'Before the Edges went abroad?'

'I believe the family was preparing to leave.'

'Wasn't it something of a coincidence that the girl should live above the stables where the family kept their horses when they were in town?'

'One would indeed call it such,' he agreed.

'Mr Hawkins, do you know a Wesley Brown?'

She had switched the line of questioning in a way that would have delighted Laurence.

'From Sion Chapel. Very slightly.'

'He came to the house twice while Tilde Miles was working for you.'

'She told you about it?'

'She said a man came to collect articles made for the Jews' basket. She felt uneasy about him.'

'Yes. He is not a prepossessing individual.'

'His manner towards her was – it frightened her.'

'He has an unpleasant manner, Miss Clark. Since I know nothing against him – on the contrary he has a reputation for doing excellent work in the chapel, but there was something about the way in which – Miss Clark, I have been a butler for many years. It is my function to maintain the smooth running of the household. This can often require a certain diplomatic skill, the ability to sum up character swiftly and accurately. Mr Brown's attitude to Tilde troubled me. I'd not have wished any daughter of my own to be stared at in that manner.'

'Was that why you dismissed her?' Tansy demanded. 'It seems very drastic, to punish her when she wasn't at fault. And please don't try to tell me that she tasted the soup!'

'I could hardly accuse Mr Brown of harbouring unchaste ideas when all he had done was look at her in a certain way, Miss Clark! I couldn't bar any future visits he chose to make nor complain about him when from all accounts his reputation is of the highest. And I could not always be on hand to protect Tilde when he called. I thought it wiser to let her go. She's a bright, willing young woman and – well, the rest you know. She flared up and told me that she had a friend to meet and went off, though I insisted she take the reference.'

'She knew herself to be unjustly accused. Why on earth didn't you tell her that it was for her own protection in case Wesley Brown called again?'

'Because girls never listen to good advice, not even when they are married. Once, many years ago, I knew a lady, a married lady, who refused to accept that a certain clergyman had more than spiritual feelings for her. She did not listen to – her husband. The outcome was very sad for she left her little family and ended – she took her own life, Miss Clark. Yet there was no way in which the tragedy could have been averted. No proof, you see.'

'Yes,' Tansy said.

She saw, she decided, more than he had wished to reveal.

'Have you seen Miss Denny since she tried to sell her cushion-covers?' she asked.

'I only had speech with her the once.'

'And the coincidence – she lived over the stable where the Edges planned to stable their horses?'

'I believe she mentioned the stable beneath her lodging was for rent. I am not usually involved with the livestock.'

'But you are tending Saffy?'

'Yes, Miss Clark. A small favour. I've known Saffy since she was a foal.'

'And you can't tell me anything more about Mary Denny?' she persisted.

'No, Miss Clark. If you will excuse me I must get back to attend to my duties.'

He bowed, put the bottle in his side-pocket and walked away, leaving her staring after him in the dim stable.

ELEVEN

Tansy had decided against mounting the stairs to find out if the elusive Patrick Denny had returned home. Instead she had waited until the footsteps of the butler had died away into the distance and then, feeling decidedly uneasy about the encounter, whisked down an alley, gained the main road and obtained a cab. Before going to her father's she wanted to wash and change her dress which, to her if not to anybody else, smelt of death.

'Miss Tansy, you just missed a visitor,' Mrs Timothy informed her, issuing from the kitchen lair.

'Who?' Tansy took off her hat.

'Mr Patrick Denny.' Mrs Timothy looked as coy as her bulk would permit.

'What did he want?'

'He came to thank you for the dinner and he brought flowers. A spray of white roses for you, a very nice mixed bouquet for me and a posy of sweet-williams for Tilde – as a token of gratitude.'

'He must have resembled a florist's shop on legs,' Tansy said drily.

'He's a very taking young gentleman,' Mrs Timothy said severely. 'Lovely manners and that rather attractive accent. I am not usually impressed with members of the opposite gender, Miss Tansy, but that gentleman has very convivial ways. Tilde was quite bowled over.'

'Was she indeed? Not too bowled over to fetch up some hot water and a good strong cup of coffee, I hope? I'll be going out again almost directly.'

Going upstairs she thought crossly that Mr Patrick Denny had no business to be bringing his taking ways here when she was running all over town looking for him.

Tilde brought the hot water, vanished and returned with the coffee. Her face was slightly flushed and her eyes sparkling.

'The young gentleman who came to dinner brought flowers for us all,' she said. 'It was very kind of him, wasn't it, Miss Tansy?'

'Very kind. Mr Denny has a great deal of charm,' Tansy said, trying to choose between a light-green dress with a short cape or a black one with bands of silvery grey in the skirt and a matching fichu.

'And he's very handsome,' Tilde said.

'Well, don't let it leap to your head,' Tansy advised.

'No, Miss Tansy.'

Tilde, Tansy thought as she dismissed her, sounded unconvinced.

She washed herself, repinned her hair, drank the coffee and decided on the more sombre black. Mr Valentine would, she guessed, have nobody to wear mourning for him.

It was dusk when she came downstairs again and as she opened the front door she found herself glancing nervously up and down the road before she stepped out onto the path. Out there, somewhere, someone might be watching.

This was ridiculous! If she began feeling like this she would never go anywhere.

She was half-way down the road, having decided to walk the longer route to the cab-stand instead of cutting through the park, when an approaching cab slowed and stopped and Inspector Jarrold put out his head.

'Miss Clark! I was on my way to see you. Have you a few moments to spare in order to answer a few questions?' he enquired.

'Yes of course. About. . . ?'

'About the unfortunate individual you and Mr Cartwright discovered this afternoon. You have surely not forgotten?'

'I have been trying to put it out of my mind,' she confessed, climbing up into the cab as he shifted to make room for her.

'Very understandable,' he nodded. 'Mr Cartwright who

reported the matter has given a very clear statement indeed, and mentioned that you were most distressed. However a few questions are in order, I believe. Are you on your way anywhere in particular?'

'To my father's. Perhaps you would like to—'

'Oh, no need to trouble him, I'm sure,' Inspector Jarrold said. 'The case is solved you see.'

'You know who killed Mr Valentine?' Tansy stared at him in surprise.

'Oh, some sneak-thief clearly tried to rob the till and was interrupted by the unfortunate victim. Perhaps we should thank the unknown assailant instead of trying to apprehend him, though naturally enquiries will continue. But I refer to the case – cases, of those two girls, Ellie Watson and Frances Jones. You were at the inquest on the latter but left early.'

'Yes, I. . . .'

'Mr Cartwright explained that the name Valentine used by an individual who placed an advertisement in the newspaper – yes, we had taken note of that – was the name of a fortune-teller sometimes consulted by ladies. Am I right in counting you among them?'

'I – did consult him this morning,' she admitted.

'Very unwise, my dear, to put one's reliance in the spurious prophecies of a charlatan. However, Mr Valentine did mention something to you which later caused you to leave the inquest before the verdict. What was that?'

'He told me there had been three murders,' Tansy said. 'When I heard that Frances Jones had been—'

'In a certain condition.'

'Pregnant,' Tansy said irritably. 'I went back to tell him that he'd been correct.'

'And found him dead. Most upsetting for you.'

'It wasn't pleasant,' she said.

'Of course he knew about the unborn child because he was the one who had killed the unfortunate girl just as he had killed Ellie Watson three months ago,' Inspector Jarrold said.

'Have you evidence for that?' she asked blankly.

'Cause and effect, my dear Miss Clark! Cause and effect! Mr

Valentine was a loner, an eccentric, probably a woman hater. He made his living by cheating credulous ladies – forgive my bluntness – out of their money by pretending to tell them the future. Of course we cannot now tell what drove him to violence against them. But he inserted the advertisement, lured his victims and having gained their confidence, killed them. Nobody knew that Frances was as you said, but Mr Valentine knew.'

'He didn't actually—'

'So the case is solved by a thief who has made it unnecessary for us to spend public moneys on further investigation.'

'Very conveniently,' Tansy said.

'Fate has a way of settling these matters,' he said comfortably. 'Now I take it that you agree with Mr Cartwright's account? You visited Mr Valentine, were told there had actually been three murders, heard the evidence given at the inquest and hurried back to the said Mr Valentine just ahead of Mr Cartwright to make further enquiries, only to find him – I mean the late Mr Valentine – dead, indisputably killed during the course of a robbery. You would confirm that?'

'Why not?' Tansy said.

It was what had happened but Inspector Jarrold had placed entirely the wrong construction on events in a bid to save public funds and wrap up a couple of unsolved murders without damage to his own authority.

'That seems to wrap matters up in a most satisfactory fashion. My cousin the chief constable will be glad to hear of it. Odd how these affairs can resolve themselves if one exercises a little patience.'

'Very odd,' Tansy said.

'No need to sign any statement then. The police station is not the most congenial setting for a charming young lady. Ah! here is the crescent. Give your father my regards and apologies for not coming in, won't you? I have another engagement. Thank you for your assistance.'

He handed her down with some ceremony.

'Good-night, Inspector.'

It was as much as she could do to answer civilly and her skirts swished indignantly as she went up the steps.

'Keeping bad company I see,' Finn remarked, admitting her.

'Stupid company,' Tansy corrected. 'Inspector Jarrold – come upstairs while I tell Pa.'

'Your pa's got a couple of visitors,' Finn said, detaining her.

'Frank and Patrick Denny?'

'Right. Shall I serve dinner soon?'

'Yes. I don't know why but murder makes me hungry,' Tansy said.

'Aye, it was the same in clink,' he said. 'On the morning someone was being topped there was extra victuals all round for convicts and screws. A way of proving you're still alive, I reckon.'

The fire had been lit and the lamps lighted in the drawing-room. When Tansy went in Frank and Patrick immediately rose, her father's gaze moving from one to the other with repressed amusement.

'No lover ever waited more eagerly for his lady than we have been waiting for you,' he said. 'We were beginning to imagine that you'd been arrested.'

'Frank told you about Mr Valentine?'

'He did. Inspector Jarrold thinks there's no need to look any further for the murderer.'

'Frank, why on earth did you tell him that I'd visited Mr Valentine this morning?' Tansy demanded, stripping off her gloves.

'I thought it best to tell him as much of the truth as possible. There was always the chance that someone had noticed you on the earlier visit.'

'Well, they didn't, and I wish that you had checked with me first. I might have put my foot in it. Finn, give me a small whisky. I am not in a sweet-sherry mood.'

'I didn't reckon on his wanting you to confirm anything,' Frank said.

'Jarrold may be a fool but he's not an idiot,' Laurence said. 'He will produce some valid statements and a neatly worked out conclusion to justify his holding the position he does.'

'Well, he's wrong,' Tansy said. 'Pa, Mr Valentine couldn't have murdered anybody.'

'We're all capable of murder,' he said mildly.

'Well, perhaps, though I'd argue that,' she said reluctantly. 'But I'm certain he didn't put that advertisement in the newspaper. He made a living from hiring out costumes and a slightly larger, I'd guess, unofficial income from telling fortunes. Mrs Mainwaring was a client and so was Tilde Miles's late mother. Tilde had never met him but she saw the advertisement, jumped to the conclusion that it was the Mr Valentine she knew about who'd put it in, and wrote to the box number.'

'She didn't retain the answer?' Laurence said.

'She threw it in the fire. She'd started work in the Edge household and I daresay she didn't want anyone there to know her business. She didn't tell me about it until I forced it out of her. She felt silly, waiting in the park for a man who didn't arrive.'

'You having fortuitously preceded him. You know, my dear, you may be right when you say that there is no proof that the murdered Mr Valentine didn't kill the two girls but nobody else called Valentine has come into the equation.'

'Surely he'd hardly use his own name to lure the poor girls?' Patrick put in.

'That's a fair point, Pa! And what happened to you this afternoon? You weren't at the newspaper offices.'

'When were you there?' Frank asked.

'After we found Mr Valentine,' she explained, 'I suddenly wondered if the real killer had followed me to the costume shop in the morning and killed Mr Valentine to prevent him giving any more information. And then I began to worry about the Russian lady who saw your sister, Mr Denny, with a young man late one January evening. So I went round to see her and on the way I looked in at the newspaper office and you weren't there.'

'Then I must only just have left,' Patrick said. 'I sat there for hours but in the end I decided to call it a day and went over to change my clothes and get ready for the meeting with your father. Oh, and I stopped off to buy some flowers.'

'For which many thanks,' Tansy said crisply. 'You'll turn the heads of both my servants at this rate. You must have been in the studio while I was talking to Babushka. That's the name she asked me to call her by. She lives in fear of agents of the Tsar.'

'I will say, Miss Tansy,' Finn interjected admiringly, 'you get mixed up with as many rum coves as any criminal I ever did see. And dinner's up.'

They repaired to the dining-table where a joint of beef with side dishes of lamb and chicken and a couple of bowls of mixed vegetables waited for them.

'So I must have been dressing while you were talking to the old lady,' Patrick said.

'And you left before I left her. Did you see anybody on your way out?'

Her eyes sharpened as he shook his head.

'Nobody,' he said, 'except the pony and that fellow who comes to tend it.'

So he had been where he said he had been. She felt herself relax.

'What fellow's this?' Laurence enquired.

'No idea.' Patrick was helping himself to gravy. 'Some big nob stables a pony below our lodgings, and this fellow comes by to groom it and take it out for a run now and then. Big man, quiet looking.'

'Mr Hawkins,' Tansy said.

Four pairs of eyes stared at her.

'The Edges' butler?' Laurence said.

'He was there when I left the old lady. He didn't mention having seen you though.'

'He likely didn't notice me,' Patrick said. 'He was putting liniment on the pony's leg.'

'Did you speak to him'?' Frank asked.

'Yes, but not to much purpose.' She briefly recounted the conversation.

'So Wesley Brown had scared young Tilde by his manner towards her and Mr Hawkins thought it best to let her go on some pretext. Sounds unlikely,' Frank remarked.

'He let slip that his own wife had been lured away and later on killed herself because of the scandal,' Tansy told him. 'I don't think that Mr Hawkins can face up to difficult situations where women are involved. He takes the easy way out. Dismiss a tweeny with a good reference on a trumped-up excuse rather than accuse a pillar of the chapel of lechery.'

'What interests me,' Frank said frowningly, 'is why he's tending a pony for the Edge family when they're abroad and presumably their mounts are in the country. They do have a country seat I assume?'

'Not too much known about the family,' Laurence said, cutting himself a slice of cheese. 'The grandfather made his fortune in India and they have a small estate in Devon somewhere. Sir James is something of a philanthropist – donated the chapel – no, that was Sir Joshua, the nabob. They own or part own several businesses.'

'Including the match factory,' Tansy said.

'Where Ellie Watson and Frances Jones and Tilde Miles worked for varying periods of time. Poor Ellie Watson was still working there when she was killed.'

'My sister would certainly never have sought employment, leave alone in a match factory,' Patrick said.

'Not in the match factory, no,' Tansy said.

'Meaning?' His dark eyes held a hint of Irish temper.

'Meaning that your sister went to the Edge house with some embroidered cushion-covers she was trying to sell. Mr Hawkins told me.'

'That,' said Patrick ominously calmly, 'is a damned lie. Pardon me, Miss Tansy, but Mary had no need to work. I left sufficient funds for her to live on, and she had museums and libraries where she could go if she found her own company tedious.'

'She told Mr Hawkins that her brother was in India and she wanted to surprise him on his return by proving that she could earn some money by her own efforts. And the old Russian lady did tell me that she sometimes saw Mary Denny going out with a parcel under her arm. Mr Denny, your sister is a lively seventeen-year-old from what you've told me. You cannot believe that she would be content to sit in a rented lodging twiddling her fingers until you decided to come home again!' Tansy said in exasperation.

'I can't believe it,' Patrick muttered.

'I'm sure Mr Hawkins was telling the truth.'

'The butler seems to get everywhere,' Frank murmured.

'So do the Edges though one never sees them,' Laurence remarked.

'There's no pudding,' Finn remarked, having eaten his own share of the meal at the end of the table in a position that vacillated delicately between the invited guest and the man-servant. 'I've some candy-sugars for you, Miss Tansy.'

'Thank you for betraying my weakness,' Tansy said sweetly.

'Always one for a bit of candy,' he informed the company at large. 'I used to say – you ought to consider them good teeth of yours, Miss Tansy. Never took no notice.'

'And my teeth are still sound! Pa, since we're pooling information maybe there's something I ought to tell you, but I don't want you fussing about it.'

'Tell me what?'

'When I came through the park the other day someone in the bushes flung a dead kitten at me. It had a pink ribbon tied round its neck.

'Nasty,' Laurence said.

'And when I got home there was a bow of bright pink ribbon tied to my door-knocker. Fortunately I was able to get it off before Mrs Timothy or Tilde spotted it.'

'Someone is warning you off,' Laurence said. 'You should have told me.'

'I didn't want you to worry or insist I come home to sleep.'

'Tansy, you're of full age and thanks to a somewhat unconventional rearing capable of looking after yourself better than most females,' he said. 'I have too much confidence in you to start reining you in now, my dear, but you must keep me fully informed and you must tread carefully. It seems to me that you are apt to take unnecessary risks – going alone to see Mr Valentine, rushing off to visit this Russian lady – you give me your word that you will take care?'

'You have it, Pa,' she said simply.

'Finn, pour the coffee and pass the brandy and port,' Laurence ordered. 'If we remain at the table we can share our knowledge of both victims and suspects. Mr Denny, have you reported your sister missing yet?'

Patrick shook his dark head.

'Surely it'd be like thinking her come to some harm?' he said uncertainly.

'If she doesn't surface in the next few days then I think you ought to report her missing. I know you regard it as somewhat shaming to have to admit you've mislaid a sister but your stiff-necked Celtic pride isn't helping us to find her,' Laurence said.

'Tomorrow's Sunday. Maybe she'll be at Mass. She likes to go sometimes though we're not deeply religious,' Patrick said.

'I'll help Finn clear the dishes.' Tansy rose.

'I thought you'd never offer,' Finn said.

In the basement kitchen where Finn reigned as supreme monarch she put down the tray and turned to see him eyeing her quizzically.

'What's on your mind?' she demanded.

'Them two lover-lads.' He jerked his head ceilingwards.

'Finn! Don't be ridiculous.'

'Mr Frank's sweet on you, Miss,' Finn said, preparing coffee. 'Needs a wife to come 'ome to. Mr Denny now – 'andsome but a bit of a fly-by-night. Fancy leaving his sister all alone. Makes your flesh creep to think what might 'ave 'appened!'

'What do you think happened?' Tansy asked.

'I say *cherchez la femme*,' Finn said in a passable French accent. 'When females start getting murdered there's a woman in it somewhere. The sugar-candy's in that jar.'

Tansy took a guilty handful and followed him back up to the drawing-room.

'I think the time's come to draw up a profile of the killer,' Laurence said when they were seated round the table again.

'Can that be done?' Patrick said.

'Let's see. He almost certainly advertises under the name of Valentine, inviting people to consult him about their problems. He must know that women rather than men are more likely to respond to such an advertisement. He obviously follows up those that appear to be prospective victims – young, poor, without close family or many intimate friends. Girls who have a craving for romance. The name Valentine is the hook.'

'He suggests a time and a place of meeting,' Frank said. 'On a public bench in a fairly public place in the evening when their work's done.'

'Or his work,' Tansy, said.

'He could be a gentleman of leisure,' Laurence said. 'Now what does he look like?'

'Middle 'eight to tall. Well built. Walks softly,' Finn said.

'Age?' Frank was jotting down notes.

'Any age between early twenties and late forties. Dresses in a conventional manner. Probably but not certainly lives alone. No close male friends. May be a homosexual,' Laurence said.

'Or impotent,' Tansy suggested, chewing on candy.

'That's also likely. Certainly has a deep-seated hatred of women.'

Patrick who looked slightly embarrassed at the turn the conversation had taken murmured, 'Ladies present.'

'I don't count as a lady when we're talking about police work,' Tansy said soothingly.

'So let's look at the victims,' Frank said briskly. 'He chooses a particular type, doesn't he?'

'Ellie Watson was seventeen, small and plain, worked in the match factory, and Frances Jones was small and plain and had worked there before she went to Mrs Mainwaring's establishment,' Tansy said.

'And Tilde Miles, whose murder your arrival almost certainly prevented, is seventeen and also worked briefly at the match factory.'

'But Tilde's pretty,' Patrick said.

'And Frances Jones was pregnant so someone must've desired her. Would that have been Valentine himself?'

'Pa, I think Wesley Brown was the father of Fanny's child,' Tansy said. 'She attended Sion Chapel and when John Mason suggested she talk to his fellow-deacon she laughed hysterically. And Mr Hawkins dismissed Tilde because Wesley Brown came round collecting for charity and made it obvious what he was after.'

'And the manager of the match factory also harasses the girls in his charge,' Laurence recalled. 'The young woman. . . ?'

'Sylvie.'

'She sneaked out to tell you that. I don't think we can cancel him out.'

'The pink ribbon?' Tansy took another candy.

'That has some deep meaning for him alone. Until we catch the man we've no possible means of even guessing,' Laurence said.

'My sister . . .' Patrick spoke hesitatingly. 'Mary's not yet eighteen. She cut out the Valentine advertisement and left it in her drawer.'

'She tried to sell her needlework at the Edge household and met Mr Hawkins,' Tansy frowned. 'But she isn't a Methodist, is she?'

'Catholics,' Patrick said. 'She likes to go to Mass quite often.'

'The Edges have been abroad for months but a pony is stabled in the mews and Mr Hawkins goes over to take care of it. Why not a groom?' Frank said.

'The young man with whom my old Russian lady saw your sister,' Tansy said. 'Could that have been one of the Edges?'

'Either Leslie Edge or his father. Dammit!' said Laurence. 'I wish we knew a little more about that family, but they live quietly, keep out of society, have no scandal about them reported.'

'I think that Mary's still alive,' Tansy said. 'Valentine left the other two girls for anybody to find. He wanted them to be found.'

'The mode of killing is very interesting,' Laurence said thoughtfully. 'No physical contact. Women-killers generally strangle or suffocate. This man creeps up behind and gives them a heavy blow on the back of the head, possibly ready to give a second blow if they don't immediately fall down. Then be ties a bright pink ribbon round their hat and walks off. No anger there. Almost like an execution.'

There was silence. Then Patrick said, 'Tomorrow I'll go to the churches that Mary likes. She might be there.'

'If you think it will do any good.' Laurence sounded curiously dismissive. 'For my own part I think your sister will turn up in her own good time.'

'That's always possible, but Mary always shared her thoughts with me,' Patrick said.

The clock chimed. Tansy, glancing at it, was aware that the hour was growing late and that neither Frank nor Patrick Denny showed any inclination to move.

After a moment she said, 'Mr Denny, it would set my mind at

rest somewhat if you checked up on the old lady who lives next door but one to your lodging. She knows nothing valuable and is surely in no danger but she is elderly and confused and if you just checked for me that her door really is locked without alarming her, of course.'

'I'll go at once, Miss Tansy.' He rose, the eagerness to please in his face. 'Mr – sorry! Inspector Clark, it's been an honour to meet you, sir. I shall keep in close touch. Miss Tansy, I hope to have the pleasure of seeing you again soon. Mr Cartwright.'

He took his cloak and hat and went away with something of a flourish.

'That was shrewd of you, my dear.' Laurence looked across the table at her approvingly.

'Pa?'

'To realize that I wanted to talk without his presence, charming though he may be.'

Tansy, who had merely hoped to avoid a possibly amorous advance in a cab, lowered her eyes and accepted the undeserved compliment meekly.

'You suspect him?' Frank said.

'I hesitate to add yet another suspect to the list,' Laurence said. 'On the face of it he is exactly what he says he is. Certainly he was in India when Ellie Watson was killed. But he is not being entirely open with us all the same. Why would he not report his sister's disappearance to the police? Any anxious brother would do that. I cannot believe that this man would feel any shame about reporting a sister missing. No, he hasn't told us the whole story about himself. Finn, I rather think this is within your province.'

Finn, who had just returned from letting Patrick out of the house, nodded.

'Criminal record. Dicey pals. Money owing. That sort of thing?'

'Exactly, Finn. Tansy, you don't intend to go around London sitting on benches, I trust?'

'I've more sense, Pa.'

'And to prove it,' Frank said with a grin, 'she is going to allow me to see her home.'

'Thank you, Frank.'

Since he was too old a friend to make lustful lunges she smiled at him cordially, feeling, nevertheless, a tinge of regret.

'Let us hope Mary Denny turns up safe and sound,' Laurence said. 'Will I see you tomorrow, Tansy?'

'Not unless something extraordinary happens. I know you like to spend your Sundays reading. Frank?'

'I'm going out of town for a couple of days,' he said unexpectedly.

'Business or pleasure?'

'Her name is Mavis and she's a stunner!'

'I never knew you, Frank, when you didn't have some panting female in tow,' Laurence said, amused. 'Someone ought to go to the funeral of that poor girl Frances Jones though.'

'I'll go,' Tansy promised. 'It won't look odd because I already made enquiries about it when I went to Sion House. I'll keep a sharp look out for who's there. Is it really true that a murderer always attends the funeral of the victim?'

'Many like to see the culmination of their crime,' her father said. 'It's not, however, an ironclad rule.'

'Will the police be there?' Frank enquired.

'No idea.' Laurence shrugged. 'From what Jarrold said to Tansy he had already decided that Mr Valentine killed the girls and then was himself killed in the course of a robbery. That ties up the loose ends and saves his department a lot of legwork. Good-night to you both.'

'Shall we cut across the park?' Frank said when they were outside.

'And I shall drape myself becomingly on a bench and you lurk in the bushes waiting for whoever comes by?' Tansy laughed, then shivered. 'It's not funny, Frank. It's not funny at all! I can't forget poor Mr Valentine. If I hadn't gone to see him he might not have been killed.'

'We don't know if your going there had anything to do with anything.' Frank tucked her fingers through his arm as they walked through the open gates. 'No, I'm not just being comforting. Think about it. You went to see him this morning.'

'Mid-morning, yes.'

'Then you went home for lunch?'

'And then I went to the inquest.'

'Mr Valentine was killed no more than a few minutes before you turned up the second time.'

'How do you know?'

'The blood on his face hadn't congealed. Anyway the police said that he'd been killed not long before. Not all police-officers are as stupid as Jarrold.'

'I didn't look closely.' Tansy shivered again.

'The point is,' Frank said, 'that if you were followed and if the murderer suspected that Mr Valentine really had the psychic power he claimed then it would've made better sense for him to follow you and kill you before you could tell anyone what Mr Valentine might have told you, or to kill Mr Valentine immediately before he could talk to anybody else. Why wait a couple of hours?'

'I haven't the least notion,' Tansy said. 'My head's going round and round because of everything that's happened.'

'Sleep on it,' he advised. 'Have an easy day tomorrow. Don't go rushing about trying to find evidence. Come on! We'll get a cab.'

'You don't have to come all the way home with me,' Tansy said. 'I'm quite capable of walking up my own front path. Truly, Frank.'

'See you on Tuesday then.'

They came out of the side-gate towards a waiting cab. Not until she was in the vehicle bowling home did she realize that for the first time in years she had passed the willow tree where Geoffrey had proposed without a single wistful pang.

TWELVE

The murder of Mr Valentine hadn't, apparently, been announced by the paper-sellers in every district, perhaps because a killing in the course of a robbery didn't compare in human interest terms with the murder of a young girl. Tilde, who would surely have been distressed at the news that her mother's adviser – the man to whom she believed she herself had written – had been killed, brought up hot water and a cup of tea in the morning with the information that Mrs Timothy's back was chronic again.

'So will you mind having a cold lunch today since she can barely drag herself around and I can't cook?' she enquired.

'Left to my own devices I can make shift to whip up an omelette,' Tansy said. 'Tilde, when you were at the Edge house, do you recall the man who came to collect for the Jews' basket?'

'The moon-faced man.' Tilde grimaced. 'Creepy man he was. He looked at me as if he could see right through to my petticoat.'

'But Mr Hawkins was there?' Tansy prompted.

'Oh, he spoke quite sharply to him,' Tilde said.

'And the man left the premises?'

'Yes.' Tilde frowned slightly. 'He turned as he was leaving and gave Mr Hawkins such a sinister look. He said, "There's those who could tell if they would," and then he went. It was very odd. I meant to ask Mr Hawkins what he'd meant but I didn't like to and the very next day I was dismissed.'

'Never mind. You like it here I hope?'

'Oh yes, Miss Tansy.' Tilde's little face flushed with pleasure. 'Mrs Timothy is a very congenial woman, isn't she?'

'I suppose she is. Tilde, about Mr Valentine?'

'Oh, I know that I ought to have told you at once,' Tilde said remorsefully. 'The point is that I felt very awkward about waiting to meet a – a person who tells fortunes.'

'Mr Valentine has been – he's died,' Tansy said.

'Died? Oh, how awful!' Tilde's dark eyes had widened. 'Is that why he didn't meet me after I replied to the advertisement?'

'No. He was apparently killed during the course of a robbery at his shop yesterday afternoon,' Tansy said carefully. 'I felt you ought to know lest you read about it in the newspaper.'

'Poor Mr Valentine! The city's getting to be a very dangerous place, don't you think? Of course I never actually met Mr Valentine but it's sad to think he's dead.'

'Very sad,' Tansy agreed. 'You'd better see about breakfast. Just fruit.'

'I can do bacon,' Tilde said helpfully.

'Just fruit,' Tansy said firmly. 'And Tilde – it might be a good idea if you didn't go too far from the house over the next few days until the person who killed Mr Valentine is arrested.'

'Yes, Miss Tansy.' Tilde dipped a curtsy and went away.

After breakfast she came to clear away the few dishes with a troubled look on her face.

'I've been thinking, Miss Tansy,' she said hesitatingly, 'that it being Sunday I ought to go to church. I mean, make up the quarrel with God. I know Mamma was taken, but I've found a very satisfactory place here.'

There was a small church a few streets off. Tansy said approvingly, 'Put on your hat and jacket and I'll come with you.'

It was weeks since she had attended a service. Pinning on her hat she recalled her father's repeated philosophy.

'Your mother and I were married and you were baptized in the established Church, but if you ever feel like turning Hindu or embracing Islam then we have no objection. If you don't want to join any branch of any faith that's fine too. We each make our own road to heaven.'

'I'm ready, Miss.'

In her neat dress and jacket Tilde was the epitome of demure maidenhood. The effect was spiced up by the addition of a small bunch of sweet-williams pinned to the brim of her straw hat. Clearly Patrick Denny had made an impression!

'I feel very happy today, Miss Tansy,' she said as they set out. 'Even though Mamma's gone and poor Mr Valentine's been killed, one can't dwell on past sorrows, can one? When we first met I was in the depths of despair.'

'About to drown yourself,' Tansy said.

Tilde had the grace to blush. 'It wasn't a very deep pond, was it?' she admitted. 'One couldn't lie on a barge and be floated down to Camelot.'

'Not in the middle of London. What morbid tastes in literature you have.'

'But morbid poetry is much more romantic, Miss Tansy.'

'It's better to wait until one meets a nice respectable man before falling in love,' Tansy said.

'The older generation always say that,' Tilde said.

Tansy shot her a look of outraged astonishment and decided to laugh.

'Not that you don't look awfully well preserved,' Tilde said hastily.

'Thank you, Tilde,' Tansy said gravely. 'I can see you're going to be a great comfort to me!'

They entered the small church where she and Geoffrey had planned to marry. Slipping into a pew she tried to imagine herself walking up the aisle dressed in white, her red hair veiled. At her side would stand the groom.

The trouble was that Geoffrey's remembered features kept dissolving into someone else, decidedly different but as yet indistinctly seen.

When they came out of church a long, lanky figure leaning against a yew tree straightened up and pulled off his hat.

'Tilde, walk on ahead. Good-morning, Finn. I trust,' Tansy said severely, 'you're not appointing yourself my bodyguard?'

'No, Miss Tansy. I reckon you can look to yourself. Is that Tilde Miles?' He nodded ahead to where the girl sauntered.

'It is.'

'She's easy on the eye,' he commented.

'You didn't come all the way over to Chelsea to comment on my maid,' Tansy said.

'No, Miss, I didn't. I would've gone round to your 'ouse but I figured you might've come to church so I walked over and waited. I've news about Mr Denny.'

'What news?'

'After you went last night I took me off to an old mate of mine. Used to be in the force 'imself but there was a bit of bother over 'im taking a fancy to a suspect and letting 'er off for favours received, if you get my meaning?'

'Very clearly indeed. What did your – mate have to tell you?'

'Well, Miss Tansy, since 'e left the force he has dabbled here and there.'

The sudden careful enunciation alerted her. When Finn had something important on his mind he took particular pains with his accent.

'And?' she said.

'My mate knows of Mr Denny. Seems there was a bit of trouble down in County Wicklow – political business. Nothing criminal, but Mr Denny made a few enemies and left in a bit of an 'urry.' Information given he lapsed happily into his normal tones.

'Why would that be important?' Tansy asked.

'Seems 'e was an informer. So 'e comes over to London with the avowed intention of using what talents 'e's got in the painting line in doing something less dangerous, and it stands to reason 'e don't want to get mixed up in the giving-of-information game again.'

'He was employed by the War Office.'

'Yes, Miss, but the War Office don't know everybody's business,' Finn said. 'Anyways it makes sense that 'e's not keen to go running to the force about Miss Denny.'

'If he made enemies in Ireland could they have abducted his sister?'

'It don't seem very likely. 'E weren't that important,' Finn said. 'Anyway, your pa thought you ought to be told seeing as 'ow Mr Denny 'as taken to calling on you and 'anging round in a general sort of way.'

'Mr Denny wants to find his sister without apparently advertising his presence in town to those who might want him to resume his former activities as an informer. Finn, what made you think I'd be in church today? I'm not a regular worshipper.'

'It being the anniversary of Mr Geoffrey's sad demise I figured you'd be there,' Finn said. 'I'll be getting back now.'

He doffed his hat with a fine Sunday flourish and loped away.

Tansy stood still. Today was the day that her world had ended. That was how she had seen it at the time. But the truth was that the world went on and life went on and – how could she possibly have forgotten?

She shook her head at herself and took longer strides to catch up with Tilde who was gazing at a large clump of dahlias with a slight frown.

'I think small flowers are more becoming, don't you, Miss Tansy?' she said. 'Gentlemen who give dainty posies are more sensitive than ones who present big showy blooms.'

'And Mr Denny is very handsome,' Tansy said.

'Oh, heavens! I wasn't thinking of anyone in a special way,' Tilde said, blushing bright red and walking on rapidly.

When they entered the house the scent of cooking drifted out.

'Is that you, Miss Tansy? Tilde just – oh, she's with you!'

Mrs Timothy came into the hall.

'We went to church,' Tansy said. 'You shouldn't have got up, Mrs Timothy, if you weren't up to it.'

'I am always up to it, Miss Tansy, as you know,' Mrs Timothy said, 'but my back does not always agree with me. However, I could not rest easy on my couch knowing you'd be reduced to cold cuts for lunch.'

'It smells very good anyway,' Tansy said.

'A simple ragout with vegetables and a summer pudding to follow. My back would not rise to a roast. Go along in, Tilde. You've the table to lay.'

Tansy went to take off her own hat. The fact of her having let the significance of the date slide from her memory troubled her. She salved her conscience until lunch-time by getting out Geoffrey's letters written to her during his brief months in Jamaica and reading them over.

She had kept them carefully, though for a couple of years after the news had reached her she hadn't brought herself to read them. In the years since she had perused them from time to time, wincing at the optimism with which Geoffrey had planned their future life together. They still moved her, but with deep regret rather than heartache.

When she folded the pages and slid them into each envelope and put each back in the box she had the feeling she was laying aside a might have been.

Geoffrey was dead and it was sad but she was alive. Putting the box in the bottom of her bureau she rose, smoothing the silk of her dress over waist and hips, aware of the taut frame beneath, the upwards swelling of her breasts.

Lunch was as usual a solitary meal. Unless she visited her father or accepted a rare invitation from an acquaintance her meals were eaten by herself. Today she was more conscious of it than usual, and found herself wishing that either Frank or Patrick Denny would turn up. Frank, however, was off with a stunner named Mavis and Patrick Denny was busily going from one Catholic church to the next in the hope his sister might be at one of them.

'Excuse my enquiring, Miss Tansy,' Mrs Timothy said, bringing in the coffee, 'but are we any further forward on the investigation?'

'Matters are progressing steadily,' Tansy said. 'Why do you ask?'

'Because young Tilde has stars in her eyes when a certain gentleman is mentioned and I'd be grateful if you could inform me that a certain young gentleman is not a suspect,' Mrs Timothy said, lowering her voice.

'It's exceedingly unlikely that Mr Denny murdered anybody,' Tansy said, 'but I'd still like Tilde to stay close to the house. Mr Denny has, I fear, a charm which he bestows upon many ladies. One wouldn't want Tilde to be hurt.'

'No indeed! I shall keep a close eye on her,' Mrs Timothy said.

And I shall keep a close eye on myself, Tansy thought, sipping her coffee. Because the heart-break over Geoffrey was fading with the passage of time, that was no reason to allow herself to think too readily about any other attractive man.

Instead, filled with determination, she finished her coffee, then sat at her desk and added conscientiously to the notes she had already made.

Suspects: Wesley Brown? He's certainly a creepy individual, a hypocrite from all accounts, cloaking his lusts under an appearance of piety. He almost certainly fathered Frances Jones's child; he alarmed both Tilde and Mr Hawkins by his manner to her. Did he lust after Ellie Watson or Mary Denny too?

Men who indulged their lusts and got a woman with child didn't often kill women too, surely. Murder arose more from frustration didn't it?

Tobias Simpson? He harassed the girls at the match factory, but he limped quite badly. It would be difficult for him to approach suddenly without being heard unless his limp was merely assumed. And that heavy stick he carried would make a formidable weapon.

Mr Hawkins? He had lost a wife who had later committed suicide because of another man. Had that made him distrust all women or merely fear for the safety of young innocents like Tilde? And why was Mr Hawkins acting as groom to one of the Edge ponies when the Edges were abroad?

Sir James Edge? She knew nothing about him or his son save that they had honoured the last wishes of old Sir Joshua in financing the chapel he had donated, but they obviously didn't extend their social compassion to the girls who laboured in the match factory. And for someone with sufficient wealth it would be easy enough to slip back to England without being noticed.

Mr Valentine? Could Inspector Jarrold have been right? Had the murderer already been removed? She thought of the flamboyant figure as he paced the back room of his costume shop and of his voice, soft and compelling, as he employed the vaunted gift of the seer, and shook her head. Mr Valentine had had no need to put advertisements in the newspaper when he already had a group of female clients eager to know what lay in store. And for Mr Valentine to be struck down by a thief before he could be brought to justice was a circumstance entirely too fortuitous.

Patrick Denny? She had told Mrs Timothy he was no longer a suspect but he certainly hadn't been completely honest about his activities before he had moved to London. Was it possible that Mary Denny had been harmed by some old enemy of her brother? Tansy thought it unlikely. Mary, she suspected, had simply eloped with a man her brother might have disapproved of. On the other hand, she had visited the Edge house and she had cut out the Valentine advertisement.

She pushed the notes away from her and rested her head on her hand.

What was it that Mr Valentine had said? Three Valentines. One was himself, one the false one who caused the killings – no, the false Valentine had lured the victims and the real Valentine had caused them. Mr Valentine had either been speaking in the kind of oblique, mysterious manner favoured by self-styled prophets, or he had simply been spouting nonsense.

By the time Tilde brought in afternoon tea she felt as if she was running round in ever-decreasing circles.

'You look tired, Miss Tansy.'

Tilde gave her a concerned look.

'You mean that I look thirty,' Tansy said with a wry grin.

'Oh no, Miss!' Tilde looked shocked. 'By the time you're thirty you'll be wed with a family I shouldn't wonder.'

'Thank you, Tilde. You've cheered me up immensely,' Tansy said.

'Will you be going out tonight, Miss?' Tilde enquired.

'I may take a short walk,' Tansy said. 'Oh, I won't be requiring any meal later on.'

A sudden restlessness had possessed her, an urge to leave the safe cocoon of her house and see other people going about their lives.

She finished her tea and went upstairs to put on her dark coat and her plain grey hat. There were evening services in many of the churches. She wondered if there was one in Sion Chapel.

'You will take care, Miss?'

Mrs Timothy stood in the kitchen doorway.

'Never fear, Mrs Timothy. I'm only going to evening service,' Tansy said.

Her housekeeper looked unflatteringly surprised as she pulled the door to behind her and came across the hall.

'Church twice in one day, Miss Tansy? That's not like you.'

'I didn't notice you rushing to service yourself,' Tansy retorted.

'Now you know very well that I always like to attend worship except when my back is chaotic,' Mrs Timothy said reproachfully.

'However, I know you were only joking. Tilde and I are going to sit by the kitchen fire. I must admit that her chatter does grow on one. She's been telling me some tale about a girl who died of a broken heart and had herself floated down the river. What she needed was a sensible talking to, of course, but I must say Tilde tells it very nicely.'

'I'm sure she does,' Tansy said with a smile as she let herself out.

It was still light and the streets were fairly crowded, it being that period between teatime and dinner when even the most hard-worked servant could slip out for an hour's breath of air, which constituted, in most cases, an excuse for flirting with the young men released from their own duties.

There were nursemaids too, wheeling their charges home from the various London parks, and cabs bowling along with passengers either bound for a quiet evening at home or on their way somewhere to dine out.

'I miss most of all wandering round the city,' Laurence had once said in a rare moment of self-pity. 'When I was on a case I made all the notes based on all the interviews that I'd undertaken and then I put the lot out of my mind and simply walked. Nine times out of ten I'd either meet someone or notice something that put a whole new angle on the case.'

Tansy walked, following the meandering curve of the river. She loved Chelsea, loved the feeling of being out in the country, savoured the occasional glimpse of a thatched roof or a small field with a cow in it.

Evening service wasn't likely to begin just yet. Tansy waved down a cab and gave directions to Oxford Street.

Mrs Mainwaring cropped up rather a lot in connection with the recent spate of events, she reflected. She couldn't think of the elegant milliner as a suspect, but Frances Jones had worked for her, Tilde's mother had sold hat-trimmings and scarves to her, as Tilde had failed to do. It was possible that Mary Denny had also tried to sell her embroideries there.

She reached the destination she had stipulated, paid off the driver, and turned into the street where the millinery shop was situated.

The shop itself was, of course, closed, with a dark blue awning stretched above the plate-glass windows. Several people, mainly couples, were strolling along the pavement. Some, Tansy thought with a touch of wistfulness, looked like engaged couples, freed from chaperonage for a spell to plan their futures and to choose items in the shop-windows that they hoped either to be given or to buy. It was odd, but she and Geoffrey had never done that. When they married they would have moved into the house he already owned and when he sailed to Jamaica he had left sufficient funds for her to redecorate and refurnish as she wished.

'Miss Clark!'

Mrs Mainwaring had issued unexpectedly from the narrow alley in which the building that housed her employees was situated.

Tansy felt suddenly and stupidly guilty, as if she'd been caught out in some misdemeanour. Mrs Mainwaring, however, seemed quite unperturbed by the encounter, pausing to hold out a grey-gloved hand with every appearance of pleasure.

'Miss Clark, how nice of you to think of calling upon me. Have you made any progress yet with your father in your joint deliberations? I have just been having a little talk with my girls. I have advised them to take very great care until this monster is apprehended. One cannot be too careful.'

'The police are of the opinion that the killer has already been found but was killed before he could be arrested,' Tansy said. 'Mr Valentine?'

Mrs Mainwaring's colour had dulled. She withdrew her hand, saying sharply, 'I believe I did read somewhere that a Mr Valentine had been struck down in the course of a robbery, but I fail to see—'

'You and Tilde Miles's late mother were both clients of his,' Tansy said.

'Hardly clients, Miss Clark!' The milliner's colour had returned with a vengeance and her voice had shrilled. 'Occasionally – for amusement – of course nobody would be so foolish as to be in fortune-telling even if it wasn't against the law!'

'Mrs Mainwaring, I'm not interested in your having gone to have your fortune told,' Tansy hastened to say. 'As a matter of fact

I'm inclined to think that some people can see a little further than the rest of us. The point is that neither my father nor myself believe that Mr Valentine was responsible for the deaths of Ellie Watson or Frances Jones. I merely wondered if you could tell me a little more about him. Was his name really Valentine?'

'I understand that it was,' Mrs Mainwaring said more calmly. 'He used to say that with a name like that the stage was the only place where he could hope to make a living – though to tell the truth I rather gained the impression that it was never a very lucrative one. He had saved very carefully and opened his premises for the hiring-out of costumes. He was quite an educated gentleman.'

'But not a woman hater?'

'Of course not!' Mrs Mainwaring sounded indignant. 'He liked the company of ladies – in a perfectly innocent way you understand. No, he was not a man capable of such wickedness.'

'Is Sir James Edge?' Tansy asked.

She had asked the question impulsively, without thinking too much about it before she spoke.

The two women had begun to walk together along the street. Now Mrs Mainwaring stopped dead, her gentility dropping from her like a discarded bath-towel.

' 'Ave you been talkin' to Mr 'Awkins?' she demanded.

'Not about his employers,' Tansy said. 'Tilde Miles was employed briefly as a tweeny by the Edges and Sir James owns the match factory where Ellie Watson and Frances Jones both worked. I rather wondered if – if Sir James had been a benefactor to yourself and your – late husband?'

Mrs Mainwaring stared at her for a full minute. Then unexpectedly she shook her head.

'There never was a Mr Mainwaring,' she said crisply. 'I've been bedded but never wedded, Miss Clark. I'm not ashamed of it! I've made my way up in the world, and I've given more pleasure than I ever got, I can tell you! Sir James – well, his wife is an invalid – weak lungs and nervous trouble, so they spend a great deal of time abroad. Sir James, he resolved to devote himself to her comfort but he's not a man to leave a – a lady friend in the lurch. He knew that I hankered after a respectable business so he set it up for me. Only the initial investment mind! That was nearly ten years ago and I've had no dealings with him since, but I'll tell you for free, Miss Clark, that he's a proper gentleman he is! He'd no more murder anyone that he'd cheat in business and that's the plain truth!'

There was a cab passing and she turned abruptly, waved it down and climbed into it. Tansy, feeling slightly stunned at the unexpected revelation, was left standing on the pavement staring after the vehicle.

She had had no chance to ask about Mary Denny but what she had learned had been extremely interesting. She didn't feel that too great reliance could be placed on Mrs Mainwaring's opinion but the Edges certainly seemed to crop up in the most unexpected places.

Dusk was falling at last, the warmth of the sun cooling. People were now hastening their footsteps, homeward bound.

If there was an evening service in Sion Chapel then it would probably be starting very soon. Tansy, who had half intended to find out if any of the girls working in the millinery establishment were at home and could enlighten her a little more about Frances Jones, changed her mind and took a cab to Wellinburgh Street.

Frances Jones, she thought, had taken the long walk from Oxford Street to Sion Chapel twice a week, to the Sunday service and to the Band of Hope on Wednesday afternoons. It was unlikely that she would have afforded to take a cab.

The walk back to her room early on winter evenings would have been cold and dark. Had she walked it alone or had Wesley Brown accompanied her, his bulky figure dwarfing her slighter one, his thick, clammy fingers drawing her hand through the crook of his arm?

She paid off the driver and stood looking at the patch of waste-ground in which the chapel stood. It contrasted with the neatly kept grounds of the churches with which she was more familiar. The congregation here wasn't wealthy, she surmised, and since they still depended on the patronage of the Edge family to some degree then they would be anxious to conceal or deny any scandals. There were no trees or flower borders here, only a few shrubs planted hopefully in a shallow trench where the weeds were already springing. Light streamed through the open door but she could hear no sound from within. Perhaps they were engaged in silent prayer, Tansy thought, and felt a certain reluctance to disturb them.

Instead she walked somewhat aimlessly along the side of the low wall to where it curled round to the back of the building. The light was fast fading and a few stunted trees cast crooked shadows across the uneven paving-stones. The heels of her shoes made brisk tapping noises.

For some reason she began to feel uneasy. It was foolish, of course, since her senses were alert. She wasn't seated on a bench in some deserted place, and she was certain that she hadn't been followed.

Nevertheless she was relieved when the thin sound of voices raised in a hymn issued faintly from the chapel. Turning, she walked back, but her intention of going in to join the congregation was frustrated by the sudden opening of the door as people came out in twos and threes.

'Miss Clark?'

To her dismay Wesley Brown was bearing down upon her, hat in hand, eyes already roving.

'Good-evening, Mr Brown.' She gave a small bow to avoid shaking hands.

'Are we to hope that you have decided to join our little gathering?' he enquired genially.

'No. I – I simply thought that I would check up on the time of the funeral tomorrow,' Tansy said.

'I understand it is fixed for two o'clock now. As we have no burial plot of our own we share the nearest graveyard – just two streets away. You cannot miss it.'

'You are very kind.'

She would have turned away but his voice, soft and insinuating, held her captive.

'One wonders, you know, what kind of young woman risks a solitary walk after dark to a place seldom frequented at night?'

'Are you referring to me?' Tansy demanded.

'No, no. Dear Miss Clark! How can you think? No, I meant poor Miss Jones and before her Miss – I can't quite recall her name.'

'Watson,' Tansy said shortly. 'Ellie Watson. Are you suggesting that females should be kept in purdah?'

'No, of course not, but you must admit there are certain individuals who – you follow my meaning?'

'I think that such individuals ought to be penned up after dark,' Tansy said, disgusted. 'Then all women could walk safely. Good-evening, Mr Brown.'

She took a few paces away but he seemed incapable of taking the broadest of hints. Instead he promptly matched his step to hers, his voice lower as he said, 'Since that happy hour has not yet arrived perhaps – perhaps you would permit me to escort you to the nearest cab-stand, or did you wish to look round the chapel? The main door is closed after the service but there is a back door, the key for which is kept on a shelf just inside the porch entrance. There are some interesting drawings executed by the Sunday school class you might like to see?'

'No thank you. And surely it's indiscreet of you to mention where the key is kept? Not every body is honest.'

'I hardly think you are likely to break in and burgle the place,' he said with an affected little laugh. 'And of course no money is kept on the – Oh, Mr Mason has joined us.' His voice was flat with disappointment.

'Good-evening. Did you enjoy the service,' his fellow-deacon asked, shaking hands firmly.

'I arrived too late,' Tansy said. 'You were having a silent prayer?'

'Two minutes' silence in memory of our departed sister,' Wesley Brown said. 'Miss Clark and I were just—'

'I was just going to bid you good-night,' Tansy said. 'I wonder if you could spare me a moment, Mr Mason.'

'I was just – yes, of course. I'll walk you to your cab-stand,' he said. 'Mr Brown, would you lock up for me?'

'With pleasure,' Wesley Brown said looking as if it was anything but. 'Good-night, Miss Clark.'

If a large man could be said to melt into the background he did, his feet making curiously little sound as he moved away.

'Thank you,' Tansy said to John Mason.

'Mr Brown is a rock in the foundations of our little congregation, though his manner can be sometimes unfortunate,' he defended.

'Very!' Tansy said. 'Mr Mason, has nobody ever made a complaint against him?'

'Of what nature?'

'His attitude towards – women. You must have noticed!'

'He has an unfortunate home-life,' John Mason said reluctantly. 'His wife is – she is not in sympathy with the excellent work he does with the Band of Hope and in the Sunday school. Most of our members speak very highly of him.'

A cab was coming along the road, slowing at the crossing where a gas-lamp glimmered. Tansy, briefly glancing, saw someone alight, raise a hand to the person still seated within and then lope off across the street.

The cab gained speed again and bowled off. Tansy stood transfixed. There was no doubt about it. Frank, who was supposed to be out of town, had just gone striding across the road without a backward glance, and the girl who had been driven rapidly away was the spitting image of the sketch that Patrick Denny had drawn of his sister.

THIRTEEN

'Miss Clark, is anything wrong? Miss Clark?'

John Mason's voice was suddenly anxious. Probably, Tansy thought as she pulled herself together, because even in the fitful light he had seen her change colour.

'I believe I am a little tired, Mr Mason,' she said quickly. 'Isn't that another cab coming?'

'I'll direct it to stop!'

He stepped out to wave it to a standstill.

'Thank you, Mr Mason. Good-night.'

She leaned back into the gloom of the interior, relieved that Wesley Brown hadn't reappeared. From the alacrity with which Mr Mason had rescued her she sensed that complaints about Mr Brown's attitude had been far from scarce in the past.

'Where to?'

The cabbie had pulled up the small trap-door in the roof and was staring down at her through the aperture.

'Where to what?' Tansy asked.

'You ain't given me directions, madam,' he said patiently.

She had half planned to finish her evening at her father's so that they could discuss what she might have found out during her wanderings round the city, but Laurence was shrewd. Her face would betray her.

She gave her own address and sat back, hardly conscious of the swaying of the cab as it was driven through the emptying Sunday streets.

Frank Cartwright had been with Mary Denny in a cab. That

meant Patrick's sister had been found safe and well, and the most natural course of action for Frank to take would have been to inform herself and Laurence and Patrick Denny. Instead he had taken her off in a cab, alighting too near Sion Chapel for coincidence. And Mary Denny had driven on. Where? Back to the mews to tell her brother she was safe? And what about Mavis, the 'stunner' Frank had been supposedly going out of town to see? Tansy had the uncomfortable suspicion that Mavis had been Mary all along.

'You said you wouldn't be back for supper,' Mrs Timothy said as she entered the house.

'I changed my mind,' Tansy said shortly. 'I am, I suppose, entitled to do that?'

'Yes, Miss Clark.' Only Mrs Timothy's use of her surname indicated her chagrin.

'Bring me some tea and toast, will you? Nothing more.'

Tansy went into her drawing-room and closed the door. The lamps had been lit ready for her return and a small fire warmed the hearth. She took off her hat and cloak and slung them across the back of the sofa, went over to the small table and poured herself a brandy. The liquid burned her throat as it went down and she reached into her pocket for a sugar-candy and bit down on it angrily.

While she had been racking her brains and running all over town in a bid to garner information, Frank had coolly bought himself a couple of days with an outright lie and was apparently shepherding a perfectly safe and healthy Mary Denny about. To Sion Chapel of all places!

'Your tea and toast, Miss Clark.'

Mrs Timothy was still very much on her dignity.

'Mrs Timothy, I'm sorry for biting your head off just now.' Tansy said contritely. 'It was unwarranted rudeness and I hope you'll overlook it. To tell you the truth these murders are disturbing my peace of mind more than I wish to admit but that's no excuse for taking out my feelings on you!'

'That's all right.' Mrs Timothy straightened up after placing the tray on the table. 'No offence taken I promise you. We are all a little on edge. My back, of which I, as you know, seldom complain, is becoming quite seriously chronic, but that is no reason for me to burden you. Good-night.'

'Good-night, Mrs Timothy.'

At the door Mrs Timothy turned to deliver her Parthian shot.

'Pardon me for mentioning the fact, Miss Tansy,' she said, 'but when a lady takes to drink it's often due to upheavals of the heart. Emotional not physical. I just thought I'd mention the fact.'

She closed the door softly behind her. Tansy looked at the brandy still in her glass, tossed it off in a defiant gulp, made a wry face and sat down to eat tea and toast in chastened silence.

She slept badly, slumber shot through with flashes of Frank alighting from a cab, giving his hand briefly to the pretty creature within, then loping away without a backward look.

By the time she finally went to sleep properly she had decided that since it was time Frank settled down then Mary Denny, provided she had a good reason for her recent absence, would be as good as any girl to make him a wife. The days when unmarried women danced in red-hot slippers were no doubt still confined to the realm of fairy-tale.

She had intended to go over to see her father but decided against it, giving herself the excuse that she had slept badly and woken feeling less than her usual self, but aware that her real reluctance lay in the fact that she couldn't in good conscience tell him about Frank without giving Frank himself time to call upon her with an explanation.

Meanwhile, leaving a now cheerful Mrs Timothy to initiate Tilde into the mysteries of the Monday wash, she ate a late breakfast and spent the rest of her morning attending assiduously to the household accounts.

Mrs Timothy brought in a cold ham salad for lunch, observing that it was going to be a warm afternoon.

'Though the summer's wearing away fast, Miss Tansy,' she observed. 'As I am myself if truth were to be told. However it's a comfort to me to know that when I am taken Tilde will be here to minister to your needs. She is a very willing young person, Miss Tansy.'

'I'm sure you're right,' Tansy said, deciding not to mention that Tilde herself might not want to spend her life in devoted servitude.

'Will you be going out this afternoon?' Mrs Timothy enquired.

'I've undertaken to attend the funeral of Frances Jones,' Tansy said.

'Poor girl! What a terrible way to die,' Mrs Timothy said. 'I'll lay out your black dress. At least she's got a fine day for the funeral. That must be some consolation to her, poor soul.'

Tansy hastily bit back a chuckle and chewed a piece of ham instead.

In her own mind the black dress unrelieved by any touch of colour brought back too sharply the memory of her own mother's funeral. She and Laurence would both have preferred a quiet ceremony but as the wife of a police-officer her mother had been laid to rest with a cortège of uniformed men. The day had passed in a blur of misery, and beyond attending a small and very private memorial service for Geoffrey she had avoided such melancholy occasions ever since.

When she was dressed with a spencer jacket and tip-tilted hat to complete her outfit she went downstairs and met a startled Tilde in the hall.

'Oh my!' Tilde's small hand was lifted to the region where no doubt she judged her heart to be. 'It isn't bad news, is it?'

'The funeral of the girl who was killed the other day.'

'You didn't know her?'

'No. No, I didn't. Stay close to the house, Tilde,' Tansy instructed.

'You don't think. . . ?'

'I don't think anything,' Tansy said. 'I'll see you later, Tilde. Mrs Timothy is pleased with your work.'

'Yes, Miss Tansy.'

Obviously repressing the urge to quote some lines befitting the occasion, she opened the front door meekly.

Tansy walked to the cab-stand and took a waiting cab. She would drop off at Sion Chapel, she decided, and find her way to the cemetery from there.

In fact finding her way was unexpectedly easy. As they neared Wellinburgh Street she saw the shops with drawn blinds and the assistants gathered in silent little groups in the doorways. Ahead of her she could see the tail-end of a short, slow-moving procession.

'Going to the funeral, madam? I can let you off at the cemetery gates,' the cabman informed her.

'Thank you.'

Tansy sat back slightly to conceal herself from the curious sightseers. It wasn't her intention to be regarded as a chief mourner.

By the time the cab had reached the open gates of a fairly large. tree-strewn cemetery the crowd had increased, considerably. Many were women with shawls and boots to denote their position as members of the working class, a designation with which Laurence for one had frequently disagreed.

'There's nothing wrong in doing menial work, but the rest of us labour quite hard too,' he had commented wryly. 'Mind you, it suits a malcontent to believe the rest of us are living in pampered luxury. Most working folk have too much sense!'

These women, some clutching small children, stood mutely, their faces drawn not only with grief for a young woman they almost certainly had never known but with the unspoken fear of a killer who stalked in darkness and had already struck twice.

Tansy paid the fare, alighted and wended her way through the crowd to where Fanny's coffin had been carried to the open grave.

In death Frances Jones received more luxury than she had ever known during her brief life. Her coffin was of oak with two large wreaths, one red, one white, of lilies and carnations. A minister in sombre garb stood with open prayer-book.

Tansy retreated a few yards to a large yew tree which spread its branches and created a space of shade in the glimmering sunshine.

Standing there, half-listening to the sonorous tone of the ancient ritual of burial she searched for familiar faces in the sea of black. Even those not in full mourning had managed to find black armlets and shawls.

There was no sign of either Frank or Patrick Denny. Presumably the former was still with Mary Denny and Patrick would be down at the newspaper office to see if the two Valentine letters were collected.

'Miss Clark. Good-day to you.'

The coffin had been lowered, its wreaths removed, and Inspector Jarrold was doffing his hat to her.

'Inspector.' She heard the ice lacing her own voice.

'You see we still strive to do the correct thing,' the inspector said.

'I beg your pardon?'

'In the unlikely event that Mr Valentine was not the murderer of the two unfortunate young women I elected to attend the funeral here in the hope – a vain one – that we might apprehend a suspect. It is a well-known fact that the murderer always attends the funeral of the victim. However there are only the few who knew the girl personally and those who attend burials as a form of entertainment present. Mr Valentine will be buried in about a week.'

'And have you caught his killer yet?' Tansy asked sweetly.

'Early days, Miss Clark. Early days. My regards to your father.'

'Inspector.'

Tansy achieved a small bow, her lips twitching despite the gravity of the situation. Inspector Jarrold evidently dreamed of a possible murderer who would leap into the open grave babbling a confession. But the truth was he wasn't even dreaming of that. He was quite certain that the killer had himself already suffered a violent end.

Inspector Jarrold moved away as did several spectators lingering round the outskirts of the crowd. For the first time Tansy spotted Mrs Mainwaring enveloped in yards of black crape with a group of young women in plain black gowns circled about her in horseshoe formation. Mrs Mainwaring's business acumen clearly hadn't deserted her. Each of her employees and she herself wore a black hat which was a triumph of the milliner's art.

'It's Miss Clark, isn't it?'

A tall, dignified man had stopped before her, doffing his silk-hat.

'Mr Hawkins!' Tansy stared at the Edges' butler. 'I didn't realize that you'd be attending.'

'The deceased did work briefly at the match factory,' he reminded her, 'and so I felt it only right that the family be represented here.'

'Does someone represent the family at the funeral of everybody connected in any way with the Edges?' Tansy enquired.

'No, Miss Clark, but the circumstances of the deaths of Miss Watson and Miss Jones are somewhat unusual,' he said.

'So you knew Frances Jones?'

'Very very slightly, Miss Clark. She worked very briefly at the match factory before finding more congenial employment with Mrs Mainwaring.'

'Was she dismissed from the factory?'

'No, Miss Clark. She merely wished to better herself. As far as I know she was never dismissed.'

'I wondered if either Mr Simpson or Mr Brown harassed her,' Tansy said. 'I understand you have a – fatherly interest in young girls pursued by – unsuitable men.'

'The only person I dismissed in the hope of discouraging unwanted advances from a certain gentleman was your current maid-servant, Tilde Miles. Ellie Watson was still working at the factory when she was killed and Miss Jones had left entirely of her own accord.'

'I see. Thank you, Mr Hawkins.' She looked at him gravely, then said, 'Do you know if any of the Edge family paid any brief return visit from abroad?'

'There were no return visits.' A shade of coldness had crept into his manner. 'You cannot possibly imagine that any of the Edge family could be involved in these sad affairs! Miss Clark, your imagination must be running away with you. The notion is preposterous!'

'They simply seem to be an unusual family,' she said placatingly. 'Of course I wasn't suggesting. . . .'

'One hopes not, Miss Clark. After all, as I understand it, the interest you and your father are taking in all this is unofficial, is it not?'

'You've been talking to Inspector Jarrold,' Tansy said resignedly.

'We exchanged a few words,' the butler said. 'I was unable to offer him any real help, unfortunately. In any case he gave me to understand that the miscreant is almost certainly dead himself.'

'Conveniently for all concerned,' Tansy said dryly. 'No more questions to be asked, no secrets to be revealed. Why does Mr Leslie Edge keep a pony in town, tended only by you? The Edges have been abroad for months. And why stable it in the mews when there must surely be a stable at the Edge residence?'

'Miss Clark. . . .' He stared at her.

'Well?' She challenged him with her eyes.

'I have nothing more to say,' he said at last. 'Good-day to you, Miss Clark.' He bowed slightly and walked away.

Her glance sharpened suddenly. At the open grave with its attendant pile of earth a familiar bulky figure was stooping to look at the two wreaths left beside it. Near Mr Brown two shawled women were sobbing into their handkerchiefs.

'Miss Clark. Good-afternoon.'

A voice spoke quietly at her elbow. Turning, she saw the neat spare figure of Wesley Brown's fellow-deacon.

'Good-afternoon, Mr Mason.'

'Did you reach home without further discomfort?' he enquired, shaking hands.

'Thank you, yes. To be honest with you,' she lowered her voice slightly, 'I find your colleague, Mr Brown, somewhat – unattractive. His manner – you must've received complaints?'

'Mr Brown has an – unfortunate manner,' he admitted, 'but he is deeply pious. And he has his own troubles. His wife is something of an invalid, I understand. She doesn't attend services.'

'You told me that Frances Jones wept hysterically and laughed when you suggested she confide her problems to Wesley Brown?'

'It was perhaps imprudent of me to tell you that.'

'At the inquest – did you go to the inquest?'

He shook his head. 'I find such occasions bring out the worst in many people,' he said. 'They go there for sensational gratification, Miss Clark.'

'At the inquest it was announced that Frances Jones had been with child. Did you know that?'

'It has been reported in the newspaper. One wishes such news could be less widely written about.'

'Didn't you start to wonder—'

'Miss Clark, this is a sad and solemn occasion,' he broke in, his face troubled. 'I am here, as is Mr Brown, in my capacity as deacon, an elder of our little congregation. Forgive me, but it hardly seems fitting to speculate – and Mr Brown has the highest principles. I cannot believe that a fellow Methodist. . . .' He shook his head, his troubled gaze straying towards the grave where his fellow-deacon still stood, staring down into its depths.

Mrs Mainwaring was shepherding her charges away. What Tansy could see of her face, half-hidden by a veil, looked genuinely unhappy and strained. It was clear that while working for her would be no sinecure, she cared about her young women.

'Miss Clark, can I 'ave a word?'

Sal Finnigan, her white face and black hair with her mourning dress seeming to give her a sharp edge, as if she had been cut out of paper with a small pair of scissors, had slipped from the group and came up to Tansy.

'Yes?' Tansy looked at her encouragingly.

'It's only that . . .' Sal gave a small, ladylike sniff and suddenly looked younger and more vulnerable.

'Are you all right?' Tansy asked.

'Yes, Miss, thanking you.' Sal applied a small handkerchief deftly. 'I allus makes a fool of myself at funerals.'

'Funerals are very sad affairs,' Tansy said gently. 'What can I do for you?'

'It's about Fanny. I remembered—'

'If you ladies will excuse me,' John Mason said, 'I'd better join my colleague.'

'I'm sorry. Mr Mason, this is Miss Finnigan, a friend of Frances Jones. Mr Mason is a deacon in Sion Chapel, Sal.'

Mr Mason bowed.

'Pleased I'm sure,' Sal said hurriedly as he moved away. 'Miss Clark, about Fanny. . . .'

'Yes?' Tansy said encouragingly.

The other had broken off abruptly, her head turning slightly to where Wesley Brown had just straightened up.

'I can't talk now,' she said. 'Can I come and see you after work?'

'I will be at my father's house,' Tansy said. 'The crescent opposite Adelaide Park? Wait, I have a card somewhere. Here it is. What time?'

'About nine? I'll eat my supper in the pie-shop and get a cab.'

'Very well, but can't you give me some idea?'

'Nine then,' Sal said. 'It was what Fanny said. . . .'

She shook her head slightly and walked away, increasing her pace until she had caught up with her fellow-workers.

Tansy frowned, watching the last of the crowd drift away, some quietly as if the sadness of so young a death had touched their own buried sorrows, others talking together, the drama of the occasion stimulating them.

A slim young man, hair curling darkly almost to the collar of his coat, had stepped out from another of the sentinel yews. Tansy, catching sight of him out of the corner of her eye, resisted the urge to swing round and stood immobile as Patrick Denny mingled with a last group of spectators and then was gone.

By the time she left the cemetery the sexton had begun his task, shovelling the discarded earth over what remained of Frances Jones. Tansy wondered if the Edge family would pay for a headstone.

She hailed a cab and gave the driver instructions to take her to Fleet Street.

She had half hoped but not really expected to find Frank there, but there were only the usual newspaper boys scurrying in and out, the reporters with note-pads in their hands and hats pushed back to denote their independent spirit, men with ink-stained white aprons and sleeves rolled high to display muscular, tattooed arms.

The pigeon-hole was empty. Tansy stared at it for a moment, biting her lip in frustration, then crossed to the main desk where an elderly clerk was studying a racing sheet.

'Excuse me, but have the letters for Valentine been collected?' she enquired.

'Val who?'

Keeping his finger on a line the clerk raised his head.

'Valentine. Number Six?'

'Advertisement's run its course. Letters are put in general post-box. Are you Valentine?'

'No,' said Tansy, wishing she could produce the right key. 'No, I'm not. Thank you.'

The clerk had returned to his racing form before she had concluded her words.

She left the newspaper office and walked briskly to the mews. If anyone was following her she wasn't aware of it. To know that someone was still following her would, she thought, have been almost a relief. It would at least have told her that the murderer was still fearful of discovery. Now it felt as if with the closing of the coffin lid over Fanny Jones the killer felt immune from discovery.

Her footsteps echoed on the cobbles, mellowed by the late-afternoon sunshine. Fanny had had a fine day for her burying.

The pony was in its stall and greeted her, as it probably greeted everybody who ever came, with a whicker.

'I'm sorry,' Tansy said. 'No sugar-candy today.'

The big, equine eyes continued to gaze hopefully as she went up the steep, spiral stairs. At the top the door stood ajar.

Tansy hesitated, then pushed it wider and stepped inside. The big room with its few pieces of furniture, its skylight, the sketches ranged on the long table looked as it had looked before, but from behind the door leading to Mary Denny's bedroom came the sound of hasty activity – the opening and closing of drawers, slight sounds like tissue paper rustling softly.

The rustling ceased abruptly and the door was opened wide as an extremely pretty girl came into the outer chamber and stood, mouth half open, her face whitening so suddenly against the black of her curling hair and the darkness of her eyes that she looked about to faint.

'Mary Denny?' Tansy said. 'Forgive me but the door was open.'

'I – thought you were my brother.'

The words came gaspingly, the Irish brogue stronger than Patrick's.

'My name's Tansy Clark. I know your brother. I thought he was here.'

'Not yet! I want to take my other things before he comes.'

'You're afraid of him?' Tansy asked.

'Afraid of him?' Mary echoed the words softly and suddenly laughed. 'Surely to God I love him to pieces! But he'll never forgive me when he learns about Leslie. And we'll not be parted. We'll not!'

'Leslie Edge? The pony. . . .'

'Mr Hawkins agreed to keep Saffy here,' Mary Denny said. 'He comes over and feeds her and tends her. Sir James said he'd have the animal destroyed so he did, if Leslie and I didn't part. But we want to stay together.'

Tansy nodded. The Edges, philanthropists though they were, would not take very kindly to a penniless Irish girl marrying their only son.

'I have to be going,' Mary Denny said in the same breathless tone. 'If Patrick turns up – please don't say – we made all the plans but we have to arrange matters bit by bit so we do. Please, Miss Clark. . . .'

Footsteps sounded on the spiral stairs and Leslie Edge came in.

'Mary, can you manage the bags? Who's this?'

The newcomer had stopped, staring at Tansy.

'Miss Tansy Clark,' Mary said. 'She's a friend of Patrick's. I told her—'

'Mary, you're an idiot! Miss Clark, you'll be running off to tell Mary's brother the gladsome tidings I daresay?'

'I think that it's not my business,' Tansy said. 'What you're doing isn't illegal, is it?'

'Only for men!'

Leslie Edge pulled off her hat and gave a wry and bitter laugh. She was a tall young woman, long-legged and narrow-hipped, her skirt as narrow as a pencil and her jacket having a decidedly masculine appearance. Her dark hair was cut short and her features were strong, her face attractive.

'Our beloved Queen,' Leslie Edge said, 'doesn't recognize that women may love women as some men love only men, so the law banning the practice has never received the royal signature. But that makes no matter to my family. It will make no matter to Mary's brother.'

'You didn't go abroad with your family?'

Tansy felt as if she had turned a half-somersault and was standing on her head.

'They took me abroad.' Leslie made a grimace. 'I'm twenty-four years old, of full age and in control of my own money, but they decided that prolonged exposure to as many handsome gentlemen as possible might "cure" me! Poor Mamma! I came home in January, simply for a week or two, and that was when Mary brought her needlework round.'

'Mr Hawkins said that none of the Edges had returned.'

'Old Hawkie will always tell a lie on my account,' Leslie Edge told her. 'He doesn't understand me but he always supports me. When I met Mary I felt – well, all that's private! I took an old house in town, rented it for three or four months while Mary and I decided what to do. In the end we stayed over half a year.'

'You're the special friend who took Mary to the Valentine Ball?'

'It was a public affair, but everybody was in dominoes.'

'I was Juliet and Leslie was Romeo,' Mary said. 'She hired the costumes from the old gentleman who—'

'Was called Mr Valentine,' Tansy said.

'You know a lot,' Mary began, but Leslie, her face full of bright intelligence broke in.

'Was?' she queried.

'He was killed, apparently by a sneak-thief,' Tansy said.

'Surely not because we hired costumes?' Mary gasped.

'Of course not. Don't be a goose, Mary,' Leslie said. 'I'm sorry to hear it. He was quite a character. How do you. . . .'

'It's a long story,' Tansy began.

'And Patrick might be here at any moment!' Mary, who had regained some of her colour, paled again.

'You were with another friend of mine last night,' Tansy said to her.

'Mr Cartwright, yes.' Mary nodded.

'And?'

'Why so many questions? Have my parents sent you?' Leslie demanded.

'I've never met them in my life,' Tansy said truthfully.

'Then who sent you here? What's going on?'

'Your brother has been looking for you since he came back from India. Why didn't you write to him, let him know you were safe?'

'I meant to write,' Mary said, sitting down abruptly. 'When I first met Leslie I thought I had made a good friend – nothing more. I wrote and told Patrick I was going to the Valentine Ball, cross my heart I did.'

'Without mentioning your new friend was a woman,' Tansy said drily.

'I thought he might come back and then I could explain properly, but my feelings became too strong. Surely something might happen to spoil my life and that might be Patrick, indeed it might!'

'So you ran away.'

'Only while we considered what to do,' Leslie said defensively. 'My own parents haven't exactly been understanding so why should Mary's brother be? We lay low, made plans.'

'Surely if Patrick was fretted about me he'd've put an advertisement in the newspaper!' Mary chimed in.

'He probably felt it rather demeaning to have to advertise for his sister as if she was a lost dog,' Tansy said.

'In the end we decided to live somewhere quiet. Two ladies sharing a house. There's no law against that!'

'Where?'

'The Lake District. I'm of age and Mary soon will be and I've got control of my own money. My parents. . . .' For an instant Leslie's voice faltered a little before she continued. 'Miss Clark, my parents wanted a son. When I was born and there were no further children my father taught me to ride and shoot and use a bow and arrow and he was proud of his sporting daughter, but then I grew older and suddenly I was supposed to wear frilled skirts and go to dances and fall in love with a suitable young man. And I wanted to found a school for girls where they could study mathematics and science and learn to stand on their own feet whether they found husbands or not. But I never desired a young man, and I hated sketching vases of flowers and being demure. Mamma said I was abnormal. Abnormal! And my father blamed himself for the way he reared me. He didn't understand that the rearing made no difference. I'm the way I am without anyone pushing me to it. And Mary's the way she is because she was always that way without really knowing it.'

'Where does Frank Cartwright come into it?' Tansy demanded.

'Mr Cartwright called at the house we were renting a couple of days ago,' Mary told her. 'We were very alarmed.'

'You were very alarmed. I was merely furious,' Leslie corrected.

'Yes. Anyway he said he was a reporter and he asked me if either of us knew anything about two girls who had been murdered. We said we didn't.'

'Read about it in the newspaper,' Leslie said gruffly. 'Awful business, poor souls!'

'Both were employed at your own factory,' Tansy said.

'Not mine,' Leslie said. 'My grandfather's business holdings are not part of my inheritance. Anyway we neither of us knew anything about it. He went off and then last evening he turned up and offered to take Mary for a drive and a talk.'

'You didn't mind?' Tansy looked at her in surprise.

'Mary's free to go where she likes with whom she likes,' Leslie said, with a slight smile. 'I'm not keeping her a prisoner, Miss Clark.'

'He wanted me to tell my brother about Leslie,' Mary said. 'I told him that I'd think about it, and he promised not to say anything. We drove round for ages and then he said he had other business and left the cab and I went back to Leslie.'

So Frank had had business in the vicinity of Sion Chapel. Tansy kept her own counsel and asked instead, 'Why did you come here today to collect the rest of your things?'

'Because if a reporter had tracked us down then others might do the same,' Leslie said. 'Mary agreed to leave a note for her brother and then—'

'Off to the Lake District!' Mary said with a yearningly romantic look that reminded Tansy of Tilde.

'And now you've turned up I think it is time we left,' Leslie said, picking up one of the suitcases.

'It's not my business,' Tansy said slowly, 'and you can do as you please, but it seems to me that you can't build your new life on the worry and grief of others. If you haven't got the courage to face Patrick how are you going to find the courage to live the rest of your lives together?'

'But Patrick would never understand,' Mary said pleadingly.

'If I were you I'd give him the chance,' Tansy said. 'Anyway, I wish you both good fortune.'

'I'll see you down, Miss Clark.'

Leslie moved to the door and preceded her down the stairs. In her stall Saffy whickered softly.

'We take her with us when we leave,' Leslie said, nodding towards the pony. 'Mr Hawkins is making the transport arrangements. I'd not put it past my father to have her put down if we left her here. I'll try to get Mary to contact her brother. Thank you for understanding.'

She shook hands briskly.

'I don't understand it at all,' Tansy said frankly, 'but I still wish you happiness. Goodbye, Miss Edge.'

She went out into the darkening mews, conscious of a feeling almost of envy.

Mary Denny and Leslie Edge had found each other and would, she guessed, stay together no matter how much society might disapprove. Since Geoffrey's death there had only been memories for her and the memories were growing fainter as month followed month.

A familiar figure had turned into the mews and was walking toward her.

'Miss Clark, I'm sorry. . . .'

As he drew level he stopped to bow, offering his hand.

'You were at the funeral,' Tansy said bluntly.

'I was supposed to be keeping watch in the newspaper office,' he said. 'I meant to go there but I kept thinking about Mary, wondering if she was still alive or if something dreadful had happened, and I wanted to be in that cemetery – just to see that poor girl laid to rest, and to see if just maybe there might be someone there who looked familiar, someone I might have seen hanging around.'

'You saw me,' Tansy said.

'I should've acknowledged you,' he said contritely. 'Sure but I was about to when it occurred to me that it might not be so wise to go displaying the fact we know each other if the murderer was there.'

'It isn't an ironclad rule that the killer always attends the funeral, Tansy said.

'If I only knew Mary was safe,' Patrick said. 'You know she may have been scared to get in touch with me again, surely she may. Afraid I'd be angry or disapproving or something. Doesn't she know that I'd be happy to know she was safe on any terms, so I would?'

'In that case,' Tansy said, glancing over her shoulder to where the open entrance to the stables remained void, 'you'd best go up to your lodging. And don't forget that you just told me you'd be glad to see her again whatever the circumstances.'

'You mean. . . ?' He gave her a look full of startled hope, then wrung her hand and without any word of farewell hurried past her.

Tansy walked on, not stopping to visit Babushka but reminding herself to arrange for food to be delivered regularly to the old lady. She would also make the time to visit her more often.

But first there was a murderer to be found.

FOURTEEN

'So that was the way of it!'

Laurence leaned back in his chair and motioned to Finn to replenish the brandy glasses.

'The last thing in the world I ever considered,' Tansy said ruefully.

'My dear girl, in an investigation one never rules anything out,' he chided with a faint smile. 'You didn't stay to witness the reaction of Patrick Denny to his sister's alliance?'

'I thought it best not,' Tansy said.

'No doubt he'll be in touch very soon. He owes a great deal to you.'

'More to Frank Cartwright,' Tansy said, a slight frown creasing her brow.

'You're wishing he'd kept you informed?'

'Frankly yes. Going off by himself and tracking down Mary Denny isn't what I would have expected of him.'

'Perhaps he wished to impress you with his efficiency.'

'Well, he hasn't!' Tansy said shortly.

'It's a funny business, ain't it?' Finn said judiciously. 'Two skirts together? Plain is she, this Leslie Edge?'

'Actually she's very attractive,' Tansy said.

'Don't be so conventional, Finn,' Laurence said mildly.

'It just don't go on much in my circles,' Finn said.

'Patrick Denny is an artist. Surely his attitude will be more Bohemian?'

'I suspect,' Laurence said, lifting an eyebrow in his daughter's direction, 'that young Denny's bohemianism has its own limits.

What's fine in theory may not please him when his own sister's involved.'

'Perhaps he had an inkling of the way the wind was blowing and that was why he hesitated to report her disappearance to the police?' Tansy said.

'That's likely too. You didn't ask Mary Denny about the Valentine cutting in her drawer?'

'I didn't think of it,' Tansy confessed. 'It's fairly obvious though, isn't it? Mary was worried about her relationship with Leslie Edge and thought of asking for advice.'

'Lucky for 'er she didn't!' Finn said.

'Lucky indeed,' Laurence said thoughtfully. 'In a way it's a pity that Patrick Denny was definitely still in India when Ellie Watson was killed else a case might well be made against him. A brother whose sister flouts the normal behaviour of females might well conceive a hatred of all women, especially if his affection for his sister was unusually close.'

'So what now? Any new theories?'

'Not that you'd notice,' Finn said gloomily.

'What time is Miss Finnigan coming here?' Laurence asked.

'Nine o'clock. She's having her supper first with the other girls.'

'It'll be interesting to hear what she has to say. Meanwhile. . . .'

'Meanwhile?' Tansy looked at him.

'Meanwhile we had best reconsider our suspects,' Laurence said.

'Maybe we ain't met 'im,' Finn surmised.

'I think that Tansy must at least have seen him,' Laurence opined. 'If my experience has taught me anything at all it's that a certain type of killer – the cold-blooded, calculating type who doesn't strike out in rage or passion but rather dispatches his victims much as an executioner might, likes to wait in the wings rather as a dramatist does when the actors take his words and interpret them. Yes, I think you have caught at least a fleeting glimpse of him – or her?'

'Wesley Brown,' Tansy said, reaching for a piece of sugar-candy. 'He's exactly the kind of person I can imagine creeping up behind some unsuspecting girl and hitting her over the head. His wife is an invalid so their married life may lack – well, you know.'

'Sexual congress,' her father said. 'Don't you go missish on me at this stage in your education!'

'So he harasses young women who don't have families to protect them. And when he finds out that Fanny Jones is with child he kills her to prevent a scandal.'

'But Ellie Watson wasn't with child,' Laurence reminded her.

'Mebbe she said she'd blow the whistle?' Finn suggested.

'Use your sense, Finn,' his employer said. 'Would a girl who works in a match factory be able to complain about a respected deacon and get anybody to listen?'

'But there might've been an 'ell of a stink,' Finn persisted.

'Which his fellow-deacon, John Mason, would be at pains to quash,' Tansy said. 'The Sion Chapel relies to a large extent on the contributions made by the wealthier members of the congregation who wouldn't turn a blind eye to scandalous goings-on.'

'You'd be astonished,' her father said drily, 'how many blind eyes are turned when it suits.'

'I once knowed a fellow,' Finn said, 'and 'e was the reincarnation of Dick Turpin 'e was. One look and you'd swear that your purse was as good as in 'is 'ands.'

'I suppose he was a saintly person,' Tansy said.

'Oh no, Miss,' Finn said. 'Got transported for sixty-seven jobs and an 'undred more not taken into consideration.'

'Meaning the outside may sometimes reflect the inside? It's a point to bear in mind, Pa.'

'I'm ruling nothing out,' Laurence said.

'What about that manager?' Finn asked.

'Tobias Simpson? I didn't catch sight of him but the funeral was packed.'

'The young woman from the match factory who told you about Simpson harassing the girls – Sylvie, you said? – did she say anything else that might throw light on anything?'

'She didn't want to be seen talking to me for fear of losing her job,' Tansy said. 'She did tell me that Tobias Simpson wouldn't leave the girls alone. Ellie Watson was scared of him.'

'And, unlike Frances Jones, didn't find more congenial employment. So I would definitely keep Tobias Simpson on the list. What about Hawkins?'

'The Edges' butler?' Tansy, who had been stirring her coffee, jerked her head up in surprise. 'Surely his part in all this was confined to helping Leslie Edge keep her pony safe and continue her plans to elope with Mary Denny?'

'Which doesn't leave out the possibility that he might have killed the other young women,' Laurence pointed out. 'His wife deserted him, didn't she? Who knows what that can do to a man? He's been in the city all along, and as virtual master of the house in the owners' absence abroad he could easily have come and gone as he pleased.'

'I suppose so,' Tansy said, somewhat reluctantly.

'What about a woman?' Finn said.

'Why would a woman want to kill two harmless girls?' Tansy demanded.

'I've got a theory.'

Finn held up his hand, fingers splayed.

'Which is?' Laurence nodded encouragement.

'Either Wesley Brown's missus or Tobias Simpson's trouble and strife took against their 'usband's 'abit of running after the skirts, and did something about it.'

'Wesley Brown's wife is an invalid and doesn't attend services,' Tansy said. 'I know nothing of Tobias Simpson's circumstances.'

'Mrs Mainwaring?'

'Surely not, Pa! She's terribly respectable.'

'Terribly respectable women have been known to commit murder,' Laurence said mildly. 'I admit that it's usually poison – for some reason the weapon of poison appeals to a certain type of woman. I suspect it's because since the action of poison is generally slow they can quiet their consciences by tending their victim devotedly during his expiration.'

'You attribute great subtlety to women, Pa,' Tansy remarked with a grin.

'I was married to one, Lord rest her sweet soul. Your mother wouldn't have harmed a fly, but she was subtle.'

'Too deep for me,' Finn said. 'Females in general ain't as strong as men, so poison's easier.'

'But Ellie Watson and Frances Jones were hit over the head,' Tansy said.

'What is Mrs Mainwaring like apart from being respectable?'

'Tall, average build – wiry rather than plump. I suppose she could have hit them hard enough to kill,' Tansy said doubtfully, 'but how could she creep up without them hearing her coming?'

'Perhaps she didn't,' Laurence said. 'If she is the one who placed the Valentine advertisement in the newspaper then she would know that Ellie and later Frances had replied and agreed upon a rendezvous. What could be simpler than to wait until the meeting place was deserted and then come across them by apparent accident? "My dear Miss So-and-so, what are you doing here," et cetera. She sits down next to them on the bench and, at the opportune moment, says, "Oh look!" The victim turns her head and—'

'Wham!' said Finn.

'It's possible I suppose,' Tansy admitted, 'but she seems genuinely fond of her workers. I think they're all fairly satisfied with conditions at the shop and in their lodgings.'

'Paid for by a gentleman friend. Perhaps he and Mrs Mainwaring have other business enterprises which are less legitimate. It's a possibility.'

'The park-keeper who wasn't a park-keeper was a man.'

'Are you certain? You said you hardly glanced at him in the dusk and you can't remember his voice. A woman who's tall can pass for a man. Like Miss Edge.'

'Surely you don't think. . . ?'

Tansy looked at him.

'I don't rule anything out,' Laurence said. 'It's possible that Leslie Edge made advances to other poor young women somewhat short of relatives. They may have rejected her.'

'The Russian lady saw Mary Denny with Leslie Edge and mistook her for a man,' Tansy said reluctantly. 'But, Pa, I spoke to her myself. She struck me as being genuinely devoted to Mary.'

'And Mary Denny didn't reject her. Others may have done. Girls who were or had been connected with the family even in a slight way. I don't say it is so for a moment, but I do say exclude nobody.'

'Be nice,' Finn said ruminatively, 'if it was Inspector Jarrold.'

'A police-officer! Surely. . . .'

'Police-officers can go where they choose without questions being asked,' Laurence agreed. 'Jarrold is stronger than you might think, despite the effects of good living and his wife, I know for certain, is a formidable lady. It's not impossible that wanting to shine up his reputation he commits the murders, kills Mr Valentine, then presents his solution.'

'I hadn't thought of that,' Tansy said, absent-mindedly taking another piece of candy.

'Jarrold is also a man who has a devotion to his wife that is an example to all married men, and the notion of harming a woman would not under any circumstances appeal to him in the least. Stupid he may be, but vicious he is not! I'm only trying to demonstrate, my dear, that nothing can be taken for granted.'

'I wish I could build up a picture of the kind of person who could do such terrible deeds,' Tansy said.

'A person who presents an entirely convincing picture of respectability to the world at large,' Laurence said. 'A person who nurses a hatred of women, probably a certain type of woman – young, working class and defenceless. who would be likely to reply to such an advertisement as was put in the newspaper. One who has the strength to deliver a crushing blow to the back of the skull, who has some obsession with bright pink ribbon, who either moves silently, catching the victim unawares, or takes them into his or her confidence and, having distracted their attention, acts swiftly and without the least semblance of pity or remorse.'

'A madman,' Tansy said and shivered.

'A person who has something twisted and evil in their make-up, certainly. Mad? I don't think so. This person knows exactly what they're doing, knows it's wrong and covers their tracks very cleverly, and will strike again.'

'Will?' Tansy looked at him.

'Oh, most certainly,' he said gravely. 'Once a crime is committed it becomes easier to commit another one. Quite apart from the fact that the crime must be concealed and possible witnesses removed there is the fact that the killer derives pleasure from his or her killings. There must be a great feeling of power and satisfaction to know that one has removed a human being from the world, if you're of a certain mentality. Don't you think so?'

'Since I'm not that kind of person I'll never know,' Tansy said thankfully as he finished speaking.

'Me neither!' Finn said with some emphasis. 'Knocking a feller's teeth down 'is throat is fair enough but 'itting ladies ain't on.'

'Sal Finnigan ought to be here by now.'

Tansy glanced at the carriage clock in the corner.

'Twenty past nine already.' Laurence drummed his fingers on the table. 'You're sure that you made the address clear to her?'

'I gave her your card ' Tansy said. 'She wanted to tell me something she'd heard – from Frances Jones. She was ready to tell me and then she broke off and said she'd meet me later.'

'Why did she break off?' Laurence asked.

'I'm not sure.' Tansy frowned, trying to re-create the scene in her mind. The black-clad people moving away from the graveside where Wesley Brown was bending over. Almost immediately afterwards she had glimpsed Patrick Denny slipping away.

'She rejoined her fellow-workers,' she said slowly. 'Mrs Mainwaring was ushering them away.'

'She ought to be here by now if she was so anxious to speak to you,' Laurence said frowningly.

'Want me to take a gander up the road?' Finn offered.

'If you would. Thank you.' Laurence waited until the manservant had left the room, then turned his gaze back to his daughter. 'You haven't heard from Frank?'

'Not since we were here.'

'And he was off to see a stunner called Mavis! Obviously he was after a solution to the disappearance of Mary Denny. Odd that he didn't say anything!'

'Perhaps he just wanted to come up with something on his own account,' Tansy suggested.

'To impress you. Now don't blush and bridle like a silly girl! Frank thinks the world of you. You must've realized that.'

'He's a good friend,' she said defensively.

'And Geoffrey has been dead a long time. My dear, I don't interfere in your life, but I'd not object to a grandchild or two during the next ten years.'

'I never knew you were so conventional, Pa,' Tansy said.

'Now and then. On and off. Only don't rush into anything.' His voice had sobered abruptly. 'I'd not have you decide on someone who might not be all he seems.'

'Pa!' Tansy stared at him, appalled.

'I don't believe for one moment that Frank had anything to do with the killing of those two girls,' Laurence said. 'However, nobody's above suspicion and he has the kind of job which enables him to go here and there with few questions being asked.'

'He was in Scotland for most of that period!'

'There are trains. Tansy, I don't think that Frank is the type to go round nursing a hatred for the opposite sex, but one never knows.'

'You'll be accusing me next!' Tansy said indignantly.

'I considered it very seriously,' her father said, straight-faced, 'but it seemed somewhat unlikely. No, it is only that fond of you Frank may be, but my girl's partner must love her and her alone. No stunners on the side.'

'Pa, you're talking nonsense,' Tansy said. 'Frank isn't ready to settle down and there isn't a day goes past when I don't think of Geoffrey. Here's Finn.'

'No sign of anyone,' Finn announced, bending his lanky frame into the room. 'Pretty quiet for a Monday night. Anything come up while I was out?'

'No new theories,' Tansy said. 'Pa, I think I'll take a cab over to the Mainwaring lodgings and see if Sal Finnigan's still in the local pie-shop eating supper with her friends.'

'And if she is?' Laurence looked at her.

'I'll bring her back with me. I'll come back anyway, so if she arrives while I'm gone keep her here. And I don't need an escort, Finn.'

It was perhaps unreasonable of her but her father's most recent remarks had stung a little. Had he secretly wished for a long time that she had grown into a more conventional woman who would marry a suitable man and provide him with grandchildren? Was he regretting the manner in which he and her mother had reared her? If so then it was a little late!

She put on her hat and went briskly down the stairs, leaving a somewhat bewildered Finn in her wake. As luck had it a cab was just turning into the crescent to disgorge an elderly gentleman in a silk muffler.

'Can you take me to Oxford Street and wait for me there?' she enquired of the driver.

'Time's getting on,' the man said grumblingly.

'I'll pay extra,' Tansy offered.

'Right, Miss.'

She had lit on one of the rare occasions when a cab-driver was weary and out of sorts and not inclined to oblige. Tansy stepped up into the cab and sat back, occupying her mind with trying to guess the various reasons why Sal Finnigan might not have kept the appointment. Almost certainly she had simply backed away from involving herself further. The possibility that she might have been prevented was something she preferred not to dwell on.

'Where in Oxford Street?'

The driver's face loomed in the trap-door aperture.

'Twenty yards further on and stop at the corner. I'll be as quick as possible but please wait.'

'It's your money,' he said sullenly, and slammed the trap-door shut again.

Alighting at the corner of the narrow street in which the millinery shop was situated she handed over half the demanded fare and hurried down past the closed shop with its display of becoming hats, towards the narrow entry where the lodgings occupied by the girls were. As far as she could see no candles burned in the windows, which meant that either the young women went early to bed, or that they were lingering over their supper. Opting for the second alternative she went on past the alley to where the street widened into an irregular square with buildings all around and with the smell of cooked meats drifting across.

It was a pie-shop pretending to be a public house, with stained glass panels in the open doors and narrow windows, and long benches drawn up alongside two tables at which a variety of young women and almost as many men were seated. A long counter displayed raised pork-pies, boiled puddings of beefsteak and oysters, and pastry triangles plump with eel. At the back, jugs of ale and cider were being sold at a brisk rate and the air was full of chattering, punctuated by snatches of song and the occasional burst of laughter, thick with the smoke of pipes and cheap cigars.

'Yes?'

A rather pretty girl seated near where Tansy had paused glanced at her.

'I'm looking for Sal Finnigan,' Tansy said. 'She has supper here every night, doesn't she?'

A couple of other heads turned and several pairs of eyes surveyed her. Tansy was conscious suddenly of her clothes, her upswept hair under the tip-tilted straw, the expensive gold watch on her jacket lapel. Even her accent jarred in her own ears. Had they been beggars, rag-shrouded, avid-eyed, grim, she would have felt more at her ease, but these young men and women were decent, respectable, clad in the clothes that many of them had made themselves, sewing on the one lace flounce, the beaded collar that would make them feel privileged, a cut above the common throng.

Then the pretty girl's expression softened and she half rose.

'It's Miss Clark, ain't it? Sal was talking to you at the funeral,' she said.

'She's by way of being a friend of mine,' Tansy said.

'Going places is our Sal!' one of the men said, pushing his cap to the back of his head with a lordly gesture.

'She set off 'alf an 'our ago, said she was keeping a promise,' the pretty girl said. 'Going to meet you, was she?'

'Yes. Yes she was. I'd best hurry back lest I miss her altogether. Thank you.'

'Stay and 'ave a drink, Miss,' someone suggested. There was mockery in the tone.

Tansy fixed the unkempt lad who had spoken with a smiling glance.

'Thanks, but maybe another time, when you're grown up,' she said.

'She's got you there, Charlie!' someone shouted.

A chorus of good-humoured cheers accompanied her into the square again.

The cab was still waiting at the corner, its driver puffing at a foul-smelling pipe.

'Where to now?' He took the pipe out of his mouth and fixed her with an unfriendly stare.

'Back to the crescent if you please.'

'Right!'

He banged the pipe against the side of his perch in a shower of sparks and barely gave her time to seat herself before he touched up the horse.

If Sal had taken a cab, and it was hardly likely that she'd walked, she'd be there by now. Tansy could imagine her father setting the girl at ease, offering her a drink and using his interviewing skills to coax out a coherent story.

'Can't you go faster?' She leaned out of the window to enquire as the horse slowed from a trot to a walk.

'He don't get extra pay!' the cabbie retorted. 'Been working twelve bloody 'ours already, and the wife's in 'ospital!'

'I'm sorry.' Her conscience pricked and Tansy forgave the ill-temper and said placatingly, 'It must be a great worry to you.'

'Means I've got to get me own supper, seeing as there ain't no female fit for the cooking of it,' was the retort.

Deciding that if she had any sense the wife would remain in hospital for as long as possible, Tansy withdrew her head and leaned back with as much patience as she could muster.

'This is as far as I go tonight!'

The vehicle was pulled up and the hoarse, unmusical voice of the driver roused her from a half-dream in which Finn suddenly confessed to the two murders and Frank married Tilde.

Stepping out Tansy looked up indignantly.

'This is the cab-stand!' she said. 'My ride was to the next street.'

'You'll 'ave to take another cab,' he said indifferently.

'There isn't one!'

'Be one along soon enough. I've got to eat – and cook it!'

He had stretched down to take the cab-fare and driven off before she could protest further.

What was it Finn was fond of saying, 'Us working class is the salt of the earth, Miss Tansy. 'Earts of gold.'

'Some hearts of gold,' Tansy muttered, gathering up her dignity and preparing to walk on.

She had taken only a few steps when footsteps behind made

her turn sharply almost colliding with the young man who had hastened after her.

'Mr Denny!'

'Patrick, please. I was on my way to your father's house to tell him that my sister is safe, though her circumstances are hardly what I would have chosen, indeed they're not,' he said.

'My father already knows. He is pleased she's safe. Did they. . . ?'

'They explained it all, though the Lord knows I can't understand it,' he said wryly. 'They're on their way to the Lake District now.'

'You could have stopped her,' Tansy said gently. 'She's not yet of age and as her brother—'

'As her brother I could've left her with a companion, so I could, and not expected her to sit with her hands folded waiting for me to sail back! But Miss Edge? I'm thinking this is a phase and when she meets a nice young man she'll . . . no?'

'I don't think so,' Tansy said.

'She never would give any of the local lads a second look,' he said. 'You don't think – if I'd taken more trouble in finding young men to. . . ?'

'Whatever you did or didn't do probably made no difference at all,' Tansy said. 'Your sister is as she is. I don't understand it either, but I liked Leslie Edge. They'll be happy.'

'You're a very tolerant person.'

'Only in my better moments. Now if you'll—'

'And a beautiful one.'

'When I walk in the park people climb up the trees to look at me,' Tansy said flippantly.

'I'm being serious, Miss Tansy. I've never met anyone who roused in me such feelings as I feel now.'

'Mr Denny, I'm very flattered but right now I'm on my way to my father's house,' Tansy said quickly, glad that they stood out of the direct flare of the gaslight and her suddenly scarlet cheeks weren't obvious.

'The way you followed me and how cool you were when you thought I had a pistol in your back! And the way your mind works – quick as a dragon-fly on a sparkling stream!'

'Mr Denny, if this is your reaction to your sister's eloping with Miss Edge – have you been drinking?'

She was abruptly aware of the unmistakable odour of whisky.

'I had a couple of drinks to bolster my courage,' he admitted. 'It was in my mind to find you at your father's house and to offer to see you home. Is there anything wrong in that?'

'Nothing at all, but having lost one companion you ought to wait a little while before you run around seeking another,' she said lightly.

'Surely to God such a thing was never in my life!' he exclaimed. 'You must know that I've a great admiration for you! I never met a woman like you in my life before. Standing on your own two feet, defying the entire world, the way you hold your head!'

'On my neck like everybody else,' Tansy said crossly. 'Please let me pass – Mr Denny!'

He had suddenly stepped in front of her, his hands reaching for hers.

'Will you not call me Pat? My mother always called me Pat.'

'I'm not your mother!'

'Thanks be to God! Miss Tansy, say that you'll sit for me. I want to capture that red hair, that—'

Tansy, exasperated beyond endurance, gave him a shove that sent him off-balance and took to her heels, diving through the nearest gate and finding herself in a few seconds in the park, the sparse lamps scarcely illuminating the darkness.

She took to the grass verge, avoiding the betraying crunch of heels on gravel.

It really was, she thought crossly, insupportable! To be wooed and won by a suitable man was one thing. To find herself grappling in a deserted street with an impetuous Irishman who'd had a couple of whiskies too many was another thing.

She had paused, standing half-concealed behind a huge lilac tree, its colour vanished in darkness but its perfume still heavy on the air. There was no sound of following footsteps and the sense of relief she felt was tinged by uneasiness. In his cups though he was it didn't strike her as typical of Patrick Denny to allow an unescorted woman to flee into a park which was ill-lit and, at this hour, probably deserted, without making some effort to follow and apologize.

The possibility that he too might be treading softly on grass somewhere close at hand was unnerving. She held her breath, hearing only the stirring of the lilacs and the plashing of a thin stream of water as it jetted from the mouth of a gargoyle set in the wall.

This, she thought, anxiety becoming anger, was ridiculous. She was a grown woman behaving like a frightened schoolgirl for no reason save that she'd received a declaration from a young man whose sister had just eloped with another woman and who probably wanted to prove something to himself.

One thing was clear. She couldn't stand under the lilac tree all night. By now her father would be becoming fretful about her and soon they would be chasing one another round in circles!

'Mr Denny!' She raised her voice into the quivering silence. 'I assume you are somewhere close at hand. I am prepared to accept your apology when you've sobered up and then we won't refer to the matter again. Now I'm going home so good-night!'

No answer came. Grimacing at her own cowardice she stepped gingerly on to the path and, guided by its windings and the fitful gaslights, walked fast towards the main entrance, resisting the temptation to take to her heels and run.

Faintly behind her footsteps moved to a different beat. Tansy stopped, head tilted. As she listened, a huge moth swooped down to brush her cheek before soaring high again. Something inside her trembled and broke.

Tansy began to run, heedless of any noise her shoes made on the gravel, careless of her sobbing breath as her stays – why had she laced them so tightly? – cut into her. She caught a glimpse of water as the pool came into view and then, without warning, the moon sailed out, its curve mirrored on the surface of the water.

Something lay on the path near the bench where she had first found Tilde. She stopped abruptly, telling herself that it was no more than the shadow of one of the branches of the willow tree as the moonlight glanced off it.

It was no such comforting illusion. She knew it even before she stooped to where Sal Finnigan lay, a bright pink ribbon, which now gleamed moon-pale, tied carelessly round her black hat, one arm outstretched.

This had been different from the others. The blow hadn't killed her at once. Moonlight revealed the long scratches her fingers had dug into the gravel. Tansy stooped lower, tracing them with her own gloved hand. The gouges were deep but not random: WIF.

The pursuing footsteps came closer. Crouching there she knew sick terror, and then Frank Cartwright panted up beside her.

'What the devil. . . ?'

'Sal Finnigan from Mrs Mainwaring's shop. She was coming to Pa's.'

He pulled her upright and knelt down, his hands feeling round the limp body and motionless head.

'She still has a pulse,' he said, rising. 'You'd best run for help.'

'I'll stay. You'll run faster,' Tansy said.

'Right!'

The one word of consent and he was running past her towards the main gates. Tansy sat down weakly on the bench. Her words had been spontaneous, the reasoning behind them genuine. Yet in some corner of her mind a blurred image was forming of a figure striking down the Finnigan girl, then making a sudden, dramatic appearance on the scene. It wasn't a picture she cared to contemplate but it persisted as she crouched on the bench under the sharp-edged moon.

FIFTEEN

The hospital had a curious metallic scent mingled with the smell of warm rubber and a sharp acid odour that made Tansy want to clear her throat. It was past midnight and the gas-lamps had been turned lower to reveal their hearts of blue flame. The slate floors were slightly damp and the walls that divided the wards from the long corridors were whitewashed, though in places the whitewash had yellowed.

Tansy sat on a hard chair and watched Frank pacing the waiting-room where they had spent the past hour.

'I wish you would sit down,' she said, unable to contain her irritation any longer. 'The doctor will come and tell us how things are when he knows himself! You're wearing out the floor!'

'I take it Sal Finnigan was on her way to see your father.'

He stopped pacing but didn't sit down.

'To see me at my father's. She was at Fanny Jones's funeral and told me she had something to tell me. She was due at Pa's at nine. She must've saved some fare by alighting from her cab at the stand and taking a short-cut, or perhaps she took a cab with a bad-tempered driver who refused to carry her the full distance, as I did.'

'Earlier in the evening?'

'When Sal Finnigan didn't turn up I took a cab out to Oxford Street to find out if she'd changed her mind. One of the other girls there told me she'd already left to meet a friend so I took a cab back but the driver would only take me as far as the stand.'

'And you walked back through the park. That was foolish. You could have gone round by the road!'

'I was trying to shake off Patrick Denny.'

'What!'

Frank sat down abruptly and stared at her.

'He caught up with me at the cab-stand and – well, he was in his cups and rather confused and. . . .'

'And what?'

'He was making rather a nuisance of himself,' Tansy said, 'so I gave him a shove and took off through the nearest gateway, which happened to be the park. Then I heard you following me.'

'I wasn't following you,' Frank said. 'If you remember I came through the main gateway.'

'Why? What were you doing there anyway? I thought,' Tansy said, with a lifted eyebrow, 'you were off with your stunner.'

Though she was still annoyed she was amused to see that he had the grace to flush slightly.

'I can explain that,' he said.

'You were tracking down Leslie Edge. I know that. Why not tell me?'

'It seemed like a highly improbable idea so I decided to do a little investigating on my own account with the intention of telling you later if it yielded any results.'

'But why give me that nonsense about spending a couple of days with a girl called Mavis?' Tansy demanded.

'I actually do know a girl of that name,' he said. 'Very fetching she is too.'

'Frank!' Tansy said warningly.

'Let's just say that it seemed like a bright idea at the time. Anyway, I went off and did a little digging into the Edge family. The first time I mentioned a Leslie Edge there were covert nods and winks from a couple of my fellow-reporters. Miss Edge prefers to be Master Edge on most occasions, though that's kept under wraps. Her father has influence and detests publicity. Anyway, I went to the Edge house.'

'You'd get nothing from Mr Hawkins! He's very fond of her.'

'So I gathered. Not from the butler, but from Albert.'

'Who's Albert?'

'The footman. Albert enjoys a pint of ale and he gets bored with not much to occupy him when the family's away, and he's a propensity for picking up unconsidered scraps of conversation while he's passing doors or lingering in the hallway. After one pint he was ready to trust me and after two he was positively loquacious.'

'And then you tracked them to the house they were renting?'

'I promised to say nothing until they were out of town.'

'You didn't consider that either of them had committed the murders?'

'I considered it but it seemed to me that they had nothing to do with any of that at all. Mary Denny had thought of seeking Valentine's advice, by the way, on the best means of telling her brother about Leslie Edge, but fortunately for her she decided against it. Tansy, I was coming to see you. I called first at your house but Mrs Timothy said you had gone to Laurence's, so I took a cab there.'

'Then why did you run back into the park?'

'I heard someone running across the gravel there. Sound carries when the evening's so quiet. It sounded like a woman running – quick and tapping.'

'That must've been me, but I started to run because someone was following me.'

'Patrick Denny?'

'I don't know.' She frowned, trying to conjure the sounds of a couple of hours before. 'I left him by the cab-stand but there were no vehicles there. I assumed he'd followed me to apologize or something, but then I began to be unsure.'

'How exactly did Denny behave in order to annoy you so much?' Frank asked.

She was spared from answering by the opening of the door and the arrival of the doctor, dapper in frock-coat and high cravat, and the matron, in black silk with a cap Mrs Timothy would have envied on her head.

'Is she. . . ?' Tansy had risen nervously.

'Miss Clark, Doctor has encouraging news,' the matron said.

'The young woman was wearing a hat with a thick, lined piece of velvet swathing the crown and falling behind in a bow with two wide ends,' the doctor said. 'That deflected the full force of the blow. She has severe concussion and a possible slight fracture of the skull but she is not in immediate danger. I have considered it necessary to report the matter to the police, however. In view of earlier attacks now under consideration I thought it necessary. Can you tell me if she has relatives who will require to be informed?'

'I've no idea. Her name is Sal Finnigan and she works at the Mainwaring millinery establishment. Doctor. . . ?'

The matron looked slightly affronted as if she had just enquired God's surname.

'Phillips, Miss Clark.'

'Sal Finnigan has information relating to the earlier incidents you mentioned. In view of that there would be no harm in taking security measures, would there? Perhaps a private ward – I would of course meet the costs myself. And no visitors?'

'I imagine the police will wish to have a constable outside her door, if that can be arranged, Matron?'

'Very good, Doctor.'

Matron looked as if cluttering the hospital up with police constables was only marginally less unwelcome than trying to find out God's surname.

'Of course,' Doctor Phillips said, 'there is no guarantee that she will recall any details of the attack when she regains full consciousness. Partial amnesia is common in these cases. Sometimes the memory recovers completely but occasionally it does not. One can only wait.'

'Thank you for giving us the details.'

Tansy shook hands firmly and glanced at Frank.

'I can stay here until the police arrive,' he said, correctly interpreting her meaning. 'I'd like to see Jarrold's face when he realizes that it didn't end with Mr Valentine's death.'

'Don't tell him too much,' Tansy whispered as the doctor went out with his acolyte a few steps behind. 'He will take all the credit if Sal really has information she remembers when she wakes up.'

'As little as possible. Tansy, the reason I told you that I was going to see Mavis for a couple of days—'

'This way, please.' Matron returned, exuding polite hostility.

'You're going back to your father's?' Frank looked at her.

'As Finn came back with you into the park when you rang the

bell and told them about Sal, I fancy he'll be over to find out how she is first thing in the morning,' Tansy said. 'No, I won't go to Pa's. You could meet me there tomorrow morning, unless you've another stunner to see?'

'Tansy, I could explain—'

From the door Matron said in threatening accents, 'I cannot have my nurses upset by comings and goings, sir.'

'Until the morning then,' Frank said. 'Can Miss Clark get a cab from here?'

'Right outside the main doors, sir. The porter will hail one. This way, sir.'

At least Sal would be safe for the moment with Frank seated outside her door. Tansy, making her way to the front hall where the night-porter sat, wondered what freak of thinking had caused her to suspect Frank, even if only briefly. It had been the result of her irritation at his taking off on his own account to chase up Mary Denny, she decided. Of all people Frank had always been utterly reliable.

'Where to?' the driver asked as she climbed into the cab.

She had fully intended to hear herself ask to be driven to Chelsea where Mrs Timothy would certainly be waiting up for her, but instead she heard herself calmly directing the cabbie to go to Sion Chapel.

Having given the command she sat bolt upright, arguing silently with herself. To go off alone to the chapel in the middle of the night was an act of folly. Stupid, reckless folly! But even if Sal Finnigan remembered what had happened and could explain why she had traced 'WIF' in the gravel, it might be days before she could be questioned. The man – or woman – who had attacked Sal had obviously been the one stalking herself through the park. The killer had clearly made off on hearing Frank's arrival, so might still be under the impression that she was dead.

By morning the police might have released the information that she had survived. Then he or she would lie low for a time until the urge to slay became too insistent to resist.

'You sure this is where you want, Miss?'

The cab had drawn up and the driver was peering down at her.

'Yes,' Tansy said. 'Here, if you please.'

This man was evidently a good-humoured soul, or perhaps he hadn't been required to cook his own supper. He said, 'Pretty run-down round 'ere, Miss. You want me to wait?'

'There's a cab-stand not far off, surely?'

Tansy tugged open the door and climbed down.

'Yes, Miss, but it's not so easy to 'ail one at this time unless you're in the city centre. I wouldn't want to see any 'arm coming to a lady.'

'You're very kind but I shall be perfectly all right. How much?'

He named the fare, still looking as if he would like to continue the argument.

Not until the vehicle was bowling away did Tansy allow herself to look round at the ill-lit, dingy street with the shabby chapel standing on its patch of waste-ground, the half-dug flower border resembling too closely the earth piled by the side of Frances Jones's open grave.

A cat slunk past close to the wall, its shadow tigerish.

You and I both hunting, Tansy thought, and walked the short distance to the gates which stood open, rusted into their hinges.

It was, she reflected, a perfect place for a man with murder in his heart to strike up an acquaintanceship with a poor, friendless young girl.

The front door was locked and bolted, securely padlocked. Finn would have had it off in a second but had never passed on his skills to his employer's daughter.

Tansy stood back, frowning at the door. Someone had mentioned at some time that a key to the back door of the chapel was left in the porch. She couldn't recall who had made the remark but she did remember that the key was on a shelf. There would be no bulging collection-box or valuable church ornaments in this modest place. Reaching up she felt with her fingers along the narrow ledge within the porch but there seemed to be nothing.

The sound of a door closing at the back of the chapel sounded like a pistol-shot in her overstrained mind.

She was out of the porch without conscious memory of leaving its shelter, and in a few quick strides had reached the half-dug ditch where she crouched down, intent on making herself part of the unmoving landscape.

The bulky figure of Wesley Brown came down the side of the chapel and into the porch. She could see nothing, but heard his little grunt of satisfaction before he emerged. Then he appeared again on the outer step, his head turning slowly from side to side before he pulled his shovel-hat down more securely on his brow and went on down the path. He passed so near that she could hear him humming under his breath and her flesh crawled a little at this evidence of satisfaction.

She waited until the soft padding of his feet had diminished before she raised her head cautiously. He was just turning the corner, presumably heading for the nearest cab-stand. Tansy stood up, brushing soil from her skirt, and flexing her cramped limbs.

Then she went swiftly and as noiselessly as possible up to the porch again and stretched her arm up to the ledge. Her fingers closed on the cold metal of a key and she slid it into her palm.

The faint glare from the nearest gas-lamp didn't reach round to the back of the chapel, where only the thin sliver of moon revealed the outlines of several large paving-stones placed at angles as if someone had been considering whether or not to build on an extension and decided against it. The back door was a narrow one with dully gleaming windows at each side.

Tansy felt for the lock with her hand as the moon vanished momentarily behind a cloud, located it and inserted the key, feeling a sense of relief as it turned as noiselessly as if the lock had been newly oiled.

The door swung inwards into a narrow room with light from the re-emerging moon filtering weakly through the windows to reveal cupboards, a pot-bellied stove in one corner with mugs stacked on a shelf at the side, and a floor of plain deal wood with an inadequate carpet spread over the central section.

There was a lamp, its wick still smoking, on a lectern against the near side-wall and a box of lucifers close by. Striking a light and rekindling the lamp she wondered, irrelevantly, which girl had dipped the stick into the boiling liquid that spattered and burned and sent its poisonous fumes into the air.

The room sprang into a semblance of life, though its dingy walls, the few pieces of furniture and complete lack of comfort would have made it a poor excuse for a life. Obviously it was used as the place where extra hymn-books were stored, where tea was brewed up during the meetings of the Band of Hope. One or two crayon drawings obviously made by children were pinned to a board.

What had Wesley Brown been doing in here? A man who believes he has just committed the latest in a series of brutal killings must, she thought, have a sense of almost unbearable excitement within himself and could surely not go home tamely to his wife! She looked round, aware of an odd perfume lingering in the air and stinging her nostrils. What the devil did it remind her of?

She had smelled it before, and she racked her brains to try to recall the exact occasion. Yes, of course! Years ago! She had come downstairs to find her father talking with one of his colleagues. The visitor had been lighting a pipe, not puffing it, but letting the smoke curl up.

Pa had said, 'That's the scent you want to remember, Dalton. Opium! The pipes may be damped down and the supply hidden but that scent lingers on the air. Find that scent and you'll find the den.'

Opium was legal, though rarely used these days, but a certain class of criminal used the drug regularly as a ploy to lure young girls into a life of prostitution. Tansy bit her lip, trying to decide into which category Wesley Brown fell.

Despite her situation she felt a quiver of amusement at the thought of other members of the congregation, kindly ladies who made the tea at the Band of Hope, noticing the lingering scent in the air and innocently attributing it to the aroma of left-over pipe-smoke.

There were a couple of ledgers on the shelf below the one holding the mugs. She lifted one and set it on the lectern. It contained lists of names and addresses stretching back over ten years. Clearly these were the various members of the congregation. Weddings were followed by baptisms and in several cases death-dates were included. The various preachers who had taken services were also listed, together with details of deacons and their families, officials who ran the Band of Hope, and, near the end, a list of contributions to the Society for the Conversion of the Jews.

Order and method were, of course, the watchwords of the Methodist movement and nobody could have faulted this record, written neatly in a variety of hands.

Here was the name she sought. Her hands shook suddenly and her breath came short. Here was the solution, jotted down some years before in all innocence and clear for anybody who cared to read.

She made a mental note of the address and put the ledger back on the shelf. Then she went, moving automatically, her mind still reeling, to the door, extinguishing the lamp and locking the door behind her as she emerged into the night.

She could find a cab and return to Laurence's house, knock him and Finn up and present her findings, but by morning word that Sal Finnigan had survived and might well remember the circumstances of the attack would almost certainly have filtered out. The Valentine game was coming to an end and there was the distinct possibility that the killer might evade justice by choosing to disappear and begin again in a different place under a different name.

The moon was flirting, coming and going in and out of the dark clouds that swirled the sky. A little wind had risen to stir the air and ruffle the weeds that clung to the cracks in the pavingstones.

Tansy walked fast because she knew that if she allowed herself to stop and think she might turn tail and flee for help. If she did that the police would be informed and Jarrold would issue his instructions, and when all was said and done all she had was one strong piece of circumstantial evidence through which any decent lawyer could drive a horse and cart.

What was needed was a confession, an acknowledgement of guilt. Further than that she hadn't dared to speculate.

The little church and the long wall of the cemetery where the members of Sion Chapel also buried their dead lay on her right. Was Frances Jones sleeping quietly under the newly turned earth or did she strain towards the light, wanting revenge for herself and Ellie Watson?

Tansy shivered as she crossed the road and turned to the left into a long, narrow street with tall houses on each side, leaning together, their roofs touching like hat-brims over gossiping heads. The gas-lamps showed lovingly whitened steps, drawn curtains, a pot-plant here and there, house numbers carefully painted, the street itself swept fairly clean save for odd bits of scrap-paper blown by the night breeze and rustling in the gutters.

This was the haven of the respectable, god-fearing poor, rising above the cheerful vulgarity of the lower class, not yet achieving the snug serenity of the middle classes. This was a street in which outward conduct was of supreme importance and where the slipping of a standard threatened the whole community.

The house looked as clean and inviolate as its neighbours. Behind the drawn curtains Tansy detected the glimmer of light.

She went up the steps and pulled sharply twice on the bell. As she stood down a pace she heard the drawing of a bolt and then the door itself was opened.

'Oh!' The woman framed in the doorway gave a little gasp. 'I thought it was my husband! I'm waiting for him, you see.'

'I'm sorry to disturb you at such a late hour.' Somehow Tansy found her voice. 'My name is Tansy Clark. Your husband hasn't mentioned me?'

'No. I'm afraid not.'

The other still held the door somewhat nervously.

'You must be Valentine?'

'Such a foolish name! I like to be called Val you know. Nothing has happened to my husband, has it?'

There was a sudden note of anxiety in the voice.

'Not as far as I know,' Tansy said. 'Actually I came to see him on a matter of some importance. I don't suppose. . . ?'

'Please, won't you come inside and wait?' The door was held wide as the woman stepped back. 'My husband isn't usually as late as this, but then he has so many charity projects. I say to him – Oh, let me light another lamp to cheer us up!'

The room into which Tansy was being ushered was so clean that it made the eyes ache. The green and white patterned carpet and curtains looked laundered; the rows of little gilt cherubs that were ranged on shelves in an alcove glittered sharply; every cushion was carefully plumped up and placed at an angle; not a smear was on the highly polished table and chairs, or on the mirror, set within an oval of wax leaves and hung over a small dresser on which three pieces of crystal sparkled.

'Everything,' said her hostess, 'is such a mess! We have a woman who comes in daily to clean, but I am always obliged to do it all over again when she's gone. Do sit down. Wait! Let me get a cover for the chair.'

She darted to a drawer, opened it and brought out a neatly folded square of embroidered linen which she placed carefully on the seat of a high-backed chair with highly elaborate legs that splayed carved feet, heavily decorated with oak leaves in four directions.

Tansy sat down gingerly, tucking her feet back but uneasily conscious of her dusty outfit.

'Tansy.' The other paused and looked at her reflectively. 'That sounds like a herb. Such a pretty name.'

'It's a yellow flower that grows wild in the hedgerows.'

'Oh, wild.' The voice had a dying fall. 'I cannot say that I altogether approve of hedgerows. Undisciplined, don't you feel? Now parks are quite another matter. All the paths neatly raked and the flowers standing in rows like little soldiers. When my husband and I were first married we hadn't the means to go away on our honeymoon, but we used to walk out to various salubrious parts of the city – Kew Gardens, Kensington, a dear little park named after one of the queens – Adelaide, I believe. But there were often leaves fallen on the grass and too many children disturbing the pond with boats and fishing-hooks so we decided not to go there again. A place for everything and everything in its place, Miss Clark! Now what can I do. . . ?'

While she rattled on, Tansy had regained some of her own control and contrived to study her closely, while maintaining an expression of eager interest on her face. Before her stood a slight, girlish figure, in a dress of frilled ribbon with a huge bow on the bustle and short sleeves with matching ribbons cascading down over her arms. It was the kind of dress an eighteen-year-old might wear for her coming-out party, but under the dyed-yellow curls the face was not so heavily rouged and powdered as to conceal the network of fine lines, the sagging flesh beneath the chin.

'Do you often wear pink?' she asked bluntly.

'I never wear anything else,' Valentine said brightly. 'When I first met my husband I was wearing this exact shade and he said to me then – you will excuse me for repeating a compliment – he said that I looked like a rose just coming into bloom. Now I won't tell you how long ago that was because you'd never believe it – people never do! "You must have been wed in your cradle" they say. Of course I was accustomed to a much finer style of living when I was a girl. But Papa's business failed and then – all in the past I say. I used to be quite a social butterfly, but these days – I really fail to see why people should wear gloomy colours just because they are religious. Do you?'

'No, I—'

' "So you go along to your old services", I said to him. "I won't dress like a frump and look like all the old biddies singing their heads off and criticizing everybody else!" '

'Do you ever read the advertisements in the newspapers?' Tansy contrived to stem the flow.

'The newspapers? No, I can't honestly say that I do.'

For some reason a tide of dull scarlet rose from the low neckline and flooded the powdered face.

'An advertisement was put in on two separate weeks—'

'Reading is such a waste of time, don't you think? One never made a fortune by reading a book. In fact, I seldom read at all! I – oh, that will be – of course he has his own key but he likes me to be waiting up for him.'

'Is he often this late?' Tansy asked.

'Seldom. Very seldom. Happily married gentlemen very often prefer to come home to their wives as early as possible, but when help is required or someone needs – excuse me, Miss Clark, but that must be him now!'

Tansy, who was feeling slightly dizzy after the deluge of chatter with which her hostess had inundated her tensed and rose from her chair as the other opened the door wider and cried merrily,

'Here you are then! A lady called to see you. I took the liberty of asking her to wait and we have been having the most delightful chat. Miss Clark, I don't know whether you said or not, but I don't know if you and my husband are actually acquainted.'

'I know Mr Mason,' Tansy said.

Despite her resolve she could feel herself trembling slightly.

'Would you like me to make some tea, dear?' Valentine asked. 'Or is this a private affair? I know how you like to help without making a great to-do about it. I often scold him, Miss Clark, for not pressing for more appreciation of the work he does.'

'Miss Clark has run out of time, darling,' John Mason said. 'I'll see you to a cab, Miss Clark.'

'But we've only just begun to talk,' Valentine complained, pouting in a way that would have been appealing had she been a young girl.

'Another time,' Tansy said, repressing a curious pitying impulse as she allowed herself to be ushered into the hall. 'Good-night, Mrs Mason.'

Stepping down into the street she left behind a stream of aimless chatter spreading like a river that grew wider but never deeper.

John Mason closed the front door and paced beside Tansy along the street.

'Valentine can't read very well,' he said in a conversational tone. 'There's nothing seriously wrong with her mind. She was simply allowed to do anything she liked when she was a child and she chose to do nothing.'

'Then why. . . ?' Tansy stopped as he picked up her unspoken question.

'I was not aware of it when we married,' he said. 'Like many young men I was dazzled by prettiness. Thirty years ago her chatter seemed to me to be enchanting.'

'Sal Finnigan isn't dead,' Tansy said.

'Not dead, but. . . .'

They had reached a gaslight and he paused beneath it, his face turned towards her, wiped free of everything except surprise.

'She's in hospital,' Tansy said, 'and will recover fully. You were in too much of a hurry when you struck her down. You didn't make certain.'

'The ribbon kept slipping when I was tying it round her hat,' he said, 'but she made no movement. I did, in fact, decide to return, just to make sure. Not something I usually do, but I was a little flustered that night. I feared she might have met you already, but when I had walked round to the cab-stand I saw you arguing with a young gentleman. My natural instinct was to intervene to save you from further insult but I would have found it difficult to account for my presence in the neighbourhood at such an hour, so I merely followed you and then I heard someone running from the other direction. Obviously the body had been found, so I turned and went very quietly away over the grass.'

There were no words that came easily. Tansy looked back at him, trying to fathom the thoughts behind the quiet, pleasant features, angled now by the light into a simplicity of black and white.

'You didn't come straight home?' she said at last.

He shook his head and continued walking, his tone as calm and self-possessed as if he were giving her directions to an unfamiliar part of the city.

'I wonder if you can imagine what it feels like to be married for thirty years to a woman like Valentine?' he asked. 'To come home night after night to inane, empty chatter. Never to be able to sit down quietly with a book without knowing that before one has digested the first page that same voice will interrupt? "Silly John, always reading! You'll addle your brain while poor me has to endure it!" Month after month. Year after year!'

'In the cemetery,' Tansy said, keeping her own voice steady, 'Sal Finnigan came to me in the cemetery. I guess she'd suddenly remembered that Frances Jones had once mentioned that your wife's name was Valentine – mentioned it in passing, so to speak. Sal began to tell me and then stopped abruptly. She was looking towards the grave and I assumed she had taken fright at seeing Wesley Brown there, but of course I had just introduced you to her, and as you walked away it was you that she was looking at, and not Mr Brown as I believed.'

'I heard what she said.' He nodded slightly, looking rather pleased with himself. 'I have an acute sense of hearing. It renders poor Valentine's chatter even more excruciating. You were to meet her at your father's house. I was not certain where your father lives so it became incumbent on me to follow her.'

'By cab?'

'She walked part of the way, then took a cab but apparently she didn't have sufficient money on her for the whole fare, so she alighted a couple of streets before she reached the park. By then I was, of course, starting to recognize my surroundings. I left my own cab which had been travelling behind – it was not, I believe, my intention to harm her. After all it was proof of nothing that my wife's name was Valentine! But she must've glimpsed me or felt herself being followed because she seemed to panic suddenly and ran. Into the park. Very foolish. I naturally followed.'

'And struck her down.'

'In full flight! She never even sat down.'

There was suddenly a grim jocularity in his tone. Tansy opened her mouth to say something, but he whipped round on the instant.

'Don't interrupt me, Miss Clark! For once in my life let me tell a tale through to the end!'

SIXTEEN

They had reached the end of the street and ahead of them the wider road was edged by the cemetery wall. It was, of course, possible to run, but where? There were no cabs in sight, not even the rumble of wheels in the distance, and no night walkers who might lend assistance. Her stays would impede her breath once she had fled a little way and there was also the fact that, despite her fear, Tansy felt an overmastering urge to hear the tale. Had Pa felt like that, she wondered, when after hours of questioning a suspect had confessed?

'Do go on,' she said aloud, politely. 'You were saying. . . .'

'That thirty years is a long time to live without any intellectual companionship at all. And then the idea came to me. I would advertise, hope to meet someone with whom I might enjoy a friendship. Nothing more than that.'

'Surely in the chapel. . . ?'

'They are worthy folk, but simple, not with my intellectual capacity. I intended to enter the ministry, you know. I believe that I might've made a reputation as a powerful and inspired preacher, but the moderator likes to see the wives as well as the candidates and with a wife like Valentine, fluttering in that vulgar pink, constantly talking nonsense – I became a deacon instead. The stipend is very small but I had a little money when my father died and we have lived in what I flatter myself is modest comfort. So I placed the advertisement.'

'Calling yourself Valentine?'

'I have always found ladies more responsive to intelligent conversation than my own gender. Valentine is, in my opinion a name with pleasant connotations which would encourage a lady to feel more confidence in contacting the advertiser. Ellie Watson answered the advertisement, along with several others. She wrote that the manager at the factory where she worked would not leave her alone. The letter was short, ill-spelt, but confiding. Her distress at being molested demonstrated that she was a moral young woman who would be glad of a mentor. We could read books and discuss them together and I might guide her into bettering her lot.'

'You met her outside the library in Kensington.'

They had reached the cemetery gates and she instinctively resisted when he seized her arm and pulled her within.

'We can talk more privately here,' he said.

She was taller than many females and healthy, but his grip on her arm had been surprisingly strong. She trod obediently at his side, seeing the headstones rear up around like silent listeners.

'I sent a brief reply, telling her to bring it with her as a means of identification,' he said. 'I asked her to meet me after dark because you may find this difficult to believe, Miss Clark, but there are those who will place the worst construction on a perfectly innocent friendship. If one has nefarious designs on a young woman one does not set a rendezvous outside the library! She came a little after the arranged hour. I think she might have experienced some difficulty in slipping away.'

'What went wrong?' Tansy asked.

'The worst luck in the world, Miss Clark!'

He had freed her arm from his grasp and leaned against a tall headstone but there was nobody to help her, nowhere to run. Tansy stood motionless, accustoming her eyes to the darkness for they were beyond the reach of the flaring jets of the gas-lamps now.

'A friend of hers – acquaintance rather – who had worked briefly at the same factory a couple of years before had apparently kept in touch. The friend, Frances Jones, was a member of Sion congregation, and though Ellie Watson was not a Methodist she had come to one or two meetings of the Band of Hope. While I stood cogitating she saw me and so, in order to allay her natural alarm, I had to acknowledge her. She became very agitated when she realized I had placed the advertisement and kept insisting she was a good girl – as if I had the same evil designs on her as did the factory manager. I could not allow her to create a scandal so I had to think fast. Fortunately thinking fast has never been a problem for me. I said "Oh, here is Miss Jones now," and hit her with my walking-stick as she turned away her head.'

'Your walking-stick?'

'It belonged to my late father. The handle is solid oak, very heavy. It is a particular treasure of mine but I only carry it when I have on my Sunday suit. It adds the finishing touch.'

'And the pink ribbon?'

'Valentine always rolls up a length of her own ribbon and puts it into my pocket – to remind me of her when we are parted. You see what kind of a female I married! I had a sudden impulse to tie it about her hat. I cannot tell exactly why.'

'And then you killed Frances Jones. Did she recognize you too?'

'That was quite different, Miss Clark!' He sounded offended. 'I am not a natural murderer. After that first occasion I swore to myself that such a thing must never happen again. Never! For nearly three months, Miss Clark, I worked at the chapel, went home to my wife and her babbling, night after night after night after–'

Something stirred beyond the tombstones. A stray dog or a prowling cat, she surmised, and felt her shivering increase.

'I decided to put in the advertisement again,' John Mason said. 'I am not sure whether or not I would have answered any of the letters or even troubled to collect them, and then I found Frances Jones weeping in the chapel. She had been seduced, Miss Clark. By my fellow-deacon. Oh, she did not need to tell me! Her laughter when I suggested she consult him told me the whole story. I promised to give her advice and help, to meet her outside Kew Gardens.'

'You didn't answer her letter. The Valentine advertisement was in her Bible.'

'I wasn't aware of that! I met her outside Kew Gardens with the honest intention of advising and helping her, but as I walked there I thought of the terrible scandal that would ensue if the fact became known. The chapel would lose subscribers. The Edge family would be affronted. My own post might be at risk. And what hope had Frances Jones with a bastard babe? I again distracted her attention as I had done with Ellie Watson and as she turned her head – the second time was not easier. It did, however, afford me considerable satisfaction, because I had solved the problem you see.'

'And Tilde Miles?' Tansy was beginning to feel a trifle sick.

'I went down to collect the Valentine replies. The letter from Tilde Miles was beautifully written, quite eloquent in fact! I sent word she was to meet me in Adelaide Park. Unhappily I was slightly delayed but I got there, and then you came through the gates, though I was unaware of your identity at the time. I couldn't allow any witnesses.'

'But that's not true!'

The odd, almost dreamy feeling that had been creeping over her as his low voice droned on vanished and she interrupted him sharply.

'I beg your pardon, Miss Clark, but lying is the Devil's tool,' he said stiffly. 'It is not a vice in which I indulge.'

'You killed Frances Jones *after* I found Tilde in the park,' Tansy said rapidly. 'You hadn't gone to the park to talk to Tilde! You'd gone there with the express purpose of killing her just as you'd killed Ellie Watson, because it satisfied you, made you feel powerful! In fact you'd arranged to kill two that night, hadn't you? Tilde, whom you'd never met, would meet you in Queen Adelaide Park and be killed very swiftly, and then you'd whisk over to Kew Gardens and meet Frances Jones who was waiting patiently there. Two in one night! That was something to be savoured privately as your wife chattered on, wasn't it?'

'I'm a very busy man, Miss Clark.' The indifference in his tone was chilling. 'I can't be expected to recall the exact order of my activities.'

'And you killed Mr Valentine too,' Tansy said. 'You killed him because you hoped that people would think the murderer had been killed by a sneak-thief.'

'I regretted having to do that,' he admitted. 'However, you must share the blame for that, Miss Clark. You came to Sion

Chapel making enquiries about Frances Jones. Your father was a noted police inspector. I sensed that you might get the bit between your teeth and start interfering. So I followed you. Not all the time, of course, since my charity work precludes that, but I am a man who can blend easily into the background. In a way, I wished that I could engage you in conversation; intelligent females are rare. However, that wasn't possible so I followed you discreetly when and where I could. I tied a pink ribbon to your door-knocker. A little joke. I am not without humour.'

'And threw the kitten you had killed at me as I walked through the park.'

'No, Miss Clark!' The words came out explosively. 'I would never harm a defenceless animal! I am an animal lover, Miss Clark. It has long been a source of grief to me that my dear wife cannot cope with the mess that even domestic animals are prone to make. The kitten was dead. It was already dead! I would never harm a dumb creature, Miss Clark!'

'What harm did Mr Valentine ever do to you?' Tansy demanded.

'You visited his establishment. I had never heard of him before. The name astonished me, truly it did! At first I regarded it as a coincidence, but then a light burst upon me and I descried the hand of the Lord! Here was someone who might have placed the advertisement in the newspaper, might have been driven to – but he might have witnesses who could swear he had been elsewhere at the specific times. I went into the shop and he was behind the counter, putting something into his till. The bell tinkled as I went in. He looked up, expecting a customer, and I approached, smiling, and strode up to him. He merely looked at me, Miss Clark. I struck him down. It was a most regrettable necessity.'

'And this evening, after you struck down Sal Finnigan?'

She had to keep him talking, until morning if necessary though her whole frame was filled with cold terror.

'I went for a walk to clear my head. I find that long walks are conducive to a quiet mind. I did not, of course, stay in the vicinity. Otherwise I would have realized that my blow had not been effective.'

'And Sal Finnigan will tell the police.'

'Tell them what? She didn't see me clearly. She has no reason to suspect me.'

'But Sal was on her way to tell my father that she did suspect you,' Tansy said. 'Frances Jones had mentioned to her some time ago, and she suddenly recalled it, that your wife's name was Valentine. She began to scrawl the word "wife" in the gravel before she lost consciousness. I thought she meant Wesley Brown's wife—'

'Wesley Brown would never kill anyone,' John Mason said. 'He has neither the courage nor the intelligence.'

'He's an unpleasant character,' she agreed. 'I fear there are many like him. Fortunately there are fewer like you.'

'There have been one or two,' he acknowledged. 'However we are, on the whole, rare beings. Now, we have a little problem. I apologize for referring to you in such terms. You are certainly more intelligent than the general run of females, but reckless. Like those poor, silly young women who went off to meet a stranger in a deserted place at night. Reckless, Miss Clark!'

Not only reckless but stupid, Tansy privately agreed. What on earth had possessed her to rush off to Sion Chapel to check up on whose wife was called Valentine? And having found out why had she gone off to the house? It had been, she thought bitterly, her own pride, her irritation with Frank who had concocted a tale to deceive and had found Mary Denny.

'Not so reckless,' she said aloud. 'You cannot believe that I came here quite unaccompanied. You cannot believe that I would be so foolish. Or perhaps you can! Is that why you've boasted to me, used me as a captive audience? Thinking nobody else could hear?'

'My dear Miss Clark, we're quite alone,' he contradicted. 'Except, of course, for the dead, and the dead cannot listen.'

'But I can,' Frank said, rising so suddenly from behind one of the sentinel headstones that Tansy felt as if someone had punched all the breath out of her body.

Frank looked taller in the half-light of the emerging moon, and the pistol in his hand was very black and very steady.

For an instant John Mason stared, the whites of his eyes visible in the gloom. Then he uttered an inarticulate cry and ran, leaping over the surrounding graves, flinging away his walking stick as he went.

'The roads are blocked,' Frank said, pocketing the pistol. 'Are you all right? Not going to faint or anything?'

'No, of course not!' Tansy said crossly.

'Then why are you sitting down on a grave?'

'Because I didn't know anyone was here.'

She struggled to her feet with the help of his hand.

'You didn't think that I'd believe for one moment that you intended to go meekly home to bed, did you?' he asked, still holding her hand in his warm clasp. 'Give me credit for knowing you better than that, Tansy girl! I asked the porter where you had told the cabbie to go and then as soon as the police arrived, accompanied, incidentally, by Finn, we left two of them guarding Miss Finnigan and explained the rest – or as much as we knew of the situation – as we went to Sion Chapel. You were already at the door of Mason's house. To be honest I was ready to break in at once but Finn reckoned that he wouldn't murder anyone in his own house, so we spread out and waited and then Mason bowled into the street.'

'You could have caught him then and saved me a very unpleasant experience indeed!' she said indignantly.

'It isn't a crime to have a wife called Valentine,' he reminded her.

'But you didn't know he was going to confess.'

'He didn't confess, he boasted to you, sooner or later he'd've had to boast to somebody, preferably a woman in order to prove how very clever he was, how far above other men. Happily the assistant commissioner has more brains than Inspector Jarrold. He can walk and think at the same time. Are you sure that you're all right?'

His hand left hers as his arm slid round her shoulders.

'You all right, Miss Tansy?'

Finn was loping towards them as they left the cemetery.

'Cold and tired but completely unhurt,' she hastened to say.

'It's been quite a bit of a night,' Finn said, shaking his head at the recent memory. 'Your pa will want to 'ear all the details, I can tell you! I'm not easy shook up as anyone who knows me can testify but I don't mind saying my 'eart was in my mouth until we saw you come walking out large as life with Mr Frank 'ere.'

'And I'll be on Pa's doorstep large as life first thing in the morning,' Tansy said. 'Right now I have to get home before Mrs Timothy has a nervous breakdown. She will either conclude that I've been murdered or that I've gone to the bad!'

'I told the cabbie to wait for me at the other side of the church,' Frank said. 'Wait for me, Finn. I'll go back with you to Laurence's.'

'You're welcome to ride back with me,' Tansy said.

'Meaning I'm forgiven?'

'For telling lies about stunners called Mavis? No, of course not. What possessed you to be so underhand?'

'I was rather hoping you might be slightly jealous,' he confessed.

'Jealous! Frank, we're close friends, but your private life has nothing to do with me,' she said.

'I've been hoping for some time that it might have.'

They had turned down the narrow path that divided the small church from the cemetery.

'So you tried to impress me by rushing off to track down Mary Denny by yourself and you pretended you had some romantic assignation to make me jealous? Frank, we're not school-children playing games.'

'I'll argue you into a different opinion tomorrow. Good-night, Tansy.'

Without warning he bent his head and kissed her. It was a swift, hard kiss that was over before she could either repulse or return it, and then he was helping her up into the interior of the waiting cab.

This, she thought weakly, sinking back into the darkness as the sounds of running feet and whistles that had echoed vaguely in the background died away, has been a remarkable night!

A tipsy Patrick Denny had tried to make love to her, she had found Sal Finnigan struck down in the park, she had gone off alone to find out if her theory about a wife named Valentine was correct, she had found the right wife and the killer she hadn't even considered, and Frank had suddenly kissed her in a manner which, if not swooningly romantic, was certainly decided.

She found herself smiling suddenly without quite knowing why. Outside a false dawn was fast approaching, greyness rising in swirls of mist from the pavements, a bundle of rags stirring as a beggar turned over in his sleep.

'Driver, there's a shorter way than this!'

She reached up to rap sharply on the trap-door.

It was drawn back and John Mason's face appeared in the aperture.

'We're not going back to Chelsea,' he said simply, and shut the trap-door again.

Shock coursed through her in waves. She sat motionless, fighting for breath.

Frank had told her that the roads were blocked. The police had sealed off the routes of escape. She had heard running feet and the blowing of whistles long after they should have ceased, but had scarcely noticed them as she recovered her self-possession and felt the security of her friend's sheltering arm.

By now someone must have realized that Mason had slipped through the cordon. He must have attacked the waiting driver, dragged him into the shadow of the church wall and taken his place, muffled to the eyebrows on the driving seat. Who ever troubled to look closely at a cabbie?

Cold terror was yielding to anger. How dare this man, in himself quite ordinary and insignificant, cause this fear in her? How dare he, saddled with a stupid wife, take his revenge on quiet and defenceless young women who had actually turned to him for help?

Because they didn't talk to him. The sentence, flashing into her mind, seemed to have been dropped there by an unseen hand.

Ellie Watson and Frances Jones and Sal Finnigan had been killed before they could utter more than a word. Valentine Mason, who hardly ever stopped talking, was still alive. Somewhere in his twisted mind John Mason perceived constant chatter as the rein upon his impulses.

The cab was going very fast, threatening to splinter a wheel as it banged the kerb on its rounding a corner. Empty pavements, shuttered buildings, aureoled gas-lamps whizzed past.

Tansy wanted to open her mouth and scream. She wanted to wrench open the door and fling herself out, but both options were denied her. If she screamed nobody would hear above the thudding of hoofs and rattling of harness. If she wrenched open the door she might succeed in leaping out but she would certainly be seriously hurt, possibly killed.

She cowered in the corner, hanging on to the window-strap, the cab lurching over cobbles and paving-stones as if it had a will of its own.

Then, abruptly, with a splintering of wood the rear wheel broke off its axle and the horses slowed from a frantic gallop to an uneven, dragging trot as they sensed the change in the vehicle they were pulling. She could hear the swishing of a whip and Mason's voice, no longer urbane but savage, raw with frustration as he screamed at the animals to go on.

The cab had slithered to a halt, leaning at an angle. Tansy reached for the lock that clicked shut the doors at each side and wound up the windows just as the cab gave a final lurch and Mason's face, livid and staring, appeared suddenly at one window, his hand tugging at the handle.

There was a narrow gap between the top of the window aperture and the window-pane. His fingers scrabbled in the space and his expression was contorted into one of almost childish rage.

In a moment he would remember the trap-door in the roof of the cab. Though he had no hope of squeezing through the space he could, she thought, drop stones through and anything else that came to hand, could bombard her as she crouched there. He would, she thought, staring at the dilated eyes, almost certainly enjoy it.

What would Pa expect her to do? Not cower here, staring at the face which had lost all semblance of humanity, that was certain! Pa would expect her to go down fighting. And the only thing she had as a weapon was her tongue.

'You,' she shouted suddenly, 'are a coward, John Mason! You don't have the courage to control your wife, so you try to control other women, ones who can't talk back because you never give them the opportunity! That's it, isn't it? You're afraid of women.'

'Don't you say that. Don't you say that. Don't you say that!'

'You're repeating yourself.' By some miracle she succeeded in steadying her voice and loaded it with scorn. 'The truth is that you're a fraud, John Mason! You haven't anything interesting to say. You don't really think that you'd ever have made a minister, do you? Why, you're not capable of holding anyone's attention for two minutes together! And your wife had to put up with your conceit, didn't she? If you had satisfied her she might not waste her life in constant chattering about nothing at all! She has to fill up the empty space you made of your marriage!'

'Be quiet! Be quiet!' His voice was a despairing wail.

'I'll reckon she knows the kind of man you are,' Tansy shrilled. 'She knows that deep down you're terrified of females. She knows that, doesn't she? I'm astonished she didn't throw you out years ago!'

He was moving now, shaking the locked door and making the cab lurch drunkenly from side to side. From the tired and steaming horses came a high, frightened whinny.

'Why don't you run off and do some charity-work? There's not much else you can do beyond collect donations and swagger round as if you had a position in society instead of being a failure!'

His walking-stick, raised high, splintered the window. Slivers of glass flew out but the window itself held. There were other sounds – the galloping of hoofs, whistles being blown loudly, running feet, shouting voices.

Uniformed men were dragging him away. His fingers clung to the edge of the glass for an instant and then were gone.

'Tansy, are you hurt? Are you all right?'

Frank again, hair dishevelled, face flushed and anxious. Tansy slipped the lever on the door and, as he wrenched it wide, stumbled into the pale, cool, early morning, felt his arms go round her and burst into humiliating tears.

'Hey, Tansy girl! This isn't like you.'

His voice was soothing but it put the steel back in her. She straightened up, fumbled for her handkerchief and wiped her eyes roughly.

'I'm not used to being abducted by madmen and driven through the streets at breakneck speed either,' she said tartly. 'The real driver? Is he – he's not. . . ?'

'Knocked out,' Frank said. 'I found him within a minute or two. We were never far behind. Mason was too clever simply to try and get through the police cordon, but there'll be a few red faces down at the station later on I reckon. Tansy, you were screeching like a banshee.'

'He couldn't stand up against verbal bullying,' Tansy said. 'The girls he killed because they were quiet. He made them substitutes, I think, for the wife he was afraid to hurt.'

'I'll drive you home. You look exhausted.'

'You can drive a cab?'

'How d'ye think I arrived here so quickly? You were being followed most of the way but you didn't know it. Come on. I've an idea that a certain Inspector Jarrold will be wanting a statement later, not that he will give you any credit for anything you've done. I'll see you back to Chelsea, and then go to the hospital. Sal Finnigan may be conscious.'

'And you want to be first with the story. You're a man of many parts, Frank Cartwright!'

'And you're a woman of infinite variety, Tansy girl.'

'I feel as if I've been dragged behind the horses,' she said tiredly.

'You look very pretty even if your hat is crooked and your nose pink.'

'Oh, surely not!'

'Don't fret about it. It's your beautiful soul that fascinates me.'

He was teasing to alleviate the horror of the night just passed. She stood up straighter, set her hat at its usual angle and said, 'I'm quite recovered now, honestly. Frank, you may find a cab for me but I'm quite capable of riding home alone. Go and get your newspaper story. I shall snatch a few hours' sleep and then go to Pa's for luncheon. Will you be there?'

'I'll always be there,' Frank said, and kissed her hand.

Weariness was dragging her down. She was vaguely conscious of being handed into a cab, of a uniformed constable asking her if she felt well enough to manage, of Finn arriving, late and indignant, with his grammar flying completely out of the window as he assured her he'd give Laurence all the details but not sufficient to distress him. Then she was in a cab, being driven Chelseawards.

She leaned her head on her hand and watched the waking city roll by. How many men emerging muffled and capped to start a day's work, or women already at work on their front steps would be aware that a drama of life and death had been played out just beyond the walls where they slept?

Later on there would be discussions, face-saving exercises on the part of Inspector Jarrold, discussions about the mind of a respectable man who derived relief from his frustrations in the act of killing. Something would have to be done about Wesley Brown too, who couldn't be permitted to abuse his position as deacon. And a quiet word from her father to Sir James Edge might ensure a change of manager at the match factory.

That was for later. Stumbling out of the cab and producing her purse she was stopped by the driver.

'Mr Cartwright paid the fare, Miss. Lucky I chanced along. Looked like there'd been a bit of an incident back there.'

'Yes,' Tansy said. 'Yes, a bit of an incident. Thank you.'

She had scarcely set foot on the path when Mrs Timothy flung wide the front door.

'Thanks be to the Lord! Your pa sent a little lad over to say that you might be late, otherwise I'd've been in a taking and no mistake! As it is my back is telling me, that it's suffering something chronic. I sent Tilde off to bed and then I composed myself to wait. Have you been helping your pa to help the police to catch that dreadful—'

'The man who killed those two young women is in custody, Mrs Timothy. I'll tell you all about it later,' Tansy said, cutting short the flow as she entered the hall. 'Right now I simply want to sleep. Wake me at eleven and I'll have a bath before I go to my father's for lunch.'

'What shall I do about Mr Denny?'

'Who?' Tansy stared at her.

'Mr Patrick Denny, Miss Tansy. Turned up an hour ago, saying he had to speak to you. He looked that woebegone I let him wait in the drawing-room but last time I looked in at him he was fast asleep.'

'Not any longer, Miss Tansy!'

Patrick Denny had opened the drawing-room door and stood,

haggard, unshaven and romantically handsome enough even for Tilde's taste, on the threshold.

'Mrs Timothy, I'm sure Mr Denny would appreciate some very strong coffee and a light breakfast,' Tansy said, going into the drawing-room. 'I'll have mine later.'

'Miss Tansy, I came to apologize,' Patrick Denny said in a rush. 'I've walked the streets for hours, so I have! The Lord knows that no man has more reason to be ashamed of himself than I have! I'm not a drinking man but hearing about my sister – my conduct towards you was unpardonable! I shall take the pledge, so I will! Miss Tansy, my sentiments towards you remain unchanged. I wouldn't want you to think that it was the drink talking or that I don't have – has something happened? You look very tired.'

'A great deal, Mr Denny, but that can keep,' Tansy said. 'I need to rest now but when Mrs Timothy has given you some breakfast and you have – tidied yourself, perhaps you could go to my father's house? We are all meeting there for lunch.'

'It will be my pleasure, Miss Tansy.' He achieved a slightly unsteady bow. 'I am quite sober now, but have a somewhat heavy – it is very good of you to – only say that I have not offended you beyond bearing!'

'Not in the least, Mr Denny. I'll see you later then.'

He was, she thought as she went slowly up the stairs, a most attractive man. Not perhaps quite – but to have been kissed twice in one night after years of deprivation must count for something!

By her bed Geoffrey's well-beloved photograph gazed out at her as it had gazed since she had received the news of his death. Tansy went over and picked it up, put her lips to the cool glass for possibly the last time and slid the portrait into a drawer. Geoffrey was gone. Life lay ahead, with two very attractive suitors in it, and she was only thirty.

She pulled off hat, jacket and shoes, shook her hair free from its pins and lay down to consider possibilities, falling into a deep and dreamless slumber before she had even begun. There would be time later for choosing or not choosing. All that mattered now was that a few ghosts had been laid.